MR. SELLER'S POND

MR. SELLER'S
POND

SHERRI GRIMAUD

Charleston, SC
www.PalmettoPublishing.com

Mr. Seller's Pond
Copyright © 2021 by Sherri Grimaud

First Edition

Hardcover ISBN: 978-1-64990-959-6
eBook ISBN: 978-1-64990-638-0
Paperback ISBN: 978-1-63837-007-9

For my family,
with gratitude and love

ACKNOWLEDGMENTS

First, an enormous thanks to all those at Palmetto Publishing who helped with designing and preparing this book and to Erin, whose kindness and excitement carried me through the process with ease.

I would also like to thank Jessica for her sharp, graceful guidance with editing my work. Her ability to see exactly what I feel is uncanny. I am convinced that without her help this story would not have blossomed into what it is. Thank you for talking to me as though the characters are real and for wonderful, helpful advice.

A special thanks goes to my sister, Kim, who believed in my story from the very beginning. Her excitement and enthusiasm inspired me to continue exploring my ideas and push me through to the end. I also want to thank her husband, Jim, for his willingness to help with finalizing the process.

To my parents, thank you for giving me the freedom to launch my imagination from a loving and carefree childhood. The years on the farm are kept in the sweetest section of my heart. I also want to thank my seven children and their amazing spouses. I'm so lucky to have each and every one of you in my life! There's a special kind of wisdom that springs up inside of me from all that I'm learning from you. Thank you for the love, laughter, and continual support.

I also want to thank all twelve of my grandchildren and any others that may one day grace our lives. You inspire me continually and bring joy to every moment I breath.

Finally, to Allen, thank you for every single day.

CONTENTS

CHAPTER ONE

GRANDMA CATHERINE

The overhead fan circled slowly in the crowded muggy room, and other than the occasional whiff of the sweet bouquets, I struggled to endure the strong woody odor of the pews we were sitting in. The reverend's voice was soft and deep like a gentle stranger seeking to console a lost child. I stared intently at the flowers as he spoke about my grandmother, Catherine Marie Ames.

My eyes began to ache, and tears welled up as I remembered the countless hours I spent with grandma. A well-worn book in hand, she would read to me in the room that overlooked her backyard. She taught me how to bake bread and make no-bake cookies. I would miss our many late nights together, watching old movies and eating ice cream. I'd tease her about putting ice cream on top of saltine crackers. She would just smile at me through ice-cream and cracker-filled teeth.

Why did this happen? Could it be that it isn't even real? The people, the flowers, and the foreign voice that never seems to end...

Hot tears streamed down my face, and the colors of the flowers melted together like crayons left on a hot stove. Grandma had taught me so much since we moved here a few years ago—how to write poetry, weave Indian baskets, and cross-stitch. At the thought of cross-stitching, my heart ached again with a sudden realization. We would never be able to finish her latest project, a beautiful cross-stitch of an old tree that she had designed herself.

Anger rushed through me. *How could she leave?* I thought bitterly. Everyone told me I was artistic and talented, just like Grandma Catherine. We had such fun together. *Doesn't she know that I still need her?*

"*Timber. Timber.*" A familiar voice tugged at my thoughts. "Timber, it's over dear. We need to go now," I heard my mother say gently.

I sighed, wiping away the tears. "Come on Ryan. Come on Kate," I said as I reached for my younger brother and sister, who sat between me and Aunt Nell.

Mother's arms felt clammy against my hot skin as we began walking down the aisle. My legs ached with a deep desire to run out of the building, but people thronged around me. There wasn't a way out. Family members, friends, and even complete strangers were in every direction. Faces of all shapes and sizes stared at me with sorrow and despair.

2

Then there was Zelly, who was sitting by the chapel doors in her wheelchair. I sighed with relief. Zelly was grandma's oldest and dearest friend. Her gnarled, nubby hands jerked wildly as she reached out towards me.

"Timber, my dear," she said in her shaky yet familiar voice. "I'm sorry about your grandmother. I will miss her probably as much as you will."

I couldn't reply as I swallowed down the tears that felt wadded in the back of my throat. Seeing Zelly was good but also hard. Grams and I visited her in the old folk's home every Thursday afternoon. I would sit and listen to them talk about the good times they had when they were kids. Catherine and Zelly had been best friends since first grade, having lived in Springfield all their lives. Grandma told me many times during the past few months that she thought Zelly's mind was slipping from her, especially as she rambled on with crazy stories. Mother mentioned something about early symptoms of dementia. But I got a kick out of listening to her anyway.

"Will you still come see me on Thursdays, my dear?" she asked from behind red, puffy eyes. But before I could answer, Zelly pulled me close, as if to whisper something in my ear.

"I know what will help you, Timber," she whispered. "Find the eye. The golden eye. It fits in the tree at Mr. Seller's Pond."

My eyebrows raised and I felt the corners of my mouth move to a slight smile. These were the kind of words Grandma would abruptly put to a stop.

"Okay, Zelly," I said with an exaggerated whisper. "I will do that!"

Zelly smiled with relief.

"And I'll be there on Thursday, too."

"Good," Zelly said, nodding.

"Timber, we're leaving," Mom called from across the room. Aunt Nell grabbed my arm and gently tugged me toward the chapel's exit.

Huge, dark clouds hung heavy during the graveside ceremony. The moment Grandma's body was lowered into the ground the sky cracked with thunder and rain fell for the rest of the day.

***

I slowly inhaled the cool morning air. I didn't want to wake up yet, and I refused to open my eyes.

I could hear Ryan running into Kate's room, the phone ringing, and voices mumbling throughout the house.

"Timmy dear," Mom's voice came from the other side of the door.

My nickname "Timmy" was given to me by my father many years ago. I used to love it, but now it felt childish, and I cringed every time anyone used it. I tolerated it only from my mother.

"Honey, that was Jill on the phone," Mom said, gently cracking the door open. "She's on her way over. You need to be getting up."

I turned over in my bed. My eyelids felt heavy as I watched the sunlight peek through the window, casting a warm array of golden hues throughout my room.

I loved my room. Directly above me was a fishing-net which I had pulled and draped over the entire length of my bed. Because we didn't have an extra bed frame, the mattresses lay directly on the floor. I set up an old, weather-beaten fence as my headboard that held various antiques Jill and I had found in the shed. Against the wall was an old, rusted milk jug, and in the corner, I placed long, earth-tone feathers in the huge pot I made in Mrs. Eckert's art class.

A month and a half ago I turned fourteen and grandma gave me something I always wanted. I paused and stared at it, hanging motionless in the doorway. She told me whenever it made noises, I could think of her. The gift was a set of hollow bamboo beads that were connected at the top and hung down in strands, almost touching the floor. If I opened the door and came through, the beads would clank against each other like a deep, wooden wind chime. Even a slight breeze from the window could catch the hollow, woody sounds and send the clamor bouncing around the room. If I closed the door, the beads were perfectly still and I had total privacy, yet they also acted as an alarm if someone tried to sneak in.

My heart ached as I remembered Grandma coming to my room. She loved being here almost as much as I did and would often say how comfortable she was, as if in her own home.

"Timber, you need to get up," Mom said, interrupting my thoughts. She opened the door and pushed the noisy beads aside. "Aunt Nell and Uncle Martin are meeting me at grandma's house at 10 o'clock. As hard as it may be, we still have to sort through her things and get the house ready to sell."

Martin was grandma's older brother and Nell was his wife. I was always glad when they came to visit. We had countless fun times together, all of us and grandma.

I moaned and glared at Mom.

"So, this means I'm in charge of the kids?"

"Yes, Timmy," Mom said as she sat down on my bed and touched my arm. "But at least Jill's on her way over to help."

I perked up and raised my eyebrows.

"Jill's mother told me she didn't have to go to school today. We thought you might like the company. Besides, school is almost out anyway. I told her you might want some help babysitting."

"Good! That will make it more fun," I said as mom stood up and walked to the doorway. "But do you really have to sell grandma's house? That means someone else will be living there, Mom."

"Timber, you know we have to," she said as she flipped the beads aside and hurried down the stairs.

Although I didn't want to get up, I pushed the sheets off and jumped out of bed. I lifted my long, thick hair over my ears as I stretched my right arm toward the ceiling.

I noticed my reflection in the mirror on the back of the closet door. My straight, light brown hair fell gently to my shoulders and I stared at my large blue eyes. Relatives would go on and on about my "breathtaking beauty," but I didn't know what all the fuss was about. I turned sideways and looked at my waist in the mirror. I knew that I wasn't fat, maybe even a little on the thin side. But that was probably because I walked everywhere, and when I wasn't walking, I was riding my bike. I also didn't eat much junk food except for the occasional Lifesavers—my favorite candy.

I looked at my face in the mirror. I didn't really like the freckles on my nose, but Grandma told me they looked like sprinkles on top of the sweetest sugar cookie ever. I gently rubbed the faded spots and forced a smile. I did have a large mouth with perfectly straight, white teeth—thanks to braces and regular use of Creststrips. I laughed and shook my head. I still don't know what all the fuss was about!

I turned my gaze to the wall beside my closet door where two barn-wood picture frames hung. One had a picture of me with my mom, my sister Kate, and my brother Ryan. My mother, Mary Ann Rhoads, was tall and just a little overweight, but she had a beautiful, kind face and wide brown eyes. She was easy to get along with and had a playful personality, but she has also had to work extremely hard for our family since the divorce five years ago. My dad wasn't in the picture. He hadn't contacted us since the split.

Kate, my younger sister, was six years old and the spitting image of my mother with her long, straight brown hair that hung just over her shoulders. Ryan was five, a little pudgy, and had a head full of curly brown hair. Because my mother worked full time at Mr. Walters Drug store, I was the family's built-in babysitter—even more so now that Grandma was gone. Even though Kate and Ryan could irritate me at times, for the most part, we were a close family.

The other picture was of Grandma Catherine and me. I gently took it off the nail and slid down with my back against the wall until my knees were up to my chest. I held tightly to the frame and then looked closely at the picture. It was taken just a few days after we moved here.

My family moved to Springfield around two years ago after the house next to grandmas went up for sale. To me it was perfect! Springfield was a small town located in the Midwestern State of Missouri. The area had green rolling hills that were covered with dense full-grown trees. In fact, the street we lived on had huge, mature trees that reached up and over the road like a wide shady canopy. Whenever the sun shined, pockets of light seem to work their way through the leaves and dance playfully upon the pavement.

Our old white house was large, with a cement porch out front and a swing. There was a main floor, a cellar, and an upstairs where all the bedrooms are. My favorite part was the wooden staircase that had a half-circle turn at the top. Mom painted it light blue after we moved in. I used to feel like a princess dancing up to my room as if I were in some ancient castle. Now that I was older, I was glad that my room was directly above the porch so I can see if any of my friends are going by. The backyard was large with a built-in sandbox and a wooden swing mom put up in the huge Hickory Tree. There was also a large building against the back fence we called the granary. It was full of old junk that I love to rummage through.

I heard a light tap against my door.

"Hey Timber," Jill said as she cautiously peeked her head through the beads. "Your mom said I could come on up."

It felt good to hear Jill's voice again after the long, hard week.

"Hey, you," I said sleepily as she walked into my room.

"I'm sorry about your grandmother. She was really awesome. And everyone I know is going to miss her, Timber. Even me."

There was an awkward pause as her eyes glanced around the room, then looked at me, like she was trying to read something in my face.

"Umm, we did go to the funeral, but I don't think you saw us."

Jill's voice was low and reserved.

"Mom and I came late."

"That's okay Jill," I said. "I'll miss my grandmother. But I'm really glad the funeral stuff is over."

There was a moment of silence, as if Jill weren't sure what to say. She put her hands deep in her pockets and swayed back on her heels. Then her tone changed a little. "Hey, your mom said I get to help you babysit," she said. Her eyes got bigger, and then she continued in her usual high-pitched voice. "Well, it's cool that I get to miss a day of school, even though there are only a few days left. But I heard down at Rumsfield Park they're setting up the fair."

Jill always had a way of cheering me up, and I welcomed the temporary distraction from the sadness I'd been feeling.

"No way!" I said excitedly, tilting my head to the side. I felt a surge of excitement that took me off guard.

"I thought we could take Kate and Ryan and go down to watch," Jill said. Her hands were moving now as fast as her voice was. "Last year it was awesome how they set up the Ferris wheel, and there was this man— he was trying out his stilts— and he even let Robby try to walk with them."

Robby was Jill's annoying older brother.

"It was so funny when he went headfirst into the water tank at the dunking booth," she laughed and then continued in her eager, breathless way of speaking. "There was this other man who gave us a cup of shaved ice. He said he was just trying out his machine, so we didn't have to pay for it."

"Okay, okay," I interrupted excitedly. "Let me get dressed and then we'll go."

Jill ran downstairs while I quickly put myself together for the day.

Jill was my all-time best friend. She just turned fourteen years old, too. Her birthday was a month before mine. Jill was a little taller than me and had layered, sandy-blonde hair that hung down past her shoulders. She had huge green eyes and a little mole on the lower side of her right cheek. Her face was somewhat round, and she was slightly bigger than me. However, if there was someone thought to be breathtakingly beautiful, it would be *her*, not me.

Jill's mother often talked to Mom about us being the cutest pair of friends. But the thing I liked most about Jill was that we have so much in common. We both loved arts and crafts, antiques, trying new things, and *especially* boys. However, our personalities were quite different, too. I tended to get nervous in uncomfortable situations. Some people might think I'm shy—although mom would probably disagree. When I'm home or around familiar things, I'm a little louder.

Jill, on the other hand, could be in a crowd of strangers and she was loud, hyper, and loved to talk. She was most comfortable being the center of attention. She was never reserved and had a passion for impulsive activities. If there was not enough variety in her life, she simply created more—often without thinking everything through.

After eating a quick breakfast, Jill and I took the two kids down to Rumsfield Park and, sure enough, there were people setting up for the fair. I decided we should stay out of the way, so we sat on a large wooden fence at the edge of the park.

"I can't get up there, Timber," Ryan whined, his arms holding tightly to the third rung of the fence.

"Here," Jill said.

She reached under his arms and lifted him up.

Kate and I were already perched on top of the fence like two hungry birds searching for the first worm.

"Look, Timber," Kate said excitedly, pointing toward some trucks that were parked across the field. "There are the horses to the merry-go-round. Oh, can we come back—please, please, please—and ride the horses when it's all set up?"

"Yeah!" Ryan joined in as he got situated on the fence.

"Oh, probably," I answered. "But it will be a few days before everything is ready, and we'll have to ask mom."

"I can't believe school's almost out, Timber," Jill said, changing the subject. "What kind of things are we going to do this summer?"

"Swimming!" Ryan yelled.

I tapped Ryan's leg and gave Jill a hard stare. "Whatever we do we'll probably have to drag these guys along with us."

"Hey," Kate pouted. "That's not so bad!"

"What are those things in the back of that truck?" Kate asked as curiosity overtook her. She was as fascinated as I was with all the commotion in front of us.

"I'm not sure," I responded.

There were people coming and going in every direction, hauling brightly colored equipment into the large open field. Some headed back to their trucks while others worked almost in a synchronized way as they put together pieces to the rides and built up the booths. I felt like I was caught in a Kaleidoscope of moving shapes and patterns.

"That's okay if we have to take care of Kate and Ryan," Jill said.

"Hum!" Kate pouted and glared at me.

"But let's plan some kind of adventure!" Jill continued. "My uncle Ray was telling my dad about some caves that are out north of town, past the old water tower. You know, the place next to that big hill people like to go sledding on during the winter."

"Isn't Crystal Cave about five miles out that way?" I asked.

"Not quite that far," Jill responded. "Anyways, there's a story about a man that lives out in that area somewhere. He's supposed to be really old. Nobody has seen him in a long time. Who knows, maybe he's not even alive anymore."

Kate and Ryan turned and looked intently at Jill; their eyes were huge as they listened.

"They say that children have disappeared out there, too," Jill continued in a slow, creepy voice. "And it's a mystery what happened to them. My dad said the old man probably stole the kids and has them hidden in those caves. Wouldn't it be cool if we found the lost kids? Or even the old man's hiding place? We might become famous."

"I don't know if I believe any of that," I said, noticing the worried looks on Kate and Ryan's faces. "I think you're exaggerating a little, Jill."

"Well," Jill said, shrugging her shoulders, "that's the story I heard."

I glared at Jill and quickly changed the subject.

"Or we could make a lemonade stand like we talked about a few weeks ago," I said, in a happier tone. "In the back of the shed there's a pile of old wood. Do you remember seeing that Kate?"

"Mom said she was going to take that stuff to the dump," Kate responded.

"Well, whatever we do," Jill added with a slight gleam in her eye. "We'll have to have *lots and lots of fun*!"

"*Oh brother!*" I said as I rolled my eyes in amusement toward Jill.

Jill burst out laughing, almost losing her balance on the fence.

Kate and Ryan giggled without even knowing why.

"I remember those famous last words of yours, Jill," I said sarcastically. "And then we got caught by Mr. Ford."

"What happened, Timber?" Kate asked between giggles. "What did you get caught doing?

"Well, it was Chad's birthday, and I gave in to one of Jill's brilliant ideas. The plan was to sneak into the closet of our classroom when Mr. Ford took our class out of the room. We would hide out for a few minutes until they all got back. Then we would jump out and surprise Chad by singing happy birthday. How was I supposed to know the class would be gone for a two-hour presentation in the auditorium?"

"*I* didn't know either, Timber," Jill interrupted.

I continued, "What made it worse was that after they left, the closet door locked on us and we couldn't get out."

Kate and Ryan burst out laughing again.

"The thing that got me through two hours with Jill in a hot closet was her famous last words, "It will be *lots and lots of fun!*"

"What happened then?" Ryan asked.

"How did you get out?" Kate questioned.

"Well, when the class came back, we had to knock on the door of the closet—from the inside," I said. "Everyone died laughing, except for Mr. Ford. He wasn't happy at all."

"It was still kind of funny," Jill piped up.

"Yeah, now that it's over," I added with another quick laugh.

A loud beeping jolted us from our laughter. Losing our balance, we gripped the fence at the same time to save ourselves from falling. The sound was right next to us but as we turned, we saw another large truck backing up in the clearing just a few feet away. I caught Jill's eyes and we all burst out laughing again, thankful to still be on the fence.

It was fun talking and laughing at Rumsfield Park. I almost felt guilty getting excited about summer, but then again it was the right thing to do. Grandma would always be in my heart and I would deeply miss her, but I know she would want me to continue with life and enjoy it like she did. At least I have a supportive family, my best friend Jill, and many wonderful memories of me and my Grandma Catherine.

CHAPTER TWO

GOLDEN EYE

The final bell rang as I grabbed my backpack, which was stuffed with my extra supplies. It felt strange going back to school on the last day of the year. Mom thought it would be a good idea to get my things and return my books, but if she only knew. Everyone stared at me all day long. They must have heard about grandma and the funeral! I kept to myself most of the day and carefully watched the clock.

I couldn't wait to leave. I quickly headed through the long hallway toward the brown doors that led outside. It was hard not to notice the buzz of excitement coming from every corner of the school; desks were being scooted around, children exploded with laughter, and voices hollered goodbyes up and down the hallway. Normally, this was an exciting time for me as well, but this time I just wanted to get it over with.

"Hey, Timber!" Jill's voice blurted out from somewhere in the commotion. "Wait up!"

Finally, I saw her blond hair bouncing through the crowd. I hated how we only had one class together. I could have used more of her cheery mood today.

"Hurry up," I said. "I have to find Kate and Ryan."

"Did you hear what Chad said to Brandon?" Jill asked as she helped me push open the big heavy doors.

As the doors swung open, a warm gust of air whipped around us. The field behind the school was large and I squinted in the afternoon sun.

"I heard him say he might call you tonight."

"What?" I gasped, giving her my full attention.

"Yep, that's what he said, and he was asking Brandon how he could get your number."

"What did he say?" I asked, almost whispering.

"I heard him spelling out your last name and said something about you not having a dad at home."

"Oh, that's great!" I said sarcastically. I hated the whole single-parent life I was stuck in. "Do you actually think he'll call me? And what does he want?"

Jill stopped suddenly and turned to me with a mischievous twinkle in her eye. "I can run back and ask him," Jill said as her big green eyes grew larger.

"No way!" I said. "I don't want him to think I like him."

"But you do," Jill said, lifting her hands out in front of her. "And I think it's about time you let him know. Besides, it's the last day of school, Timber."

"Jill! Stop it right now!" I exclaimed. "If he is going to call, then he will call! We should just leave it at that!"

My face felt like a hot, red pepper. This was the most emotion I had felt all day.

I spotted Kate and Ryan bounding toward us across the field. It was a perfect way to change the subject.

"Kate! Ryan!" I called as they ran up next to us. "So, how was your last day of school?"

"Great!" they both said together.

We headed through the gate and started home.

For two blocks, Jill and I listened to Ryan and Kate. We couldn't get a word in as they talked about their day and how excited they were for summer.

I saw our old brown station wagon coming up the street. It was Mom.

"Kids," Mom said as she pulled up beside us. She had her work apron on, and I knew exactly where she was going.

"I'm sorry, but I've got to go to work. Betsy called in and her boys have the chickenpox. Don asked me if I would take her shift. I know it is a few days earlier than I had planned but since we have Grandma's house done, I thought I might as well.

"That's okay, Mom," I said.

"I'll be home by eleven, tonight," she said, her voice weary. "Get your chores done. And Timmy, there's some microwave dinners in the freezer."

"All right," I said. "But Mom, Jill and I were wondering—since school is out—could she stay the night tonight?"

"Sure, if it's okay with her mother," Mom answered. "Call me if you need anything."

Ryan and Kate gave Mom a hug and ran on ahead.

"Oh, and Timber, Aunt Nell wanted me to say goodbye. She and Martin had to go home. It's a long drive to Mannheim from here. Anyways, we also found some notes on some things that grandma wanted you to have, so we put them in your bedroom. All the extra boxes and furniture we just put in the granary out back."

"What kind of things?" I asked.

"You'll love them," Mom said with a gentle yet eager voice. Then she looked at her watch. "I really need to get going, honey."

"Okay," I said, nodding.

"Hey, I love you, Timmy," Mom said with a smile. Her eyes looked sad and tired, like she didn't really want to leave. I could tell grandmas death had taken a toll on her as well. "Take care kids," she said as she drove off down the street.

Jill and I walked along the old, cracked sidewalk that led toward the house. We quietly looked up as we passed grandma's empty home. Everything felt different since she was gone.

"Timmy," Kate whined as she flung open the squeaky screen door on our front porch. "Mom told me I could have the last ice cream bar, but Ryan took it."

The smell of old wood was thick in the air as Jill and I tossed our backpacks on the floor next to the front door.

"Ryan, give her what's left of it, right now!" I yelled.

"No, I got it first!" Ryan said stubbornly. With a large smile, he took another bite.

"Then I'll have to get it from you," Jill said playfully. She leaped from behind me and grabbed for Ryan, barely missing him as he ran screaming off.

"Get him!" Kate screamed, almost gleefully.

"Hey, Jill!" I hollered as I walked through the kitchen. "I'm going upstairs to see what Grandma left for me. You ought to call your Mom and see if you can stay the night."

"Okay," Jill gasped as she came running through the kitchen door. She turned quickly and held it shut while Ryan pounded hard on the other side.

Jill smiled and revealed the melting ice cream bar from behind her back. Just then, Kate came running in through the back entrance of the kitchen.

"My ice-cream bar!" Kate squealed with delight, snatching the treat from Jill's hands.

Curiosity got the best of me as I quickly headed past the noise and ran up the wooden staircase to my room.

"You guys, behave!" I yelled down the stairs. "And hurry up, Jill!"

For a moment, I felt like grandma might be sitting on my bed, just waiting for me to get home.

Hollow wooden sounds bounced against the doorway as I quickly flipped the beads aside and entered my room.

On my bed was a box with a cream-colored shawl draped over the top. I recognized it. It was the one grandma got from her mother. Quickly, I picked it up and wrapped it around my shoulders.

I gasped as I turned to look in the mirror.

There to the side of my room was grandma's brown wicker sewing basket.

"Oh, Grandma," I said in awe, as if she was standing right beside me. I dropped to my knees and tears began to well up in my eyes. I gently touched the top and slowly moved my fingers down the bumps of the old worn wicker. Some strands were torn and beginning to fray. I had forgotten all about her sewing basket. I loved the sound of the wicker lid as it rubbed against itself when she would open it. But what I loved most was that it was old. Grandma told me that it was a family heirloom that had been handed down for many generations. I didn't know how old it was, but I knew it was a real antique.

The heirloom stood about three feet tall and resembled a small table. It had an elegant shaped basket on the top, about twelve inches deep and twenty to thirty inches wide. Four wicker legs were connected and curved out and down toward the floor. On the lid was a cursive cross-stitch of my grandma's name:

I stood up, wiped the tears from my eyes and rubbed the brown threads of the crossed-stitched letters. I slowly opened the squeaky lid. Everything looked the same. There were little wooden compartments that were filled with different sewing items. In the middle was a handle to lift the whole top layer out. I quickly sat the top layer on the floor and looked in the basket. This part was for storing other sewing items and was made differently than the outside of the basket. Grams told me that when she was a little girl, one Christmas her father built the inside and added the extra compartments for her.

Suddenly, I remembered a box that was at the very bottom of the basket. It used to be attached to the wicker and had a tarnished padlock on it. The lock reminded me of what might have been on a pirate's old treasure chest.

I smiled as my heart began to race like the paws of a playful puppy.

"Surely, it has to still be there," I said out loud.

I began to pull different kinds of material out and carefully set them aside.

There it is! I said to myself. In the back corner of the basket was a small wooden box securely fastened to the sides and locked with the old grey padlock.

"It's still locked," I whispered in amazement. "What could be in there?"

Without warning, Jill burst in through the door, beads flying everywhere. I jumped, almost out of my skin!

"...And leave me alone!" she screamed as she held the door shut with both hands. "Your brother's driving me crazy!" Then she saw me. "Are you okay?"

I must have looked white as a sheet.

"Yeah, you just scared me to death," I said, trying to catch my breath.

"Sorry. Hey, mom said I could spend the night tonight."

"Cool. Now come look at this," I said.

"Wow!" Jill exclaimed. "What is all this stuff?"

"My Grandma left me her old sewing basket, and there's this little box in the bottom that's still locked."

Jill looked in amazement as she gently held on to the side of the basket.

"One time, when I was helping grandma clean the basket out, I noticed this locked box. She told me to leave it alone and not open it. When I asked her why not, she got kind of upset with me and said '*never.*'"

"Why would she say that?" Jill asked.

"I don't know, but it makes me wonder what's in there."

"Ooh, a mystery!" Jill exclaimed. "Well, break it open!"

"I don't want to do that," I said. "Grandma gave this to me, and I want to keep it nice."

"Well, maybe there's a key around here someplace," Jill said as she began looking around the sewing basket. "But Timber, your grandma's not here anymore—you could still break it open."

I looked in every compartment but found no key.

"Maybe it's in this box over here," Jill suggested as she grabbed the side of the box that was sitting on the bed. "Hey, listen to this," she said and began to read a note out loud. "'Dearest Timber, If I should ever die, I would like you to have my sewing basket. This means a lot to me! Take good care of it and pass it on to someone who has a good heart. (Make sure you can truly trust the one you give it too!) With love, Grandma Catherine.'"

Jill stopped and looked up at me.

"Well, she did want you to have the sewing basket, so a key has to be around here someplace."

Jill and I quickly began looking through the box. Under a picture on the top was the folded cross-stitch grandma and I had been working on.

"The cross-stitch," I said in amazement.

I gently picked it up and opened the material. The roots and trunk were finished along with part of the upper branches and some of the leaves. I felt an emptiness open inside my chest. Grandma had worked hard on the pattern of this tree long before we had even started stitching it, and it still wasn't finished.

"I remember seeing that!" Jill said, "That's a cool-looking tree. Hey, maybe we can work on it together? If you want my help, that is."

I nodded as something else in the box caught my eye.

"Oh," I gasped as I saw the hair of the porcelain doll I loved so much.

I set down the cross-stitch and picked up the doll.

"Grandma had this sitting on the end-table next to the fireplace," I said.

I clutched the doll to my chest, closed my eyes, and carefully flipped through my memories. I loved the doll's sweet little face and the long, curly brown hair. I had always wanted hair like this, and I used to sit and twirl the ringlets while grandma and I would watch movies together.

"Timber!" Jill whispered with surprise.

I quickly opened my eyes to see Jill's face light up with excitement.

"What?" I asked.

"The doll!" she said, pointing.

I quickly pushed the doll away from my chest and turned it around. There, hanging from a string around the neck was a small, silver key.

"Do you think...?" I asked in astonishment.

Jill and I dropped to our knees at the same time and I pulled hard at the string, trying to get the key off the doll's head.

"This was never on the doll before," I exclaimed.

The string snapped and the key dropped right into my lap. Quickly, I picked it up and held it for both Jill and I to look at. We made our way to the sewing basket and Jill took hold of the pad lock.

The key fit perfectly, and I turned it easily to the right. With a click, the top of the lock popped open.

In amazement, I gently pulled the lock out of the latch and lifted the old wooden lid.

"I feel like grandma almost *wanted* me to find the key."

"*And* open the box!" Jill added.

We both peered into the box and saw a brilliant golden cloth, which was wrapped around a small object.

"What do you think it is?" asked Jill.

"I don't know," I said as I picked up the bundle. "Something hard is inside of it, though. Feel how soft the cloth is."

Jill gently felt the material between her fingertips.

"Let's set it down on the bed and unwrap it," I suggested.

Jill looked puzzled, rubbing her fingers in a circular motion over the cloth.

"What is this?" she asked, staring at the soft golden wrapping between her fingertips.

"I don't know, but it's so…silky," I said. I began to gently unwrap the golden material.

There, in the center of the cloth, was a large, exquisite needle. It was unlike any other sewing needle I had seen. It was big—an inch wide and at least six inches long. On the surface was etched beautiful, swirly lines and shapes that covered the entire needle. The crevasses of the design were deeper and darker in color.

"It looks like pure gold!" I whispered slowly.

"Look, Timber— there's some kind of writing on it," Jill pointed out.

"Right there, inside the *eye* of the needle."

"The eye?" I said as I tilted my head to the side. "That's funny. At Grandma's funeral Zelly told me to get the 'golden eye' and put it in the tree at Mr. Sellers Pond. And that it might help me somehow."

Jill's eyebrows rose.

"What?" she asked incredulously.

I picked up the needle as gently as I would a newborn kitten and turned it slightly to see the lettering more clearly.

"I've *never* seen letters like that before. It looks like ancient writing of some kind."

"What do you think she meant by that?" Jill asked.

"Oh, Zelly was just babbling like she always does."

"I've never heard of a pond around here," Jill said. "Maybe she meant a lake or something like the Lake of the Ozarks."

"Jill, I'm sure she wasn't thinking straight. Grams used to tell me that Zelly is losing her mind, especially whenever she'd talk about stuff like that."

"But what if she wasn't losing her mind," Jill said as her green eyes grew larger. "What if her old age was simply giving-way and she was blurting out things that were supposed to be kept a secret?"

"I don't know, Jill," I said, shaking my head.

"Maybe there *is* a pond around here that we don't know about," Jill continued as her voice hurried with excitement, "like a hidden pond. We could find the pond and do what Zelly said and put the golden eye in the tree."

"Jill," I said firmly. "You're getting a little carried away."

I paused for a moment as I remembered something strange.

"But wait. It was kind of weird how Grandma used to always cut Zelly off whenever she would talk about a 'Mr. Seller.' In fact, one time at the old folk's home when Zelly kept going on and on, Grams gently touched Zelly's mouth and looked sternly at her, as if she were telling her to be quiet. And then she looked at me and rolled her eyes, like Zelly was just losing her mind. I remembered thinking how odd that was."

"Timber, I think there is a mystery here that we know nothing about. The needle is like pure gold. Why would your Grandma have it locked away in a box at the bottom of a sewing basket and tell you never to open it? And then leave the key to the lock around the neck of the doll that she left for you?"

"I know," I said as I picked up the porcelain doll.

"Hey look!" I held up a note attached to the underside of the doll's skirt and read it out loud. "'Timber, if anything should ever happen to me, I want you to have this doll that you love so much! Take special care of it, and someday give it to someone you trust. With love, Grandma Catherine.'"

"Why does she keep saying for me to give it to someone I can trust?" I asked. "I'll never give these things away."

"Maybe she means before you die, like passing on a family heirloom," Jill said. "Hey, when did she put the notes on everything? I thought she died of a sudden heart-attack."

"She... did," I said, questioning the events of the past few weeks. "I've heard how some people put notes on things when they get older because they know they'll die eventually. Maybe that's what she was doing."

"I think we need to talk to Zelly," Jill suggested.

I nodded in agreement.

"But first, we need to put this needle away and hide the key. And Jill, promise not to tell anyone about this. It seems like Grandma wanted it that way."

"Sure!" Jill said as she tilted her head to the side. Her big green eyes were like saucers. "And you know what else I think? We just found our summer adventure and it's going to be *lots and lots of fun!*"

Jill and I began to laugh as I quickly folded the soft, silky material around the ancient golden needle.

CHAPTER THREE

OLD LEATHER BOOK

The cool air settled on my face as I snuggled into my sleeping bag and stared off into the night sky. The backyard felt different in the dark, even a little scary. I could tell the neighbor's dog knew we were here because he was sniffing against the wooden fence and moving restlessly through the bushes.

"What is that Timber?" Ryan asked sleepily.

"Oh, that's just Jake next door. I'm sure he hears us out here. Now go on to sleep, Ryan. Kate's already out. Besides, if we want to get a head start to the fair tomorrow, then we need to sleep."

"Okay," he replied. "Did Mom give you enough money so we all could go?"

"Yes, Ryan."

"Even Jill?" he continued as he flipped his pillow over and changed positions in his sleeping bag.

"Even Jill," I said. "Now go on to sleep."

"That was nice of your mom to let us sleep out here in the backyard," Jill said.

"I know, isn't it great?" I agreed as I heard Ryan yawn. "Look at all those stars. I wonder how many are actually out there."

Ryan moaned as he moved his head back and forth.

"Ryan," I said gently, checking to see if he was asleep.

I turned to Jill. "I'm sorry I couldn't explain earlier. I am trying to keep this a secret. Remember when Mom came home? You went downstairs with the kids to get the sleeping bags. But Mom and I were talking about Zelly and she had heard that Zelly wasn't feeling well."

"Oh," Jill said slowly. "That's why you looked at me funny and agreed to take the kids to the fair tomorrow."

"I wanted to tell you, but Kate and Ryan were always around. I have an idea though, for tonight," I said as I disappeared into the bottom of my sleeping bag.

"What's that?" Jill asked, waiting for me to reappear.

I lifted a heavy, long black flashlight above my head. "This is what," I said.

"Okay," Jill said, confused.

"Remember how Mom said Aunt Nell and Uncle Martin helped her move Grandma's extra things out to the granary for storage?"

Jill's eyes grew big as a smile spread across her face.

"Let's go!" I said.

"But quietly," Jill whispered as we both stood up.

I shined the flashlight on the ground in front of us as we crept softly through the cool grass of the backyard.

The granary was a building at the back end of our property. Whoever put it together was very creative. Two old boxcars from a train had been set parallel to each other with a large space between them, possibly to store farm equipment. The front of the boxcars was facing the house and the back was against the end of our property. A tin roof was built up and over them with the pitch of the roof directly above the middle of the two boxcars. Large machinery could drive through the opening at the front. Long pieces of wood had been shabbily nailed on the back wall of the building for a barrier against the weather. I never could figure out why it was called a granary because grain was not stored in it. Mom called it that, so we called it that too.

The light from the flashlight cut through the darkness as we entered the large, open space under the roof. My eyes remained fixed on the flashlight's beam as I moved it along the inner walls of the building. At the back of the building were pieces of antique-looking farm equipment. Along the side was a rusted lawn mower, an old green couch, and a pile of rakes. Then I moved the light to the huge sliding door of the boxcar. The red paint was old and flaking off beside the enormous, rusted metal latch.

"Here Jill, hold this," I said, pushing the flashlight into her side. I put both hands on the lever of the metal latch and pulled down. It didn't budge.

"Pull harder, Timber," Jill whispered. She held the light on my hands, and I exhaled a deep breath of air.

I tried again, this time pulling with all the weight of my body. The force of it made my feet lift off the ground. When the lever finally dropped, my feet slammed hard against the dirt floor, sending a flurry of dust into the air.

Jill began to cough.

"Oh," she said. "I honestly didn't think it was going to open."

"Me neither!" I exclaimed, clearing my own throat.

While the dust settled, I grabbed the edge of the sliding door. It was positioned on two huge rollers fit into special grooves. I pulled with all my might, but it wouldn't move. Jill set the flashlight down on the ground, and the light shined across our feet as she helped push while I pulled. The wheels squeaked as they moved, and finally the large door opened all the way.

I shined the light into the boxcar and saw all of Grandma's things, a lamp and shade, furniture, mirrors, and many brown boxes.

"Here we go," I said as we climbed into the rusty, old boxcar.

Jill grabbed the flashlight and laid it on top of a tall dresser while we began opening boxes and sorting through leftover items. Some were full of material and craft things; others were full of kitchen supplies like plastic lids and bowls.

"Hey, look at all these books I found," Jill said in amazement. She stood over three boxes that she had opened.

"Yeah, I know. Grams really loved books!"

"But something is different about these books, Timber," Jill said holding two of them up in the light. "They're all about trees."

"What?" I asked.

"She must have really loved trees," Jill said incredulously, sifting through the books.

I grabbed the flashlight and stepped over some boxes to get to Jill.

"Look at these," Jill said, handing a few more books to me.

"Well, I knew she liked trees because she had pictures of them hanging around her house and the cross-stitch. But wow!" I exclaimed, shining the light over all the boxes. "I never knew about all these books and that she, like, *studied* trees."

I quickly opened three more boxes.

"These are all about trees, too!" Jill gasped.

We stared in amazement.

"Well, I think," Jill said as she began digging into the box closest to her, "if we find anything that's even a little suspicious, we should probably examine it more closely."

"Right," I agreed.

Jill and I found many books about trees. Some were about how to take care of trees, how to harvest the fruit from trees, the bugs and animals that live in trees, and how to cut down a tree the right way. There were even special encyclopedias about trees.

"Jill, look at this," I whispered. I held up a thin, tattered book that was made from old leather.

Jill sat down beside me.

I had never seen anything like it before. It was old—ancient, even— like something a Native American girl had made and carried around in her pouch for a hundred years. I began to unwind a thin leather strand that was twirled around a circle-shaped piece of leather in the front. I slowly opened the book. On the first page was a faded pencil drawing of a tree.

"Hey, this looks almost like the cross-stitch," I whispered softly.

Underneath the drawing it was signed and dated:

Winston Michael Wilson, June 1828

"Wow," I said slowly, "This is really old."

"Eighteen twenty-eight?" Jill gasped. "And who is Winston Wilson?"

"I don't know."

I slowly turned the old, crinkled page. There was another drawing of a tree and scrawled in the margins of the page were tiny little rocks and notes in the same handwriting.

"Hey, look at this," I said as I turned another page. I slowly read the words out loud:

Trees_____ plant_____next_____them
Every time! —Winston

"Some of the writing is smudged off," I said.

"It must be like a notebook or a journal that was kept," Jill stated.

"Yeah," I whispered as I carefully flipped through a few more pages. "I wonder why Grandma had it? Well, it sure has a lot of drawings of trees."

"*That's* a big surprise!" Jill said sarcastically. "Hey, look there," she said, reaching quickly for the book. The flashlight dropped to the floor with a heavy thud, and everything went pitch black.

"Jill!" I yelled.

Panic gripped at my chest. The darkness felt like it was crushing in on me.

"Why did you do that?" I whispered frantically as I dropped to my knees, groping around for the flashlight in the dark. I could feel Jill doing the same thing.

"Sorry," Jill said. "But I saw *your name* on the next page."

"What?" I squeaked out. "My name wouldn't be in this book."

"Here's the flashlight," Jill said.

I could hear shuffling then a click.

Light penetrated the darkness and my eyes throbbed against the sudden change.

I took a deep breath and moved to sit down on a wooden crate. I opened the leather book again. Jill held on tight to the flashlight that illuminated the pages in front of us. I carefully turned them one by one until the handwriting looked different.

"Right here. This is grandma's writing," I said astonished.

Jill's voice cut me off as she began to read the words out loud. "'Give this book to Timber someday—you need to tell her *soon* about Mr. Seller's Pond!'"

"What?" I gasped. "I don't understand."

"It looks like a note she wrote to herself," Jill said.

"How could she be writing about Mr. Seller?" I asked slowly, as if some unseen person would answer me from the dark corner of the boxcar. "I didn't even think this was real."

I lifted the book closer to the light and turned the pages slower than before, only to discover more hand-drawn pictures of trees and rocks. Some of the trees had perfect diamond-shaped leaves, and rocks were sporadically drawn alongside the water's edge. The drawings were beautiful and brilliantly detailed. And always, each page included little notes scribbled out on the edge. The words were clearer and looked exactly like Grandma's handwriting.

"Wow..." Jill said in amazement staring off into the darkness. "Zelly was telling the truth. She's not crazy after all."

"Grams always told me that Zelly was losing her mind when she talked about Mr. Seller," I said slowly. "And all that crazy stuff—I thought it was just babbling nonsense because she's so old.

"Well, it wasn't nonsense," Jill said with certainty. "Zelly told you to put the golden eye into the tree at Mr. Seller's Pond, right?"

I nodded slowly as Jill fixed her big green eyes upon mine.

"No wonder your Grandma studied trees. And this is her handwriting. It looks exactly like the writing on the notes in your bedroom."

Jill started counting off with her hand.

"One: She left you the doll that had a mysterious key around its neck. Two: You told me the key never used to be there. Three: That key opened the compartment at the bottom of the sewing basket, which Grandma also gave to you, right?" I nodded, and Jill continued, "Four: In there, we found the golden needle. And five: The note in this old leather book brings it all together."

"But why would she keep this from me?" I asked, confused. "I don't understand. This is so unlike her."

"Maybe she couldn't tell you, Timber."

I noticed how the flashlight cast strange shadows on Jill's face as she talked.

"Or maybe she was waiting for the perfect time to tell you. She died of a sudden heart attack, Timber. She didn't plan to leave."

There was a long silent pause as we both stared at each other.

"In a way," she continued, "this is all kind of exciting! It's like a puzzle that she wants you to put together. And each piece is a clue. Timber we need to find out why Grandma Catherine kept this secret from you. We found the golden eye that Zelly told you about. Now we just need to find Mr. Seller and ask him about his pond."

"I wonder if Mom knows about any of this," I said.

"I don't know, but I think we should try to figure this out on our own," Jill said. "Then go to your Mom only if we really need to. Besides, it sounds like your grandma wanted to keep this a secret. I bet your mom doesn't even know about it."

"Yeah, you're probably right. Well, we should keep this old book in the sewing basket."

"With the golden eye," Jill added.

"Tomorrow we have to take the kids to the fair, but maybe after that we could go to the old folk's home and talk to Zelly about this."

"That sounds great!" Jill agreed.

***

Rumsfield Park was a busy place the next day as the town of Springfield opened summer with the noise and commotion of the fair. People were busy walking everywhere, and rides of all kinds were constantly in motion. The Ferris wheel stood high in the sky with bright blinking lights that continued to move around the circular frame. A group of teenagers were laughing about something while children with pink cotton-candy raced to get in line for another ride.

I leaned up against the silver gates that surrounded the Octopus ride and watched the fair workers buckle Jill, Kate, and Ryan into their seats. It had been a long day, and we decided that this would be the last ride before we headed home. Usually I loved the fair, but all I could think about was Grandma Catherine's secret.

A loud humming sound began as the Octopus ride raised itself and started moving. Loud music blared just above the piercing sounds of the screamers who were tucked away into little black buckets.

I reached into my purse and pulled out the small leather book and a half empty roll of Lifesavers. I had to bring the book, just in case I had some time to look at it again. I unrolled a green candy and popped it into my mouth as I flipped through the pages. I stared at the pictures of the trees and looked at the handwriting of Winston Wilson. *Did grandma know this man, or did she just find his notebook?* I wondered. *Who is Mr. Seller? Will he let us explore the trees around his pond?*

"Timber!" Ryan screamed as he zoomed past where I was standing. I smiled and waved—not that he would be able to see me, moving that fast.

I wondered how we would figure out all of this while watching Kate and Ryan all summer. The ride began to slow down and then stop.

"Do we have to go?" Kate pouted as they walked through the gate.

"We've gone over this Kate, and we have to go home," I said. "It's been a long day!"

"It's been an awesome day, too!" Jill exclaimed in her usual excitement. "But Timber's right; we need to go. Besides, I'm starting to get hungry."

We walked past the two large trucks that were parked beside the entrance to the fair.

"Hey, let's stop at Mom's work," Kate suggested. "Maybe she'd make us a shake."

"Can we?" Ryan asked, grabbing my arm.

"Okay, but mom doesn't want us to visit her if we are loud, so you have to behave."

Ryan looked at Kate with determination in his eyes.

"I bet I can beat you there!" he exclaimed, then bolted off toward the sidewalk that was just outside the entrance gate.

"No, you won't!" Kate yelled as she raced off behind him.

"Hey you guys, be careful crossing the streets!"

Jill and I followed behind the kids as we walked to Mr. Walter's Drug Store. Mom's work was only about four blocks away from the fair grounds.

"All I can think about is Grandma Catherine's secret," Jill said, low enough so that no one could hear.

"Yeah, me too."

"What should we do first?" Jill asked. "And how can we do it with Kate and Ryan?"

"I've been thinking about that also. Mom expects me to watch them all summer now that grandma's gone."

"Maybe we'll just have to tell them," Jill said.

"I don't know," I said warily.

"I think we ought to find a phone book," Jill suggested. "And see if there's a Mr. Seller that lives around here."

"That sounds great!"

When we reached the drug store Kate and Ryan already had ice cream shakes. They were sitting on the stools that lined the counter in the middle of the store. It felt muggy and hot as we walked in.

"Hey Mom," I called out as I saw her propping the fan against the opened back door.

"Girls," Mom said in her usual happy voice. "I'm so glad you stopped to visit."

She quickly walked up to me and Jill and gave us a hug.

"Sorry that the air-conditioning isn't working!"

"I know. It's hot, huh?" I responded.

"It's been kind of a slow day here too, with all that's going on in town. But I've got some news," she said with excitement in her voice. "Remember how we went to the Rawlings cabin on the lake last year?"

I nodded, unsure where she was going with this.

"Well," Mom said, "tomorrow Betty and Mark are leaving for two weeks with their kids and wondered if you guys wanted to go with them again? I need to stay home and work. But you guys can still go and have some fun. You could even bring Jill if it were okay with her mother. Besides, there have been a couple of people interested in Grandma's house already."

Mom paused when she saw my jaw drop. She continued, this time cautiously, "I'm meeting them there tomorrow afternoon, so I really couldn't go anyways."

I felt nauseous at the thought.

At the same time, Jill's eyes lightened up as if she wanted to say something.

"We get to go to the lake!" Ryan yelled.

Kate squealed with delight. "Can we go Mommy, please?" she begged.

"Mom, I don't really want to go," I said slowly. "Jill and I have a lot of things we wanted to do around here this summer."

Mom's eyebrows pulled together. "Are you sure, Timber?"

"I know how much fun it was last year, but we just want to hang out here," I said.

"Kate and Ryan could still go, couldn't they?" Jill blurted out, as if she couldn't hold her lips together one more second. "They would have a blast with Betty's kids! Aren't they about the same age?"

"Yes," Mom said, eyeing Jill suspiciously. Her eyes shifted to me. "You girls wouldn't have something up your sleeves that you might need to share with me, now, would you?"

"No!" I said quickly. "Umm. Well, I was kind of wishing that I wouldn't have to babysit all summer long."

"Yeah, I know, Timmy," Mom said as she gently grabbed my hand in hers. I could tell she was thinking about grandma being gone.

"Well, I guess it would give you two a little time to be alone and give Kate and Ryan a vacation."

"Can we please?" Ryan and Kate begged at the same time.

"I'll talk to Betty," Mom said as she walked to the back of the store.

I turned to Jill, but she was already headed off towards the front.

"Can I please look at that phone book?" Jill asked the woman behind the counter.

"Sure, honey," she said.

I grabbed Jill's arm and began looking over her shoulder as she flipped through the pages full of names. I knew exactly what she was doing. Excitement fell upon me as I thought about Kate and Ryan being gone for two whole weeks. But still, there wasn't any time to waste!

"Seller...Seller... S... e... l...," Jill quietly sounded out the spelling. "Here it is. There are actually three people with the Seller name."

"Here, let's get some paper and a pen," Jill said.

"No!" I whispered as I reached into my purse. "I'll write them down in the leather book. This is *our* notebook now. Plus, we can keep all the information in one place."

Jill grabbed a pen from the counter and handed it to me.

"I'll write the names here," I said, flipping to the pages in the back of the book.

"Okay," Jill said as she began reading off the names and addresses.

"I can't believe there are actually three people who have that name," I whispered with excitement. "This might be easier than I thought."

"Let's find a phone and call these people."

"Girls," Mom interrupted. "Betty said that would be fine, so I need you to go home and help the kids pack. They will pick them up in the morning before I go to work at 8:30."

I quickly closed the leather book and put it back into my purse.

"Sure, Mom. Anything to help," I said trying to stifle the excitement in my voice.

"I don't know about you two," Mom said cautiously. "I could swear you're hiding something. This would not have anything to do with a boy named Chad, would it?"

"Mom," I whined.

Jill quietly chuckled to herself.

"No!" I continued, "We're just excited about summer."

"Hey, Kate and Ryan," Jill called out to the kids. "Let's go home and get you guys packed for the Lake."

The kids went running out the front door.

"I'll see you two later," Mom said.

The evening was busy for Jill and me as we helped the kids pack their things for two-weeks. Jill had to go home after it got dark, so I put Kate and Ryan to bed then headed to my room. After putting on a comfortable oversized t-shirt, I laid back on the pillows at the head of my bed and held the tattered notebook to my chest. Somehow, I felt more connected to Grandma than I had since she went away.

A warm summer breeze brushed gently over me from the opened window. I closed my eyes and drifted off to sleep.

CHAPTER FOUR

FINDING MR. SELLER

I awoke to the rich, morning light that filtered through the orange curtains in my windows. Kate and Ryan were leaving for two whole weeks to go to the Rawlings cabin, and Jill and I were free to work on Grandma's secret. Just the thought of it sent a shiver of excitement down my spine.

I clenched my fists and stretched my whole body under the sheets as I listened to the sounds of an early summer day. Birds chirped outside the window and a slight breeze rattled the leaves of the tree above the front porch. A motor hummed in the distance, then grew louder and louder until it stopped right out front.

Were the Rawling's here already? I shot out of bed and made my way to the windowsill. Parked in the front of the house was a big, tan camper with a wide brown line down the side. *They were here!*

Kate's high-pitched voice screeched from downstairs, and I heard the locks click to open our front door. I was just as excited as Kate was. Jill and I had an adventure to get started on, so I quickly threw on some clothes, tucked the old leather book in my back pocket, and headed downstairs.

Mom only had fifteen minutes to get to work, so we quickly packed the kids' things into the camper and said our goodbyes. We watched as the Rawlings drove away.

"Now Timber," Mom said as she climbed into the front seat of the station wagon, "what are you and Jill going to do today?"

"I'm not sure yet," I said.

"Well, speak of the devil!" Mom said in a playful voice, as she glanced up the street.

"Jill!" I hollered.

"Hey, Timber!" she shouted back.

Jill walked up to the car. Her hair was pulled back into a high ponytail, and she wore shorts and a white t-shirt with the sleeves rolled up. She looked ready to work.

"Well, you girls have a fun day," Mom said as she started the car. "And promise me you will stay out of trouble."

"We will!" Jill and I said at the same time.

"Maybe we'll stop in and get a soda later," I suggested. I knew Mom would like to hear that.

"That sounds great!" she said as a big smile spread across her face.

Jill and I waved as she drove off.

"This is so exciting!" I said.

"I know. Did you bring the notebook?"

"Yeah. It's right here." I quickly pulled it out of my back pocket.

"So, which Mr. Seller do you want to try first?" Jill asked.

"Well, I thought we should probably stop in and talk to Zelly, if she's feeling better."

"But isn't Elva Street right on the way?" Jill pointed out. "I think it's just a few blocks down from the school."

"You're right," I said. "Let's go there first!"

We headed off down the street, on the old broken sidewalk that led toward the school, carefully checking the green street signs as we crossed each road. The sunlight flickered through the trees and across the paper as I began to read.

"The first one is on West Elva," I said.

"Elva!" Jill called out as she pointed across the road. "There it is!"

My heart began to pound in my chest, and I quickly pulled the book closer to my face so I could read it better.

"It's 170 West Elva."

"That house number is 110," Jill said in a high-pitched voice. "It must be at the end of the block."

I hurried to keep up with Jill as she took off running down the street.

When we arrived, we noticed an old rusty mailbox with worn, grey numbers on the side that read 170. Jill and I stopped and stared. The property looked rundown and even somewhat neglected. The grass had not been trimmed in a long while, and the white paint had begun to peel off the house like loose sheets of thin paper.

Jill opened the gate, and we slowly began to walk up to the porch. I noticed old tires barely hidden in the long grass with bicycles leaning up against them. At the edge of the porch was a large tin bucket with wildflowers growing out of it. Hanging on the screen door was a colorful painted sign that said *Welcome*.

I looked at Jill and took a deep breath. I could feel my nerves tightening up in my stomach.

"The name is Monty Seller, right?" Jill asked quietly.

I nodded. "What's he going to think when we ask him about a pond?" I whispered.

"I guess we'll find out," Jill said as she knocked on the wooden screen door.

We waited with great anticipation.

From inside the house came a slow, heavy clomping sound. Like someone—or something— was making its way up a long hallway and then stopped.

The door opened.

There stood a tall, pleasant-looking black man with huge, muddy boots on.

"Well, now," he said in a low, deep southern accent. "What can I do for you two young ladies this mornin'?"

"Hello sir," I said in a quiet, unsure voice. I couldn't help but notice his messy boots and the trail of mud all the way down the hallway. "Um, we're looking... um, for."

"Are you Monty Seller?" Jill asked in a loud confident voice.

I was relieved!

"Why, yes, I am," the man replied, grinning ear to ear.

"We're sorry to interrupt you," Jill said as she tilted her head to the side, looking at the floor behind him. "But we heard of a man whose name is Mr. Seller and that he has a small pond here in Springfield."

The man burst out a deep belly laugh as he leaned his head back toward the ceiling.

"Well, I've never owned a pond," he said, still laughing. "But ya might say I do now!"

I glanced at Jill. Her head was leaning forward, a confused expression on her face.

"We had a water line burst in this ol' house last night. The whole backyard is full of water *and* mud," the man said as he looked down at his feet.

"Oh," I said.

"But no, I've never owned a *real* pond," the man continued. "And I'm sorry to say I've never known anybody 'round these parts who has!"

"Alright," Jill said. "Well, thanks for your time! And good luck with the water line."

"Thankya!" the man said jovially. "Y'all have a nice day now, ya hear!"

The man shut the door.

"Well, one down," I whispered to Jill as we jumped off the porch and headed down the street. "Did you see that house?"

"Yeah, that place gave me the creeps!" Jill exclaimed. "But the man was nice enough.

"He was," I agreed.

"Hey Timber, isn't one of the other addresses on Grandview?"

I opened the leather book again. "Yep, it says here that Brady Seller lives on 1060 Grandview Drive."

"How about we try that one also before we head back to the old folk's home?" Jill said.

"Sure!" I agreed. This was kind of fun. One of these names had to be the one we were looking for. I just knew it. I kicked a rock that was on the sidewalk and watched it jump along the pavement in front of us.

Jill and I turned at the same time, looked both ways and crossed in the middle of the road. We walked by Bellevue, Pacific, and then Koakane and finally Grandview.

"Well, *Brady*, we're on our way!" Jill blurted out.

We decided to run since we weren't quite there yet.

"Finally!" Jill exclaimed. We both put our hands on our knees and gasped for a deep breath of air.

"There it is!" I screamed pointing to a small yellow house with white trim around the windows. Neither one of us could miss the large white sign that was placed in the middle of the yard. It had big red letters on it that said *SOLD*.

My heart dropped. "Sold?" I asked.

"Yeah," Jill acknowledged. "And it looks like no one lives here anymore."

"Let's look around back," I suggested.

We quickly walked around the little house and peered over a short white fence. The back yard was small and lined with overgrown bushes. Right in the middle of the yard was a little concrete birdbath. It looked like it hadn't been used in years and was covered with dirt and twigs.

"Well, there's our pond," Jill said sarcastically. She chuckled to herself.

"I guess this Mr. Seller wasn't the right one either," I said.

We turned and walked slowly down the sidewalk to the end of street.

"What are we going to do now?' I asked, kicking another rock that was on the edge of the sidewalk a little harder than I meant to.

"Oops!" I said as I watched it skid straight past a parked car and almost hit a man walking toward us. "Sorry!" I hollered out, ducking my head a little.

"Are you kicking rocks at me?" he asked in a playful voice.

"No," I said. "I was just goofing around and accidentally— Hey, you're a mailman!"

He laughed out loud as I looked at Jill.

"Why, yes I am," he exclaimed. "And it's bad enough that I have dogs chasing me!"

"You might know!" Jill blurted out as her green eyes sprung wide open. "We're looking for an address."

I opened the leather notebook. "Fred Seller on 624 Pleasant Drive," I said. "Do you know where that is?"

"Sure, I do. That's out next to Burly Road at the edge of my route."

He paused for a moment like he was in deep thought and then nodded. "Fred doesn't live there anymore," he said. "Well, I'm not sure, but I think he and his wife got divorced a few years back, and he moved out East. She still lives there though."

"Do they have a pond?" Jill and I eagerly asked at the same time.

"Slow down girls—a pond?" he asked confusingly.

"We are trying to find Mr. Seller's Pond," I said slowly.

The mailman looked bewildered as he pulled his blue bag up higher on his shoulder.

"I know there's not a pond in that area. It's all residential back there. But there is this place called Pete's Puddle out towards Burton if you're looking for a place to go swimming."

"No," I said, shaking my head.

"We just heard about a pond," Jill added as she began tugging on my shirt. "But hey, thanks anyways!"

"Well, you girls have a good day," he said. "And be careful how you kick those rocks around."

I smiled as we started walking down the sidewalk. "You have a good day too, sir," I said.

Without saying a word, we crossed the street and headed back the way we came.

"Now what?" I whispered, gently kicking another pebble.

"Let's think about this," Jill said. "There are no more Mr. Sellers in town. Maybe there used to be, and they moved away over the years."

"The pond would still be here, though," I added.

"You're right, but maybe we're looking at this the wrong way. Instead of trying to find the man, maybe we should just try to find the pond, like on a map."

"Or on the Internet," I added as my eyes caught Jill's with a quick glance. "Would your mother let us use her computer?"

"Sure, she would," Jill said. "That's a great idea, Timber!"

We made our way back through town to Jill's house. As we headed up the stairs of the front porch her mother rounded the corner of their home.

"Hello kids," she said in her usual cheery voice.

Jill's mother was tall and had long blond hair that was tucked under a wide-brimmed hat. She was wearing flowered gloves and holding gardening tools out in front of her. There was a smudge of dirt on her nose that seemed to match the one on her wrist.

"Hi Mom," Jill answered.

"What have you been up to?" she asked.

"Oh, not much." Jill said. "We were wondering if we could use your computer to look up something on the Internet."

"Sure, you can, and help yourselves to the leftover pizza that Robby ordered for him and Ray. They're getting ready to go camping for a few days up at Stockton Lake."

It felt good to be out of the sun as we sat down in front of the computer in Jill's living room. The pizza tasted delicious. I watched as Jill typed away on the computer.

"Look at this," she said, stopping to take a bite of pizza. "There aren't rivers or lakes around Springfield."

The screen showed a perfect map of Missouri. Springfield was in the lower, left-hand side of the state. There were bright blue lakes and squiggly lines all over the map except for around Springfield.

"What?" I said in disbelief. "How can that be? We just crossed a little stream earlier today when we ran over that one bridge. That had to have come from someplace."

Jill touched the screen with the tip of her finger following the only blue line going past the lower side of Springfield. "Look," she said as her finger moved up the map, "I think that comes from the Pomme de Terre Lake, clear up past Louisburg."

"I can't believe there are no small lakes anywhere around here." I said, discouraged. "How are we ever going to put the 'golden eye' in the tree at Mr. Seller's pond, if there isn't a man by that name or a pond?"

Just then Robby and their cousin Ray came crashing through the doorway, dumping sleeping bags, backpacks, and two coolers on the floor. Robby was tall and had a head full of natural brown curls and big brown eyes. He was usually kind to me but often ended up teasing both me and Jill.

I looked at Ray and remembered meeting him once at a school ball game. Jill told me that he sometimes visited from Chesapeake, a small town about ten miles west of here.

"So, what are you two up to?" Robby asked.

"Have you ever heard of a pond that is around Springfield?" Jill asked in frustration.

Robby put his hand on Jill's head and ruffled her hair into a crazy mess, ignoring her question. "So, I see you've been eating our pizza?" he said.

Jill tilted her head to the side and glared at Robby, her thick blond hair sticking out all over the place.

"Okay," Robby said as his expression changed to a more serious one. "You want to know about a pond?"

"Yeah," Jill said, smoothing her hair back over her head.

"Why? Do you want to go swimming?"

"It doesn't matter, Robby," Jill said. She was obviously annoyed. "I just wondered if you have ever heard about one."

"Nope!" he said.

"Just don't go looking around the outskirts of town," Ray blurted out.

Jill and I looked directly at him.

"Especially *north* of town," he warned. "You've heard about that old man that lives in some caves out that way, haven't you?"

"Yeah, but I thought that was just some kind of story," Jill said.

"It's real!" Ray exclaimed. "My parents told me I could come to Springfield and visit you guys anytime. But they always warn me to stay here at the house and not wander off, and if I go anywhere else, I need to check with them first." Ray's eyes were big and intensely serious as he continued, "The man who lives out there is extremely dangerous! Years ago, there was a boy that went out there and never came back. At least, that's what my Grandpa told my parents. They think the man out there killed him. No one has been able to prove it, but everyone thinks it's true."

"Hey," Robby piped up. "Maybe we ought to get my twenty-two and go hunt him down."

Ray's face went white as a sheet. "You'll never catch me out that way. Rumor has it that the old man took the boy and skinned him alive. All they found were his socks and shoes and his bike. They say there was blood all over the trees."

"When did this happen?" I asked. My voice quivered slightly. "I've never heard those details."

"It was when my Grandpa was a boy," Ray said. "He told me it was in all the newspapers."

Jill reached over and turned off the computer. "Well, we are *not* going out there," she said.

"Who told you about the pond?" Robby asked.

"Oh...well, a friend of ours," I said, not wanting to divulge any more details. *Besides*, I thought to myself, *what*

*would they think if I told them my dead Grandmother left me
a note, or that a senile old lady whispered it in my ear?*

Robby shrugged. "Why don't you just go ask your
friend where it is?"

I looked at my watch, then up at Jill. "That's not a
bad idea."

"Yeah," Jill agreed.

We grabbed our things and headed for the old
folk's home.

"Do you believe what Ray was talking about?" I
asked Jill.

"Well, I've heard that story off and on. But I didn't
know the boy was murdered and that blood was in the
trees. That's really creepy."

"Yeah," I said. "Grandma lived in Springfield her
whole life, but she never said anything to me about
that."

"Anyways," I sighed, "we need to just ask Zelly if
she will tell us where Mr. Seller's pond is."

"That's all we can do." Jill agreed.

Jill and I noticed the old folk's home at the same
time. People were coming in and out of the building
and others were planting in the flower beds out front.

"This place is always busy," Jill observed.

"Timber!" A familiar voice yelled from the parking lot.

I turned and saw Uncle Martin getting out of his
orange, rusted pickup. There was a refrigerator and
stove propped up in the bed of the truck with blue
straps securely tied to the sides.

"Hey, you!" I hollered. Jill and I ran across the street to meet him. "So, what are you doing back in town?"

He put his arm around me to give me a hug and nodded to Jill. "I had to show Catherine's house to a couple that really want to buy it."

My heart dropped. "Really?" I asked dejectedly.

"And since your mother had to work today, I came down to show it to them," Uncle Martin continued, not noticing my disappointment. "Oh, and I also had to pick up these appliances from the house."

My mind pictured a little old couple moving into grandma's house. I felt a surge of anger and thought to myself, *they better not try to get to know me!* I already resented them for wanting to buy something that obviously did not belong to them.

Jill interrupted my thoughts. "Are you going to visit Zelly, too?" she asked Uncle Martin.

"Yes, I thought I'd just stop in really quick to say hello," he said as we walked to the front doors of the building. "I hope she's doing alright since Catharine's death and all."

"Yeah, me too," I said.

"We all have to adjust, huh, Timber?" he concluded.

The lady at the front desk motioned for us to come in as she hung up the phone in front of her. "Zelly will love to see all of you," she said with a smile. "We will be serving dinner at five-thirty, so you have plenty of time to visit."

"Thank you," Martin replied. "I'm going to stop at the restroom before I head back to Zelly's room." He held his hands out in front of him. "I need to wash up from loading those appliances in my truck."

"Okay," I said.

Jill and I walked back to Zelly's room.

"How exactly are you related to Martin?" Jill asked.

"He's my grandmother's older brother. I think he's five years older than her. When we moved here a few years ago, Martin had just had heart surgery. Grandma talked a lot about him, and I even went with her to visit him in the hospital in Manheim. He's doing really well now."

"Well, that's good," Jill said as I pushed open Zelly's heavy brown door and peeked in.

I knew the place well. The shades were drawn, giving the room a warm, yellow tone. Pictures were hung all over the walls, and a big dresser with a mirror was on the opposite side of the room from her bed. Zelly was sitting in her orange tweed rocking-chair in the corner. In front of her was her silver walker, which sat on a beautiful burgundy rug. Her head was tilted back, her eyes closed as if she were sleeping.

"Zelly?" I whispered, careful not to startle her as Jill and I came into the room.

"Timber," she replied and smiled opening her eyes. "Come on in dear. Both of you come in and sit down."

Jill and I quickly sat down on her bed. Zelly reached out and grabbed my hands. "I'm so glad you came to visit," she said in her shaky little voice.

"I hope we didn't wake you," I said.

"No, no. I was just resting and thinking about Catherine."

"I think a lot about her too, Zelly," I said.

"I miss her so much," she said. "If only I had the strength...."

"The strength?" I questioned. "Strength for what?"

Zelly leaned her head back and grabbed on tightly to the arms of the chair. Her eyes looked up toward the ceiling, almost in a daze, as she took a deep breath. "If only I had the strength to leave this place," she continued. "I would go!"

"Go where?" I asked.

"To the pond."

My heart leaped. Jill leaned forward with a shocked look on her face and my thoughts raced with excitement.

"Where *is* the pond," I blurted out. "Zelly, we want to know about it."

Zelly's head jerked forward and she looked a bit surprised.

"Grandma left me a note," I continued quickly. Zelly's eyelids abruptly shut tight. As she opened them her head shook gently back and forth.

"We just need to know where the pond is, Zelly," Jill piped up.

Zelly shook her head again and her eyebrows pulled together. She looked like she just woke up from a nightmare.

"No!" she said slowly in a harsh tone, as if she had made a huge mistake. She put her hands to the sides of her head and then repeated herself. "No! There is no pond!"

"But Zelly," I said, shaking my head. "I know about the pond."

"No, you don't!" Zelly screamed. Her face grew angry and her eyes looked dark. She stood straight up and grabbed her walker. I leaned forward to help steady her shaking body. Jill stepped forward too.

"Get out of my way girls!" Zelly yelled as she wobbled toward the door. "There is no pond! There is no pond! Now get out of my room!"

My heart started pounding like a drum.

"But Zelly," I said in a sweet tone, hoping to reel her in.

She looked wild with anger— a look I had never seen on her face before. Jill stood frozen in the corner of the room. Shock had obviously overtaken her, which was something else I had never seen before.

"No. No!" Zelly continued.

"Okay Zelly, we'll leave," I said as I motioned to Jill. "I'm so sorry."

Zelly grabbed the handle of the door and yelled while she opened it, "Nurse! Someone! Get these girls out of here!"

My body went cold as I grabbed Jill and pulled her past Zelly. Martin was just about to enter the room and stopped with a surprised look on his face. I could feel the tears welling up in my eyes. I had hurt the one person that kept me most connected to my Grandmother.

"What's going on here?" Martin asked.

"Get those girls out of here!" Zelly yelled again.

"Calm down, Zelly," I heard him say as I held on tight to Jill and ran all the way down the hall and out the front doors. I could feel the tears streaming down my face. I ran to the nearest bench and dropped, heavy with anguish.

"It's okay, Timber," Jill said gently as she wrapped her arm around me.

"She got so mad," I cried. My mind would not stop racing. I wiped my tears and pulled my knees up to my chest. "There are so many questions. Who is Mr. Seller anyways? Is there really a stupid pond? Why wouldn't she just tell us? She got mad at me!"

"I don't know, Timber," Jill said, knitting her eyebrows together. "That was really weird!"

"Timber," Martin said as he walked toward us. "Are you okay, honey?"

"Yes," I responded as I took a deep breath and wiped the tears from my face.

"What happened back there?"

"We just started talking about her grandmother," Jill said.

I knew Jill was trying to cover for us and was not going to tell Martin the whole truth. But I felt like he should know some of the details.

"We *did* start talking about Grandma," I said. "But we asked her about a few other things that seemed to really upset her."

Martin put his hand on my shoulder and said, "Timber, don't take this too personally. Zelly and Catherine have been friends since they were just kids. Catherine's death might be harder on her than any of us really know, and she is not in the best of health. She might even think more about Catherine when she sees you, since you two always came here together."

"Well, we did say some other things…" I repeated.

"Like what?" he said.

"Grandma left me a note about Mr. Seller's Pond," I said as I glanced at Jill. "And we just asked her where it was."

"That upset her?" Martin asked.

"Yeah," I said.

"Well, that is strange," he shrugged. "I don't know anything about Mr. Seller's Pond. But I do know that some people have a really hard time dealing with life after someone close to them has died. Give Zelly some time."

He paused a moment then said, "I'm going over to the drugstore to talk to your mom. Do you want to come?"

"Sure," Jill and I said together.

"The nurses are settling Zelly down, and I told them I'd be back after a bit," Martin said as we walked to his rusty old truck.

Jill and I went around the other side and I pulled up the handle of the door. I noticed the dirty floor as I climbed in and the smell of dust and old vinyl. I scooted over for Jill to climb in beside me.

"Sorry about how dirty it is in here," Martin said as he turned the key and revved the sputtering engine. "I use this old gal whenever I need to haul things around."

I looked down in search of a seatbelt but couldn't find one.

"Yeah, she doesn't have any seatbelts either. I know it's not too safe. But I always say if it is your time to go, then it's your time to go. Kind of like Catherine I guess," he said as he drove us out of the parking lot, resting his hands on the biggest steering wheel I had ever seen.

"That's okay," I said wiping some dust off the side of my leg.

"Mr. Seller," he said slowly, shaking his head. "Now where have I heard that before?"

I turned to look at Martin. "You *have* heard that name?"

"I remember now," he said, snapping his fingers. With a chuckle he continued, "Remember I told you about how Catherine and Zelly have known each other since they were little?"

"Yes," I said.

"Years ago, our families used to go to a farmers market and pick up fresh fruits and vegetables about every two weeks or so. The girls loved red raspberries that they used to grow here in Missouri. Mom would buy those first so Catherine and Zelly would stay occupied with something. That would allow mom time to pick the items that she needed."

Martin tilted his head to the side thoughtfully, as if he were remembering pleasant days from the past.

Jill and I froze stiff with anticipation.

He continued, "I can still see those two girls sitting up high in the trees, their cheeks stained from the raspberries."

Jill and I laughed.

"One time when we went to the farmers market, the girls were so anxious to buy their raspberries that we found them standing behind the counter next to the man selling the produce. They both had one hand full of raspberries and the other hand tugging on the man's shirt."

Martin couldn't contain himself and started to laugh.

"What was it?" I asked.

"They were so cute. All they could say was '*Mr. Seller, Mr. Seller.*'"

My mouth dropped open and I felt Jill's cold hand grab my arm.

"From that time on, our families called the farmers market 'Mr. Seller's Market.' Yeah, those were some good ol' days back then." He turned to me and continued, "So, Timber, I guess I have heard of a *Mr. Seller* after all."

"Yeah," I heard myself say distantly. I felt numb. *This had to be the Mr. Seller, grandma and Zelly were talking about!*

"It's just that the man's name wasn't Mr. Seller," Martin said, chuckling to himself. "He was simply the guy selling produce at the market."

Jill leaned forward and asked, "Where was that farmers market?"

"Oh, it was out north of town on Bellen Road. Those silly girls," Martin said, shaking his head as he parked the truck in front of the drug store.

I felt a chill run down my spine. *North of town? Bellen Road? It couldn't be!* My heart dropped as I remembered the story of the old man and the boy who disappeared. Jill's fingers gripped tighter around my arm.

Jill and I stared through the dirty windshield, paralyzed like two mummies in an ancient tomb.

CHAPTER FIVE

SIR LANCELOT

"Hey girls," Martin said for what must have been the third time, tapping on the window. "Aren't you getting out?"

Fear had a funny way of gripping my thoughts. I somehow felt caught in a slow-motion dream. I realized Jill and I were both trying to sort through the facts that had just been laid out in front of us. Neither of us wanted to step one foot out north of town, but that option was something we now had to consider.

Martin tapped on the window next to Jill. "Girls?"

"Oh, yeah," Jill said and opened the door. We both climbed out of the truck.

Mom was standing in front of Mr. Walter's Drug Store. She was holding the screen door in one hand and a broom in the other.

"Come on in," she said cheerfully. "Good, you're all here."

"Yes," Martin said. "I found the girls when I stopped in to visit Zelly."

"Well, good," Mom said as she reached to put her arm around me. "I'm glad to see you. How's your day been?"

"Good," I said absentmindedly, trying to focus on reality again.

"Are you hungry?"

"Not really," I said, shaking my head and looking at Jill.

"Yeah, we just had some pizza a little bit ago," Jill added.

"How 'bout a soda then?" Mom said, as she stepped around the counter and held up the tall, ribbed glass that Italian sodas were put in.

"That sounds great," Jill responded, sliding into one of the chairs.

"I guess I'll have a cherry one."

"And I'll take a strawberry," Jill added.

I joined Jill and sat on a leather stool at the edge of the counter. We both spun around a few times and giggled.

"So, do you want one too, Martin?" Mom asked.

"No thank you," he said. "But I will take a glass of water."

Mom gingerly filled a glass of water and passed it to Martin, then continued making our sodas. "So, how did the appointment go?" she asked eagerly, looking at Martin.

"You're not going to believe it, Mary," he said. "I showed them the whole house and the yard. They want to buy it."

"Grandma's house?" I interrupted.

"Yes, Timber," Martin said.

"That's great," Mom exclaimed as if she didn't hear me. "Did you tell them how much we're asking for it?"

"I did, and they said that would be fine."

Mom stopped for a second. "Just like that?" Her hand was holding the whip cream bottle upside-down in the air. "They didn't even challenge the price?"

"Nope," Martin said and shook his head like he couldn't believe it either. Mother sprayed a cone shape of cream on the Italian soda. "Mary, they said they've wanted to live in a small town for a long time now, and they *loved* the old home. They said when they drove up to the house, they couldn't believe how beautiful the street was with the old trees that reached up and over the road. They felt like they knew *instantly* that the home was for them."

With every word Martin spoke I felt more and more anger bottle up inside of me. I didn't want some old couple living in my Grandma's home. Those trees over the street were *my* trees. I suddenly felt invaded.

"But why, mom?" I blurted out.

Moms' cheerful face dropped as she looked straight at me. "Honey, I told you before, we have to sell Grandma's house. There is no other way around this."

"I know," I said grudgingly. "It's just... she's not even been gone very long."

Mom put a cherry on top of our sodas and set them both in front of Jill and me. "Timber, it would be a miracle if we could actually sell the home to the first people to look at it." She gave us each a straw.

"Well," Martin said. "The amazing thing is his company has already moved them here from Wichita.

They are staying in a motel until they can find a place. And Mary, they want to pay cash for it."

"What?" Mom exclaimed. Her eyes grew wide.

Jill and I stopped sucking from our straws at the same time and looked at Martin.

"Great, they're rich too!" I mumbled sarcastically under my breath.

"It's true. I have already talked to the bank. In fact, I told them they could go ahead and move in since they were staying in the motel. I figured it would be okay while we wait for all the paperwork to get done. Mary, I hope you didn't mind me making that decision?"

"Heavens no!" Mom said as she squealed with delight and ran around the counter to give Martin a hug.

When it comes to money matters, my mom worries like a wild horse. For years, she has supported us three kids by herself, always anxious about our clothes and having enough food to eat. My dad never paid a drop of child-support. One thing was for sure: out of her concerns, she has grown to be the hardest working woman I have ever known. I realized how deeply troubled she must have been about Grandma's home.

"Girls," she said as she took Martin's arm. "We'll be in the back for a little bit."

"Okay," Jill and I said as we watched them walk to the back of the store.

I leaned over almost bumping Jill's head. "What are we going to do?" I whispered. She knew exactly what I was asking about, and it was not about the couple moving into Grandma's home.

"Well, first of all, I think it is fair to say that the Mr. Seller we've been looking for is the one from the farmers market," Jill said eagerly.

"That would mean there isn't a *real* person with the last name of Seller," I said.

"It makes perfect sense, Timber," Jill continued. "Catherine and Zelly must have stumbled upon the tree when they were eating the raspberries, and the pond must be out there, too."

"Yeah. That's probably what happened, but out north of town on *Bellen Road*?" I moaned.

"I know, I hate that," Jill said. "The pond wasn't on the map out that way either."

"Maybe it isn't big enough to be put on a map?"

"Maybe," Jill nodded as her eyes grew wide. "Didn't Zelly tell you to put the golden eye in the *tree* at Mr. Sellers' pond?"

"Yeah," I said.

"Well, maybe the tree is still there," Jill concluded.

"But Grandma's note said she wanted to tell me about Mr. Seller's pond."

"That's true," Jill said, pausing for a moment. "Well, even though we don't want to, I think if we went out there and looked around, maybe we could find some clues that could piece this all together."

I flinched as I heard Jill say those words and whispered softly, "But Jill, I really don't want to go out there. Those stories...they scare me."

"I know," she said. "Me too." Jill had a look of alarm in her eyes. "But you need to ask yourself, is it worth it to find out what this is all about? Do you *really* want to know what Grandma Catherine wanted *you* to know about?"

I stirred my Italian soda with my straw. "It is worth it," I said. "And I do want to know!"

"Well," Jill shrugged. "Then let's go tomorrow!"

We both took a deep breath.

"We can get our bikes, pack a lunch, and make a day of it," Jill said, trying to sound optimistic. "Besides, one thing I did hear was that nobody has seen that old bum for an awfully long time. He's probably dead, Timber."

"That would be a good thing," I said. "But I'm going to take Mom's pepper spray, just in case."

"Jill," Mom's voice came from the back of the store. Jill and I swung around on our stools. "Your mother just called and said she wants you home soon. She said something about cooking dinner and that she wants you to do your chores."

"Okay," Jill said with a hint of disappointment in her voice.

"Timber, you should probably go home, too. I would love to have that living room picked up. And did you put away all of those sleeping bags from the other night?"

"No, they're still on the back porch," I said.

Martin joined in, "I'm heading back over to check on Zelly. If you two want a ride, I'll drop you off at your house first."

"Sure," I said. Jill and I stood up and headed for the door.

"I'll be home around eleven tonight, Timmy."

"Okay, Mom," I said.

"Thank you for the soda," Jill said politely.

"Oh sure," Mom responded as she held the front door open wide.

"And Mom, Jill and I want to go on a bike ride tomorrow, if that's okay?"

"That's fine, just let me know where you'll be going."

I could almost read Jill's thoughts as I saw her glance at me. If mother only knew. We ran and jumped into Martin's old truck.

"Goodbye, Mary," Martin called out.

"Tell Aunt Nell I love her," she called back, waving.

"Sure thing," he said as he fired up the engine.

Martin drove slowly through the streets back toward my house. He talked about his old truck and the beautiful weather we had been having in Springfield. Jill said a few things now and then, but Martin did most of the talking. He seemed happy just to have someone to talk to. I listened but found it hard to pay attention. I was thinking about to-morrow. *Would we be able to find a special tree?* Trees are packed everywhere here in Springfield. *Would we run into the man who killed that boy?* I shivered at the thought.

"Are you okay, Timber?" Martin said as he pulled up to my house.

"Yeah, I'm fine. I just felt a little chill, that's all."

Jill opened the door. "I'll just walk from here," she said jumping out of the truck.

"Are you sure?"

"Her house is just down the street," I said, pointing straight ahead.

"Hey, Martin?" Jill asked, "Do you remember how far that farmers market was out on Bellen Road, the one you were telling us about earlier?"

Martin rubbed his chin, recalling our earlier conversation. "Well, there isn't a market out there now. If I remember correctly, they closed that one down because of some accident."

I felt a lump swell up in my throat. Jill looked pale as she held open the door of the truck.

"I think it was about three miles or so out that way," he finally said. "Why? Are you two thinking about going out there?"

"No," Jill said, shrugging her shoulders. "I was just wondering."

Martin seemed to accept Jill's response. "Well, okay then," he said. "I guess I best get going. You girls have a wonderful evening. Timber, you will have to tell me how you like your new neighbors. They'll probably be moving some of their things in today."

The lump in my throat felt like it became a rock and sunk to the bottom of my stomach. "I don't know if I'll be getting to know them too soon, Martin," I said.

"Oh Timber, give them a chance. You know, they're about your mom's age, and they have a son that's around your age."

"What?" Jill and I said at the same time.

"I thought they were some *old* couple."

"Well, that depends on your definition of old," Martin laughed.

"They have a son?" Jill asked.

"Yes, he's fourteen or fifteen. I forget exactly."

"Really?" I said.

"Their name is Connelly—Dave and Maria Connelly. I'm not sure about their boy's name."

Jill and I stood on the edge of the street as we watched Martin drive away.

I noticed the sun was starting to set, and I thought of the times Grandma and I would sit on our porch swing about this time of day.

"Well, Timber, I should go on home," Jill said.

"Come over in the morning about eight and we'll get started, okay?"

"Alright!" Jill said as she hurried off down the street.

When I entered the house, I noticed the living room was a disaster, just like mom said. Maybe I would clean every room just to surprise her. It was so quiet without Kate and Ryan here, so I turned on the radio and got to work.

***

"There," I said finally, as if someone was standing next to me in the kitchen. "The house is spotless, and mom is going to love it!"

As I put a frozen dinner in the microwave, I faintly heard a noise coming from Grandma's house. I ran to the piano room. It was dark outside, so I left the light off and I made my way to the window. Carefully, trying not to be seen, I peered through the curtains. I saw a large man handing a bag to a woman with long dark hair. She looked Hispanic, but I couldn't quite tell in the lowlight of the evening.

Then I saw another tall figure on the other side of the car. His hair looked kind of long, and I saw him swing his head back as if to get his hair out of his face. He was carrying in some large suitcases, making it hard to get a good look at him. I waited. The lights were on and I could see Grandma's curtains shining like they always did when she was home. But now, there was no movement in the house.

After I ate supper, I remembered the sleeping bags on the back porch. "There's always one more thing," I sighed as I yawned and leaned back in my chair.

I rinsed my dishes and stepped out onto the back porch, turning the outside light on. There they were: four rumpled sleeping bags, pillows, and a few blankets. *Oh brother,* I thought to myself. *I should have had Kate and Ryan clean this mess up before they left.* Mother always had to have the sleeping bags neatly rolled up and rolling them up was my least favorite thing to do. Besides, I could never seem to roll them up the right way.

I dragged the bags out to the lawn and zipped the first one up then folded it over once. I started rolling it as tight as I could, but when I got to the end, my weight shifted. Somehow, the part that I had already rolled up squished out from inside.

"Oh my gosh," I mumbled.

I tried again. This time I balanced myself exactly on top of the rolled sleeping bag, but I couldn't find the strings to tie the bag with. I looked under one side and then the other. To my surprise, I completely lost my balance. My face landed flat in the grass as the sleeping bag unrolled beside me. Loud laughter burst from the other side of Grandma's fence and to my horror I realized I was not alone.

There I was, looking up from the grass at the most gorgeous boy I had ever seen. He had loose, brown hair and big brown eyes. His face was square, and his skin was a beautiful light, honey-brown color.

"What are you laughing at?" I said, trying to roll off my arms so I could sit up.

"Sorry," he said laughing a little more. "But that was just the funniest thing I have ever seen."

"I hate rolling up sleeping bags," I complained. "I can never seem to do it."

"Would you like some help?" he said, dangling his arms over the fence.

My heart jumped out of my chest. *Would I ever!*

"Sure," I said calmly, hoping my voice didn't betray my pounding heart.

He gracefully hopped over the fence and walked over to me. He was tall and skinny, yet with broad shoulders. I couldn't believe how good-looking he was. I had to consciously shut my jaw as I noticed it was hanging open. I hoped he didn't see that.

"Here," he said with a slight smile on his face. "I'll roll it up and you can tie, okay?"

"Okay," I said.

He began rolling the sleeping bags perfectly tight. His straight brown hair hung in his eyes. *Focus Timber,* I said to myself as I quickly found the strings and tied them.

"So, I guess you're my new neighbor," he said in a deep voice.

I nodded. I was so nervous I couldn't seem to concentrate.

He flipped his hair out of his eyes, stopped what he was doing and said, "So, do you have a name?"

"Oh, sure," I said. "My name is Timber."

"Timber? That's cool!" he exclaimed. "Now, how did you ever get a name like that?"

I felt my face flush and was glad it was dark outside. "My Grandmother named me that," I said.

"Hum," he grunted as he looked directly at my face.

I continued, "When I was born, I guess I spent two days in the hospital without a name. Mom couldn't decide."

"With those big blue eyes, how could she *not* think of a name?"

I felt my jaw slightly drop again. I noticed his face turn a soft pink as he looked away.

"Uh, thanks," I responded. "When my Grandmother got to the hospital, she begged my mom to name me Timber. I guess she liked it. She told me it was one of her favorite names. So, what's your name?"

"I'm Tyler," he said.

We both sat back on the grass.

"There's nothing real special about my name. My parents had it picked out before they even got married," he laughed as he leaned his body forward and put his elbows on his knees. "My friends just call me Ty."

He smiled a half smile and looked up at me.

"Well then, I'll have to call you Ty, too!" I said, wondering if I should have jumped so quickly into 'friendship.'

"That's great!" he agreed eagerly.

"Just promise me you won't call me what my mother calls me."

"What's that?" he asked. His beautiful eyes stared right at me.

"Timmy," I said with a hint of resentment.

Tyler burst out laughing as he tilted his head back to the night sky. I quickly questioned my decision to give out that much information. He stopped suddenly, however, when he saw my lips puckered shut and my head tilted to the side.

"Okay," he said, muffling a laugh. He took his index finger and gently tapped my nose. "I promise to just call you Timber."

"Thanks," I said anxiously.

His voice grew deep and serious. "So, Timber how old are you?"

My heart skipped a beat. He looked so much older than fourteen. How could Martin have ever been right? I wanted to lie, but I knew I couldn't. "I just barely turned fourteen," I said sheepishly. "How about you?"

"Well, I turned fifteen about three months ago," he said as the corner of his mouth curved up into a little smile.

I nodded. *Only a year apart,* I thought. *That's perfect!*

"So, I heard our house belonged to your Grandma?"

"Yeah," I said looking down at the grass.

"So how long ago did she move out?"

"Well, she didn't move. She died about three weeks ago," I said in almost a whisper. I realized this was the first time I had said those words without straining to hold back tears.

"Oh man, I'm sorry," he looked as if he was deep in thought, then asked hesitantly, "Did she die in the house?"

"No," I said. "She had a heart attack when we were at the park. My mother rushed her to the hospital. She died there. She was just fifty-five years old." My voice began to crack. "We were best friends."

Tyler's eyes grew deeply sympathetic. "Man, she wasn't that old. That must be hard," he said as he looked down. We both sat in silence for a minute before he continued. "My cousin was killed in a plane crash two years ago. We were best friends, too. It is kind of hard for me to talk about. It's taken me a long time to get over," he said. "I guess no one ever really gets over it though. We just have to learn to keep living."

"And make new friends," I said, trying to lighten the mood as I nudged his side playfully.

He smiled the cutest grin. "Yeah," he said.

"Well, I better get these things put away."

"I should probably go. I have a lot of unpacking to do," he said begrudgingly.

I watched him jump over the fence. I felt a twinge of sadness fall over me.

"Well, I guess I'll see you later," he said, looking back at me.

"Sure," I agreed.

Later that night, I couldn't sleep. My mind was racing. I had to be the luckiest person in the whole world to have a neighbor like that! I think Grandma would have even approved. *Tyler is so cute! Jill is going to die when she sees him,* I thought. I almost didn't want her to see him—she would instantly be in love, and the thought made me jealous.

What was I thinking? A guy that cute must have a girlfriend. *But he was nice to me and seemed like he wanted to be my friend,* I reminded myself. He even commented on my blue eyes. *What if he kind of likes me?* I allowed myself to entertain the thought for a moment.

Then I remembered tomorrow. Jill and I had a busy day ahead of us. I would be my own version of Sherlock Holmes with my dependable side-kick Watson, Jill of course. We are about to embark upon another stage of our mystery and summer adventure. *At the break of dawn,* I thought, *we will brave the vast forest, find our special tree that will unlock the secrets of the universe, and do it all while dodging a dark and dreadful killer.* I laughed to myself. *Oh yeah, and Sir Lancelot will stand on grandma's porch waiting for our safe return.*

My mind drifted off to sleep as I thought I heard mom's car pull into the driveway.

CHAPTER SIX

GREEN GLOWING EYES

The sound of a loud truck and voices in the distance woke me up. It had to be early. I wrestled with the thought of opening my eyes. The diesel engine was relentless—backing up, pulling forward, gears grinding. *Oh my gosh*, I thought to myself. *Where am I, in a gravel pit? Or am I dreaming?*

Slowly, I opened my eyes to the fresh sensation of morning sun filtering in through my window. I took a deep breath and stretched long and hard. I realized the sounds were coming from right out front. I flung my covers off and dashed to the window.

There in Grandmas' driveway was a large white and orange U-Haul truck with a bright blue whale on the side. I could see clearly a short Hispanic woman standing on Grandma's porch waving to the driver of the truck. The motor shut off, and finally there was silence again. The woman ran up to the front of the truck, and I watched a tall white man step out. He put his arm around the woman, and they both looked at Grandma's house and smiled with gratitude as they walked toward it. My eyes searched the rest of the scene before me. I wanted to see Tyler again, just to make sure he was real. Those had to be his parents. That would explain his beautiful Olive skin tone and height. But scanning the area was to no avail.

I decided to get dressed, quickly throwing on a pink t-shirt and blue Jean shorts. I noticed the clock and laughed at how, for once, I was up *before* Jill came to pry me out of bed. It was 7:30 A.M. I flipped the hollow beads out of the doorway and headed downstairs.

Then I remembered the golden needle. *I should put it in my pocket*, I thought. *Just in case we might need it.* Running back, I flipped the beads again, keeping the hollow sounds resonating around my room. I opened Grandmas' sewing basket and unlocked the secret compartment. Carefully, I retrieved the golden needle, still safely wrapped in the silky material it came in.

I ran downstairs and headed to the bathroom where I quickly washed my face and put mascara on. I wanted to look *exactly right* just in case I ran into Tyler.

"Timmy, is that you?" Mom's voice came from the other side of the door.

"Yes, Mom, who else would it be?"

"Well, I know honey, I'm just glad you're up," Mom said as I opened the door. "Wow, you're looking as beautiful as ever."

"Mom," I moaned, rolling my eyes—though secretly, I was grateful for the compliment.

"Timmy, you have to meet the neighbors," Mom grabbed my arm with excitement and practically dragged me out the front door. "They are so wonderful!"

Mom waved from the porch. "Maria! Dave!" she hollered. Obviously, she had already met them, and I began to feel a little embarrassed at her eagerness to introduce me. The woman came walking over with a stack of folded blankets in her arms. She had a round, attractive face with huge brown eyes. Her smile was pleasant, and her thick brown hair hung over her shoulders. The tall man, who was rolling a dolly carrying a desk down the truck's ramp, stopped, and walked over to us. He had light brown hair and thick glasses that sat upon a rather large nose.

"Hello," they both said.

"Hi!" I responded politely.

"This is my daughter, Timber," Mom bragged. "She's my oldest. She just turned fourteen."

Maria's eyes resembled someone I had already met, and they captivated me just the same. She said, "Well, you are a very beautiful young lady."

"Thank you," I said, blushing.

She reached her hand out for mine. "I'm Maria Connelly, and this is my husband, Dave."

I quickly shook her hand.

Dave smiled at me.

"Nice to meet you, Timber," he said. "We will have to introduce you to our son. You two are almost the same age."

My heart leaped with excitement.

"Tyler!" he yelled, then turned to me and said, "He's still in the truck."

Tyler walked down the ramp carrying an open box. He was as perfect as I remembered. My heart leaped as I saw him glance my way and smile. I noticed my legs were weak, like I would suddenly drop to my knees. I smiled back.

"Good morning," he said. His voice sounded to me like rushing water spilling over a majestic waterfall.

"Hi!" I said and smiled again, internally laughing at my crazy thoughts.

"This is our son, Tyler, who turned fifteen a few months ago," Dave said, stretching his arms toward his son. His dad somehow reminded me of a lady from the Price is Right, presenting the prize.

Tyler looked right at me and asked, "Did you sleep good last night?"

His mom looked puzzled. "Have you two already met?"

"Yeah, mom," Tyler admitted. "I met Timber last night when she was rolling up some sleeping bags in their backyard."

"*Trying* to roll them up!" I said sarcastically. We both laughed at our inside joke.

"You must like science?" Mom asked Tyler. It was hard not to notice the box that Tyler was carrying. There were all kinds of tools and a large expensive microscope sticking out the top.

"Tyler loves science," his father said proudly. "He got second place at the Regional Science Fair last year in Kansas City for his study of rocks and minerals."

"It wasn't that big of a deal, Dad," Tyler moaned. I could tell he was embarrassed about his dad's bragging about him. Tyler rolled his beautiful brown eyes and looked right at me.

"Oh, don't let him fool you," Maria joined in. "He won over a thousand dollars for getting second place. It was a pretty prestigious event!"

"Wow," I said.

"It's not a big deal—really," Tyler shrugged, trying to tone down the situation. "I just like geology. You know, like, land formations and rocks. Things like that. I displayed some interesting rocks from my collection and just happened to win at the Science Fair."

"That is really neat, Tyler," Mom said.

I couldn't believe it! Tyler is good-looking and *smart! How perfect can a person be?*

Suddenly, out of the corner of my eye, I saw Jill riding her bike up the street. My heart sank. There she was, the perfect green-eyed blonde bombshell, ready to steal my new prince charming right out from under me. I watched Tyler's every move.

"Jill!" Mom yelled cheerfully. Jill rode right up to the porch and smiled as she got off her bike. "I'd like to introduce you to our new neighbors. This is Maria, Dave, and their son, Tyler."

"Nice to meet you," she said, fixing her eyes right on Tyler. I knew exactly what she was thinking. He smiled and quickly looked at me. His look melted my concerns away, as if he knew exactly what I was thinking.

"These girls are best friends," Mom said, putting her arm around Jill. "So, you'll probably see a lot of Jill around here."

"Well, nice to meet you Jill," Maria said.

Mom looked at her watch. "I'm sorry to break this up but I have to go into work a little early. It's inventory day."

"Oh. Where do you work, Mary?" Maria asked.

"I work at Mr. Walter's Drug Store. It's downtown on Main Street. We have the best prices, so if you ever need a prescription filled, come on in." Mom sounded like she had perfectly rehearsed a commercial. "We also have an old-fashioned little deli where we make sandwiches and have drinks and sodas of all kinds."

"That sounds fun," Dave said pushing his glasses up on his nose, "We'll have to stop in."

Mom continued, "I wish I could help you unload the truck."

"Oh, that's okay," Maria said grabbing hold of Tyler's arm. "That's what these big muscles are for," she laughed. Tyler blushed.

I noticed that Jill had not stopped staring at Tyler.

"Maybe Timber and Jill could help?" Mom suggested.

Jill's eyes finally broke free and glanced at me. "Ah, well, ah... we were going to go on a...a bike ride," Jill said, stumbling over her words. I sympathized with her struggle to speak—Tyler had the same effect on me.

Tyler was looking right at me. He looked hopeful. *Does he want me to stay and help?* My heart fluttered. *He almost acts like he likes me. But that can't be right...*

"No, really," Dave said. "You girls go ahead; we'll be fine unloading this."

"Where are you going?" Tyler asked me.

"We are going out north of town," I responded almost choking on the last few words.

Tyler stepped toward me and looked in his box. "I'll show you my rock collection later, if you want to see it, Timber." It almost sounded like a question, and I took note that he only said *my* name.

"Okay."

"Maybe when you get back?"

"Sure!" I said. When Tyler spoke to me, it was as if we were the only two people standing in the front yard.

"Timber," Jill said, trying to get my attention.

"Yeah?"

"I packed a lunch. Do you want to get started?"

"Sure."

"Call me when you get back girls," Mom said.

"Okay." I picked up my bike that was leaning against the side of the porch.

"It was nice meeting you," I called out to the Connelly's.

Jill and I took off down the street. I looked back and saw Tyler standing alone on the porch holding his box of science things. I waved at him and he graciously returned the gesture.

"Wow!" Jill exclaimed. "He's gorgeous!"

"I know and keep your hands off! He's mine already!" I blurted, almost surprising myself. Still, I thought it better to lay out some ground rules while I had the opportunity.

"Oh, come on Timber," Jill whined. "You know you like Chad, and he's in love with you."

Chad? I had completely forgotten about him. "Chad and I are just friends, Jill."

"Yeah, whatever," she said sarcastically, rolling her eyes. "Not to him!"

"Hey Timber," she said, changing the subject. "I have a really good feeling about today. Did you bring the old needle?"

"Yes, I did," I replied, feeling the bump in my pocket.

Jill and I rode passed many streets in town. We stopped our bikes when we saw the sign above us that read in large, foreboding letters 'BELLEN ROAD.' Jill looked at me and started pedaling harder, as if she were racing toward a finish line. I noticed the dirt on the road was harder to peddle through, and it felt like I was going in slow motion.

The trees were thick and seemed to reach to the sky on both sides of us. I counted as we came to the end of each mile mark. We approached the third one and I grew anxious as we came upon an abandoned gas station. It felt eerie to be so far out of town with not a soul around, surrounded by thick trees that seemed to trap us in. It reminded me of a weekly show from the Twilight Zone that I saw on cable once with grandma. I let out a troubled sigh and wondered if the town would still be there when we got back. *Why did you have to think about that right now, Timber?* I asked myself.

"It feels kind of weird out here!" Jill said as we both came to a stop in front of an old abandoned gas station. A gust of wind blew dust in a swirl across the lot as a large Coke sign banged against the empty building.

"Yeah," I agreed warily.

"There's like, *no one* out here." Jill said.

"Not even a car," I added.

A loud crash came from the building. Jill and I both jumped and bolted forward on our bikes. I looked back, but nothing seemed different.

"That must have been the wind," I yelled.

Jill was in front of me. It was easier to ride in a single file along the edge of the road because the dirt was not as deep there.

"Yeah, hopefully," Jill yelled back. "Hey, look up there."

There was an opening in the trees off to the left. It looked like a place where cars might have parked. Just beyond that, the road continued up a hill.

Without warning, a tall dark figure was suddenly in front of Jill. I saw her bike swerve hard to the left, barely missing it. Somehow, she kept her bike up and moving.

Fear gripped at my chest as I realized it was a person. Frantically, I turned my handlebars, but my front wheel caught the dirt and turned sharp to the right. My bike stopped abruptly, and I crashed down on the dirt road. My hands stung with pain. It took me a second to realize what happened. I saw that Jill had stopped ahead, looking back at me. Her face was twisted with worry.

Standing directly over me was a large, hunched over man in a heavy black overcoat. He was wearing a frayed wool hat that was pulled down over his long scraggly hair. His dirty beard was twisted and gnarled in all directions, and the skin on his face looked red and weather-beaten, like leather. Deep wrinkles marked the darkened area around his eyes. A rotten smell reached me, and I couldn't breathe.

"You two get out of here!" he screamed as he pointed back the way we came. His voice was deep and scratchy. He was crazy with anger. "Do you hear me, girl?" he yelled, leaning closer to my face. As he tilted his head to the side, I saw that he had green, glowing eyes that seemed to move like a rolling boiling.

I was paralyzed with fear and wondered if this was the man that killed that boy.

"Timber!" Jill yelled. But my body would not move.

"Get up!" she screamed.

The man turned and began limping toward Jill. "Go on, get out of here! Or I'll have to force you two back the way you came!" His voice was fierce with rage.

"Look," Jill yelled, putting the palms of her hands up as if to say no. "We are meeting some friends at the end of this road—we can't go back."

I realized I was still sitting on the sandy dirt, my hands throbbing. The sound of Jill's voice made the paralyzing fear begin to dissolve, and I finally took a breath. *Did she say we can't go back? Why not? I would run with all my might if I could just stand up,* I thought to myself.

"Timber, come on!" Jill demanded in a sharp tone.

"You tell your friends to never come out here!" he said in a twisted, menacing voice. "This is *my* road!" he roared as spit flew wildly from his mouth.

I jumped on my bike and began peddling as hard as I could. I reached Jill and we headed past the clearing and started up the hill. I couldn't believe we were going past that madman and not going back toward town.

Jill stopped at the top of the hill. "Timber, are you okay?"

"Yeah, I'm fine!" I lied as I slowed down and looked behind me. The road was empty.

"I have an idea," Jill said with a twinge of excitement.

"Like what, go home?" I suggested.

"No, silly. We need to hide the bikes and work our way back through the woods to that clearing. I'm sure that's where the farmers market was, and the tree has to be around there somewhere!"

"Are you serious?" I asked in total disbelief.

"Look, Timber, do you want to find the tree or not?"

"Well, yes, but—"

"We're going to have to work on your *fear* issues," Jill said in an exasperated tone. "You can't freeze up like that when you get scared." I couldn't tell if Jill had some superhuman powers or if she was running completely on adrenalin.

"I know, Jill. If I had mom's pepper-spray, I wouldn't have even been able to use it," I said, upset that I had forgotten it. "But did you see how angry he was? He looked crazy! What if he finds us? He could kill us too, Jill."

"Well, we're just going to have to be really quiet," Jill said as she quickly moved her bike off the road, "Timber, that man scared me, too. Did you see how I almost hit him?"

"Yeah," I said, moving my bike next to Jill's.

"That was weird how he seemed to come out of no-where," Jill said, looking worried. "It's like he almost *appeared* in front of me.

"Did you see his eyes?" I asked.

"I did!" she said.

"They were green, and they glowed," I continued. "They looked like they were even bubbling."

"Yeah. Something is just not normal with that guy," Jill continued, "But, I still think we can do this. Did you see how he was limping?"

"Yeah," I nodded.

We both started grabbing branches and covering up our bicycles.

"Well, we could easily outrun him."

"You're probably right," I agreed.

Jill took off her backpack and stuffed it under the front wheel of her bike tire, rearranging the tree branches. Our bikes were hidden completely out of sight.

"Are you ready?" she asked, eager to get started.

"I guess," I said warily. "But just for the record, I don't think this is a good idea."

Jill huffed and began walking into the wooded area. I reluctantly followed as we started back-tracking down the hill. The brush was dense around our feet, but we kept moving as quickly as possible. I tried to avoid stepping on branches that might make any noise, and every now and again we stopped just to listen. The sound of birds chirped sweetly overhead, and I noticed how the sun shined down through the enormous trees that hovered over us. We kept a safe distance from the road, still able to see it, but not too close in case that man was still out there.

I felt the front pocket of my shorts. The needle was safely there. I wondered how we would ever find a special tree that this fit into. Like *finding a needle in a haystack,* I laughed to myself.

Jill stopped abruptly in front of me. She put her arm back with her fingers opened wide, as if to protect me—or stop me from moving—and leaned forward to listen. We both heard twigs breaking in the brush just a little way ahead of us. As if we read each other's minds, we crouched down at the same time and wordlessly crawled under a pile of fallen branches near us.

I could smell the musty dirt. Jill squeezed my hand tightly and held a finger up to her mouth with the other, motioning for me to be quiet. I listened, trying to ignore the noise of my pounding heart. The sound of uneven, heavy footsteps was now coming straight for us. The rotten smell once again penetrated my nose. I knew exactly who it was.

The man walked around the area like he was looking for something. Jill and I waited for what seemed to be like an hour until he slowly moved past and finally out of hearing range.

"That was a close one," Jill whispered as she moved slowly from under the brush, looking to see if he was truly gone.

When I finally stood up, my body ached with pain.

"Are you okay?" Jill asked, a concerned look on her face.

"I'll be fine," I responded, rubbing my thighs.

"Hey, look," Jill said, pointing in front of her. I followed quickly behind her as we came upon the clearing. We both sat down on an old fallen tree to catch our breath.

"Hey," I whispered, "Martin said that Zelly and Catherine used to sit in the trees and eat their raspberries." Jill looked at me and nodded. "Do you think that over the years this was how they found the golden needle?"

"Probably," Jill said, shrugging her shoulders. "Why don't we climb some of these trees and look around?"

"Sure," I agreed. "But let's do this quickly."

Jill and I began searching. We climbed the trees, one after another, and carefully examined the bark and branches. Some trees were fat and round at the base with bulges in the bark, making it easy for us to climb on. Other trees were too tall for us to even reach the first branch. Each time, we found nothing that remotely looked like a place to put a large needle. Finally, we sat down on one of the branches.

"Before we try another one, why don't you get the needle out so we can take a good look at it," Jill said.

"Yeah, that's a good idea," I agreed.

I pulled the golden cloth out of my pocket as I balanced myself on the tree branch. We both looked intently as I unfolded the material. There it was: the exquisite, ancient needle.

"It's so beautiful, and it really looks like pure gold," Jill said as we both stared in amazement.

"I know, and it's heavy," I said, lifting it up and down.

Jill placed her finger on the eye of the needle and slowly began tracing it. "This part is probably the end you would put in the tree,"

"Do you think it's like a key?" I asked.

"Maybe," she shrugged.

I looked up and started scanning the area. All the trees seemed the same to me. The sun was high in the sky, but I noticed the shadows that were cast on the ground below. One shadow was rather large, and I wondered what tree it came from. I followed it back to the base of a large tree with deep, wide-spread branches. It looked somehow familiar, but I knew we had not climbed it. I loved how the roots were so big and gnarly. Many of them were exposed from the earth.

"Wait," I whispered slowly.

"What is it?" Jill said, as she followed where my eyes were looking.

"That tree, it looks like—"

"Like the cross-stitch!" Jill blurted out with excitement.

"Yes! The roots are the same!" I squealed as I quickly shoved the needle in my pocket and followed Jill down the tree.

"It has to be!" Jill yelled.

We raced over fallen branches and thick brush. Neither one of us seemed to care at all if we made a sound in the forest. Suddenly, Jill fell hard on the ground in front of me. My feet got tangled in hers and I landed on the grass beside her.

"Whoa," I said laughing as I tried to catch myself.

"Okay, what just happened?" Jill asked.

I reached back toward our feet and pushed the brush aside. On the ground was an old tree stump that had uneven wedges over the top of it. It looked like someone used a hatchet to chop it down at least a century ago.

"The tree stump tripped us!" Jill said jokingly.

I began to laugh along with Jill as we looked up at the large, beautiful tree that stood majestically over us. I reached out and put my hands on the bark. It was old, but it felt solid and strong. We climbed over the roots and used the big knots to pull ourselves up. A large branch reached over the ground and I scooted out on it, giving Jill some room to scoot beside me. Directly in front of our heads was a thick branch with a large, raised knot. In the center was a perfect oblong circle.

"Get it out!" Jill blurted with excitement. "This has to be the spot!"

I pulled the needle out of my pocket, unwrapped it, and handed it to Jill. She waited patiently as I put the cloth back. I looked at Jill's anxious green eyes. "Well, go ahead," she said holding the needle out for me to take.

I took the needle from her hand. At the exact same time, we heard the sound of branches cracking in the distance. The excitement dropped with heaviness in my chest. I looked at Jill. Once again, I couldn't move.

"Timber," Jill whispered. "Go ahead—see if it fits!"

"But the man," I said quietly.

"We found the tree, just do it Timber!" Jill demanded.

I tried to ignore the fear. My eyes focused on the needle as I turned it on end. I looked one more time at Jill and then, with both hands, I pushed the needle into the tree. To my astonishment, the needle sunk deeper into the branch, as if pulled by the tree itself. There was a loud click and then another as the needle made a half turn, all on its own. *Jill was right—it is a key!* I realized.

The world stood still—no birds chirping, no fluttering of leaves and movement in the trees. I couldn't even hear myself breathe. We both listened intently. The air that surrounded us felt heavy and perfectly still. I noticed the leaves were brilliantly illuminated as they hung completely motionless. I moved my head to search for an answer.

Suddenly, like two freight-trains crashing into each other, the wind exploded with a roar and whirled viciously around us. I frantically grabbed the part of the tree that I was sitting on and wrapped my legs around it. Every muscle in my body was pulled tight as I held on with all my might. I saw Jill thrown to the ground and branches flung wildly around her. She was groping for something to hold onto as she slid frantically over the ground. I screamed at her but couldn't even hear my own voice. I felt my nails dig into the tree bark as I tried to hold tighter and tighter to the tree. Twigs and dirt whipped against my body, and I clenched my eyes tightly shut and ducked my head. The sound was deafening to my ears as it screamed relentlessly around me.

As quickly as it started, the wind calmed and then was gone. All was quiet again, though not as quiet as the moments before the furious wind. I gasped for air and released my muscles from their tight grip. I took another deep slow breath.

"Jill?" I called out in a scratchy voice. I sat up on the tree branch and began looking around for her.

"Jill, where are you?" I asked again.

Her muffled voice responded, "Over here."

I looked to the sound and saw her at the base of a small tree about fifteen feet away. She was holding her head with one hand and pulling twigs and debris out of her messy blond hair with the other.

"Are you okay?" I hollered.

"Yeah, I'm a little scratched up and my head kind of hurts, but I think I'm okay."

I carefully climbed down the tree and sat at the base. I pulled my knees up to my chest and covered my face with my arms. Thoughts began to flood my mind as I began to feel sick. Maybe I needed to cry—or scream! Like a young child, I suddenly yearned for my mom. *I could have died!* I realized, still in shock.

Jill's hand gently touched my shoulder. "Timber, look," Jill said in a softened, awestruck tone.

I looked up at Jill. She had scrapes all over her body, like she had been dragged on the pavement. But her big green eyes were fixed on something behind us. I slowly stood up and looked around the tree.

The forest had changed. The trees were not in the same place. A few yards in front of us were two beautiful trees that stood like sentinels on each side of a pathway that worked its way back into the forest. It looked old and worn, as if it had been used for centuries. The trees and vines were different, like we had somehow stepped into a storybook. They were overgrown and perfectly symmetrical, with delicate details of exquisite green colors that twisted up and over the pathway. Little white flowers peppered the vines, somehow reminding me of the flowers at Grandma Catherine's funeral.

Rays of light shot through the branches of the trees from the warm sun overhead. It was the most beautiful thing I had ever seen. A feeling of peace began to permeate my whole body, and I felt a sense of healing wash away the dramatic prior event. The pathway seemed to beckon for me to enter.

"Let's go," Jill whispered reverently, as if she were on hallowed ground.

I gently grabbed her arm, and we entered the opening of the beautiful pathway.

CHAPTER SEVEN

CRESHTIL PASS

Magnificent trees stood tall with huge, strong arms that reached up and over us. I held on to Jill as we moved gradually forward through the breathtaking pathway. A dome of branches and clear, enumerated leaves created a spacious ceiling that arched up high above us. Vines were laden with tiny white flowers that weaved in every direction over the canopy. Shadows flickered gently over the path, and the rays of sunlight were like pillars falling upon us as we walked forward.

The path was broad and extended approximately ten feet before it bowed to the left. After making the turn, we approached the end of the path. The opening through the archway had an overgrowth of delicate, green leaves that hung from the tree above. Jill and I reached up at the same time and gently spread the leaves aside. Directly in front of us was a beautiful, crystal-clear pond.

"Mr. Seller's pond," I gasped. This is what Grandma wanted to tell me about. And Zelly—she simply forgot how to keep this place a secret. Somehow, I felt a new connection to my grandma. She had known this place and being here made me feel closer to her.

"It is so beautiful, Jill!"

"It's magical!" she exclaimed. "The tree. The golden eye!"

"And the pathway!" I added with exuberance.

"This is amazing!" Jill said looking all around. "The trees are huge."

"Look at the water," I said in awe, my voice fading into a whisper.

Jill and I walked to the edge of the glimmering pond.

"Timber, I bet Catherine and Zelly came here and got in the water."

I smiled and inhaled a deep breath of air. "I bet they did!" my voice squealed with excitement. I could hardly contain my emotions as I quickly pulled off my shoes. "Let's just put our feet in!" I said.

"Okay!" Jill responded.

My toes felt a cool, exhilarating sensation as I placed them into the pond. The water was so refreshing.

"What *is* this?" I asked.

"It's water, but… I don't know," Jill responded. She was up to her knees already. "It's different, but it feels so good!"

I reached down and felt the water between my fingertips. It was thick yet light as it rolled off my hand. "Hey look, Jill," I said laughing, as I noticed the back of my hand. "It looks like it leaves kind of a shimmer on your skin." I tried to gently splash the water with my fingers, but it just pillowed together in heavy clumps and dropped back into the pond. I tilted my head to the side and watched the water bounce slowly up and down, as if suspended in zero gravity, and then stop without even a ripple.

"Timber," Jill said placing the palms of her hands on top of the water. "Everything is magical about this place; you can't expect the *water* to be any different."

"Right," I agreed.

"Besides, it feels so good on my skin," Jill concluded, the bottom of her shorts getting wet as she stepped further into the pond.

"It's the perfect temperature, isn't it?" I exclaimed.

"It is," Jill added, in a smooth, low voice as she waded deeper into the pond. Her head was tilted all the way back and her hair was almost touching the water behind her. Both arms were stretched out and moving back and forth in a rhythmic motion. I followed Jill and moved deeper into the silky, cool water until it was at my waist. It was soothing and exhilarating at the same time. I had a sudden urge to sink up to my neck. I closed my eyes and dropped with ease into the water, focusing on how it enveloped every inch of my skin. This felt like heaven. Relaxation took hold of my entire being.

In the distance, there was noise. It came from the pathway— a pounding, uneven sound. I used all my strength to stand up and come back from the strange, hypnotic state I was in. The water gently rolled off my skin. I noticed Jill waist-deep in the pond just ahead of me, a worried look on her face.

"Get out of the pond!" roared the scratchy, wild voice from the pathway. I knew in an instant who it was, and my heart dropped as fear, once again, gripped my chest. I took a step back in the water.

The hunched over man in the black overcoat tore his way through the leaves at the end of the pathway. He stumbled forward and tried to catch himself from stepping into the water. He moaned and roared, and shook his head wildly, throwing his arms angrily in the air. He looked more like an animal than a man. Jill and I stood stiff in the pond.

"I said get out!" he screamed. His voice was loud and violent as it pierced the serene stillness that surrounded us.

"You have to get out, and you have to get out now!" he demanded. I noticed how careful he was not to touch the water, but he ranted and raved right along the edge.

"You should have never come here!" he continued to roar.

Why not? I thought to myself. He must know about this place. Questions began to whip around in my head. *What could ever be wrong here except him?*

"Keeper?" he yelled slowly. His eyes flickered as he investigated the trees around the pond. "Where are you? I know you are here, Keeper!"

My mind was racing. *What is a Keeper? Did Grandma know this man?*

"Leave us alone!" Jill yelled. "Just, leave us alone!" Her voice sounded terrified. I couldn't speak. I knew one thing, however; I was *not* getting out of the pond!

The man stopped, eyes blazing a cold green glow under dark twisted eyebrows. His back slowly straightened up from being hunched over and his shoulders pulled back as he gradually moved his arms away from his body. His form was changing right before our eyes. He shifted from an old decrepit man to what looked like a warrior preparing for battle. His merciless gaze dropped over Jill like cold fury bathed in control. Something terrible was sure to happen.

"You, try to order *ME?*" The once peaceful pond echoed with his menacing growl. "You. Will. Get. Out!" He was screaming now, even less human than before. "Or you will die!"

Jill grabbed my arm.

"Swim!" she screamed as she lunged toward the middle of the pond and disappeared under the water.

I looked back at the man. He reached his hands over his head and pulled something long and metal from under his long black overcoat. Frantically, I began to move through the silky, velvet water. The man was now aiming directly at me, and I stared down the edge of an ancient weapon. Out of sheer panic, I took a fast breath of air and dove under the water as quickly as possible. Underwater, I heard muffled sounds of piercing darts strike the water all around me. *He was shooting at me,* I screamed to myself in disbelief.

I fought to swim down and away from the darts. My mind was racing with fear and confusion.

But then something far more terrifying became apparent. The water was gently pulling me downward. My long, brown hair began to tickle my face as it moved above me. *What is happening?* I tried to swim to the top. One arm after another, I tried pulling the water down behind me, but it was to no avail; the current was simply too strong. My body was being pulled deeper and deeper into the pond.

I fought wildly, one arm and then the other grabbing hard at the water. I opened my eyes in terror, searching for something to hold onto. Beautiful, vivid colors of blue and green were everywhere. My lungs began to ache. *I need air!* Frantically I moved my head to the left and then to the right in search of Jill. *Help me, Jill!* I screamed inside of my head. *I need to breathe! Could this really be the end? Was I was going to die in grandma's stupid pond?*

Suddenly, like watching a drive-in movie, memories began to flash through my mind. I saw my father wave goodbye from the window of the old work truck, his big blue eyes filled with tears as he drove off down the long dirt road. Then I saw Grandma Catherine sitting on my bed, holding a pillow she had made, and giggling with me at some joke we shared. Next, I saw my mother with her sweet, caring face pulling a turkey from the oven on Thanksgiving Day. The table was perfectly set. Then Kate and Ryan running through the sprinkler in the backyard. Then the casket. The tree. The pond. The colors. The tormenting pain in my chest.

I need to breathe! But no, I wouldn't let myself give in to the reflex. *Don't breathe in! No! No!* Out of sheer exhaustion, I closed my eyes and gave in. Reluctantly I drew in the thick, silky water deep into my lungs.

For a moment I hung there in the cool, rejuvenating water. A mysterious feeling filtered through my lungs and rushed through the rest of my body. I had heard that when a person drowns it feels relaxing, but I didn't think it would feel this good. I took another long inhale of the water. *Am I dead?* I wondered to myself. Every cell in my entire being felt like it was experiencing something I had never known before. It completely invigorated my whole being. Then I stopped descending in the pond.

My eyes focused on the most brilliant kaleidoscope of colors I had ever seen. I was still in the water, and whether I was dead or alive, I didn't know exactly. But I could feel the cool, silky liquid going smoothly in and out of my lungs.

The caste of colors captivated me. All shades of blue filled the water, including indigo, sapphire, and an array of turquoise. I noticed how the light that descended from above captured and illuminated each color. Below me, I saw what looked like purple and red paint splashed across the pond floor. I realized they were flowers, clustered together in vibrant bunches all around the pond. Brilliant yellows and greens of every shade covered the plants that flourished on the pond floor. The leaves were delicate and detailed. I could feel the grassy tips tickling at my feet as they swayed softly beneath me.

I saw a school of brilliant orange and yellow fish swim past. They looked as if they had been dipped in a bucket of paint. I leaned my head gently to the left and smiled as I watched their brightly tinted fins moving as quickly as they could through the thick water.

The technicolor underwater world surrounding me was surreal, vaguely reminding me of an ocean special I had watched once on television. *I can't still be in the pond, can I?* I wondered. Everywhere I looked, I saw new and wonderful things.

A beautiful purple creature glided out from behind a large rock. Its fins were huge and moved like elegant, rippling ribbons in the wind. With every movement, it changed a different shade of purple. The fish turned and looked right at me with eyes like smooth black marbles. It seemed to wave at me before it glided off along the bottom of the pond.

As I began to swim after my new purple friend, I noticed how my body felt more weightless than it did when I was on the surface. I could only barely feel the pressure of the water. I closed my eyes and enjoyed the rush of liquid that flowed over my skin and through my lungs. A strange cluster of Crimson-red fish with wide

bellies and velvet black fins swiftly darted out from behind an old log that looked like it had sunk years ago.
Just above the tips of the seaweed I saw golden, spiral
creatures that made me laugh as I watched them move
like springs, bouncing their way through the thick, silky
water.

I swam ahead and came upon brilliant orange trans-
parent bubbles that clung to a tall, swaying plant. The
orange orbs suddenly went completely flat, and then,
just as quickly, blew up again into a bubble. I reached
out to touch them and felt their thin, smooth surface.
At my touch, they flattened and then puffed up again.
I smiled as my fingertips felt a soft, tingling sensation.

There was a little hill in the distance with white coral growing up and over it. *How could that be?* I thought
coral was only in the ocean. I moved my feet quicker
and pulled the water past me as I glided toward them.
It looked exactly like coral in the ocean. Something was
quite different here in the pond. Rules from the outside
didn't seem to apply to this enchanted place.

The coral was hiding shimmering, diamond-like
rocks that had symmetrical lines on them. As I swam
near the underwater hill, the white coral expanded out-
ward a few inches and changed instantly into a brilliant
pink color. It startled me. I moved my head backward
and my long hair swirled up and around my face. I noticed brilliant red and orange colors along the edge of
the hillside and glided forward to see more closely. I

found different coral that looked like intricate, colorful snowflakes.

A large, bright-blue fish with big, bulgy black eyes swam right next to me. His eyes were outlined with yellow rings. He didn't even seem to notice me as his fins gently caressed my arm. I moved around the rocks and plants with ease, like I was somehow a part of this new world. Gentle movements, brilliant colors, and life was all around me. I felt tranquil and happy in my quiet new surroundings.

Then I saw Jill. *What?* My mind had to work hard to remember. I was so enamored by this beautiful place; I had totally forgotten about her or what even happened to us. *Yes, that was Jill!* Her beautiful hair was swaying in a gentle motion around her. *Did she drown, too?* I wondered. *Maybe we are still alive.* She smiled at me and beckoned for me to come. Jill had on a light purple shirt and blue shorts that caught the water in funny ways as they moved deliberately about her body. She kicked her feet back and forth to keep herself suspended above the floor of the pond. I swam quickly to her.

The scratches on Jill's arms and legs were gone. I tilted my head to the side, remembering the wind at the tree that almost killed us. I rubbed my arm and motioned to hers as if to question her about her scratches. She shrugged her shoulders and smiled as she reached out and took my hands. The sensation of her skin touching mine was real. *We must be alive!*

Jill gestured with her head in another direction, suggesting that she wanted to show me something. We swam hand in hand as she led me down through a small opening between some rocks. We spooked a school of long, skinny brown fish, and as they scattered away, I saw them change into a rainbow of colors. Each one took on a unique color of its own as they joined back up together and continued. Jill looked back at me in amazement. We continued to swim down and around some large boulders into the wide opening of a cave. The rock that was outlining the entry had jagged little holes in it. Another school of bright blue fish darted off from in front of us.

I noticed a broken piece of wood, half covered in the dirt, along the floor of the pond. There were letters on it. I quickly made my way down and wiped away clumps of mud. Inscribed in the wood was the word PASS. I lifted it up and showed Jill. She tilted her head as her hair swayed gently over her cheeks. She looked confused. Jill pointed to something just beside me. She quickly swam to my side and pulled out another piece of wood from the lumpy mud and held it up for us to both read. The word CRESHTIL was carved into it. It looked like a sign of some kind. Jill grabbed the flat piece of jagged wood out of my hand and placed it in front of hers. Like a puzzle, it fit perfectly together and read CRESHTIL PASS. I looked at Jill in amazement. She smiled at me and laid the sign down.

Jill tugged at my hand as she led me back into the dark cave. I could see a glimmer of light coming from the far corner of the cave. As we moved closer the light grew more and more brilliant. On the floor, like a suitcase leaning against a wall, was a large rectangular stone sitting on its side. Beams of yellow light scattered out around the edge of the stone into the dark water. I looked at Jill. We both put our fingers on opposite corners of the stone and pulled with all our might. It crashed down on the floor of the cave and clumps of dirt escaped like little clouds just around the stone. Light filled the cave instantly. Jill and I looked at the opening in the wall. It reminded me of a window with sunlight shining through.

I could see colors of green and yellow through the opening. Jill motioned for me to enter. I gently touched the soft, silky film with my fingers. Something was protecting it. I pushed gently and my hand easily went through. It was dry on the other side. It felt like air. I pulled my hand quickly back into the water and took Jill's hand and pushed it through with mine. I looked at Jill's big green eyes, as if to ask her what to do. She motioned me to go through. I held tightly to her hand, closed my eyes, and pressed my face slowly through the opening.

CHAPTER EIGHT

THE NEW KEEPER

I felt dryness upon my cheeks as I pushed my head and shoulders through the opening in the side of the cave. I tried to take a breath. Instantly, a tickle rushed through my throat, like the water was somehow being quickly dried up. I coughed twice, jerked my head back and opened my eyes. I took a deep breath of air and focused on gently pulling my arms through the opening and placing my hand down on what felt like tuffs of grass. With my other hand, I held on tightly to Jill's hand and then pulled my legs and feet through. As we pushed through the opening, I felt a gentle pressure surround my skin, like a sponge was helping to dry it off. Jill was halfway through when I heard her cough too.

Although I was wet from the water, the sun overhead warmed my body. I squinted to look at my new surroundings, allowing my eyes time to adjust to the bright light. Jill and I were sitting on a patch of short, green grass. I couldn't help but notice the strong smell of wildflowers in the air as the bright yellow sun glared from above.

Strange, tiny trees were in a half-circle around us. They were small, approximately two feet tall, and I could easily see the tops of them as they trailed off and met tiny, majestic mountains in the distance. From where I sat, I could see sharp cliffs, little waterfalls, and a valley filled with lush, green plants—a miniature world compared to the one I knew. I wasn't used to being so high above the trees—there was so much sky! —and I felt like, if I stood up my head would rest above the clouds like a giant in some unknown land.

"Where are we?" I whispered. We were still sitting, and I stretched my legs out straight in front of me, careful not to touch any of the miniature trees.

"I don't know, but at least we are alive and breathing air," Jill laughed sarcastically.

We both looked back at the same time to the opening that we just came through. It looked like a miniature, rocky hillside with tiny plants growing on it. Jill reached out and gently touched it.

"It's hard—there's no opening," she said in a worried voice.

My heart dropped as I reached back to feel the small rocks. I pushed with all my strength, and slowly my hand squeezed through the rock.

I smiled as I wiggled my fingers. "The water is in there! You just have to push hard to get to it."

"Good!" Jill agreed with a big sigh.

"The pond was so beautiful!" I said, finally being able to talk and be heard. "But I thought I had drowned back there."

"Me too," Jill said sullenly. "The water pulled me down. It was terrible, Timber. I thought I had died."

"But then I could somehow *breathe* the water!" I said.

Jill smiled and nodded in agreement.

"The colors were so beautiful!" she continued with excitement. "The plants and flowers and…"

"Did you see that purple 'fish-like' thing that swam along the bottom?" I interrupted.

"And those long brown fish that suddenly turned all different colors?"

"I know, those were beautiful!"

I smiled in wonder at what we had both seen and experienced.

"The pond is amazing!" Jill concluded.

"Yeah, it was magical!" I said as I pulled my legs up to my chest and looked around the tops of the trees in front of us. "This place looks kind of magical too, Jill."

"The mountains and trees are so small," she stated.

"I just worry about getting out of here," I said.

"We will just have to *drown* again," Jill said sarcastically. "That's all!"

We both sat quietly for a moment.

"Did you know that man back there shot darts at us," I finally said. "From some kind of bow and arrow thing?"

"What?" Jill gasped as her eyes grew bigger than I had ever seen them. "He had a weapon?"

"Yeah, just after I went under the water. I saw them above me."

"I think I was already being pulled down in the pond when that happened," Jill said. "I didn't see any of that. That old bum was trying to kill us. I can't believe it!"

"He didn't look *old* when he was aiming at me," I said. "Didn't you see him change?"

"Change?" Jill asked.

Suddenly, there was an odd fluttering sound that came from the trees just in front of us. It got louder and louder, like something was coming closer. I scooted back toward the small hillside.

To our amazement, we saw little people running out from the edge of the forest. They looked like little moving Barbie dolls—but real. They slowed down as they entered the clearing where Jill and I were sitting. There were many of them, about fifty, and they stared intently at us as they gathered around.

The people stood about twelve inches high. Their skin was white with a hint of yellow and they all had straight, shimmering golden hair. Even though they were small, I could tell they were about our same age. Maybe a few of them were a little older.

The young men's hair was shaved above their ears and pulled back into a high ponytail. Long golden capes hung over their shoulders and swayed gently behind them. They wore black boots up to the knee, and their golden pants were slightly loose and fit just under long-breasted overcoats that were ornamented with rings and clasps. A dark belt was secured at the waist over the coat. Black wristbands went around their thumbs and up to their elbows.

Their faces were handsome and rugged with a square chin, prominent cheekbones, and dark, deep-set eyes. Their shoulders were broad and somewhat muscular. Arrows in a quiver were on their backs, and each had an intricately designed bow that they held tightly in front of them. They looked like young, fierce warriors ready to fight. I realized they would have scared me to death if I was their same size.

There were just a handful of young women in the group. However, each was quite beautiful and had long, golden hair that fell loosely around their shoulders and back. They each wore headbands made of tiny, twisted strands of leaves or twigs. Their faces were beautiful with delicate features and wide, colorful eyes. Like the young men, they wore black boots up to their knees but had golden tights on with little straps secured along the outer sides of their legs. These straps held tiny darts. They each had short golden skirts that moved gently around their legs, and the sleeves from their tops were fitted all the way to their wrists. Covering the tops were short golden coats with dark belts tied along the rib cage. Wristbands also went around their thumbs and up to the elbow but were instead adorned with tiny golden leather straps and shiny buckles. Each girl had a small handheld bow in one hand. They looked just as fierce and strong as the others.

Two young men and one young woman stood out in front of the others. One of the boys looked taller and slightly older. His hair was a darker shade of gold. He had a deeply concerned look on his face and kept looking back at the tiny hillside that Jill and I just came through.

"Where's Catherine?" he demanded in a small, yet strong, voice.

Jill and I looked at each other, astonished.

"They speak," Jill whispered. "And English, too!"

"Where is Catherine?" the older boy repeated.

"Who?" I asked. The name registered in my mind, but I could not imagine my grandma knowing these little people.

The boy looked frustrated as he craned his neck to look around us. "Catherine! Where is she?" he said as he raised his hands in the air, along with his bow.

"You knew my grandmother?" I asked slowly in amazement.

The girl standing with the two young men moved forward quickly and asked, "Are you Timber?"

I gasped. "How do you know my name?"

The other young man's face lit up. "Catherine speaks about *you* all the time," he said with a smile. He was a very handsome young man and had a long braid of hair that hung down off to one side of his face. It wasn't pulled back with the rest of his hair, and it had a tiny little charm on the end of it.

"You must be Jill," he said, looking at her.

"I am," she said as she pushed her wet hair out of her eyes.

"Now tell me, where is Catherine?" The older boy asked firmly, turning back to me.

I had a sickening feeling come over me as I realized these little golden people knew my grandmother but did not know about her death. I remembered how I felt when I was first told.

Jill looked at me with her big green eyes, and whispered, "Tell them, Timber."

The group of little people waited anxiously for me to speak.

"My grandmother…is dead."

The girl instantly covered her mouth with her hand and inhaled a deep breath of air.

"No!" the older one said as he shook his head in disbelief.

The boy with the braid stepped back, almost tripping on the ground behind him. Others in the group gasped and shook their heads in disbelief. Some of them dropped to their knees.

"No! She wouldn't die!" The taller boy said as his voice began to crack behind his broken expression.

I felt the pain of her death crash upon me again like an unwanted waterfall of hot emotions.

The taller boy held his hand up to my face and pointed his finger at me.

"She would *never* let this happen!" he yelled as he looked back to the others in his group. "She was coming to... stay!" His face was torn with emotion as he stumbled backwards then stood abruptly.

"We need to get her into the pond!" he said sharply, yet full of hope. "Right now!"

"What?" I asked, looking at Jill. I felt sick and confused.

"When did this happen?" he screamed through tear-filled eyes.

I could see his pain and could not bring myself to speak another word.

"Well?" he yelled.

"About three weeks ago," Jill said slowly. "She was buried in the Springville Saltwater Graveyard."

The boy looked horrified. He shook his head in disbelief as he swiftly ran off into the small trees behind them.

"Stroder!" the girl yelled as she held out her arm and began to move toward him.

The boy with the braid gently grabbed the girl's arm. Others from the group looked bewildered and started to move back to the edge of the trees. They looked as if they didn't know what to do.

"I'm sorry," I said, tears welling up in my eyes. "But my grandmother *really is* dead."

Another boy from the group yelled to the others, "We will follow Stroder."

The boy with the braid nodded and put his arm around the girl that stood frozen beside him. She had a dazed look in her eyes as the others disappeared into the little forest.

"How did this happen?" the boy asked quietly. I could tell he was trying to hold back tears as he looked up to my face.

"She. Um. She had a sudden… heart-attack," I responded.

He looked confused.

"Her heart stopped," Jill said as she tapped her hand on her chest.

"Just like that?" he asked.

"We were all surprised," I said. "It's been very hard for me."

"It must have been," he said with a tiny yet deeply caring voice. "We know how close you and Catherine were."

"Did she come here often?" I asked.

The girl looked up at me in amazement. "She's the Keeper!" she exclaimed.

"The…what?" I asked, confused.

"What is a Keeper?" Jill questioned.

The girl looked quickly at the boy and then at me.

"How did you get past the Drimlor?" she asked. Her expression was filled with alarm.

"What's that?" I asked, looking at Jill.

The girl pushed away from the boy with the braid and said in disbelief, "Didn't Catherine tell you anything? How could she leave and not even tell you about us or the Watchman?"

"Look," Jill interrupted. "Catherine died because her heart stopped. She didn't know she was going to die! And I'm sure she didn't want to die either!"

"And how did you even get here?" The girl asked as if she didn't hear what Jill had said. Her huge blue eyes grew fierce with frustration. She flipped her golden blond hair over her shoulder and looked back and forth from the boy to me. "And how do you think you're ever going to get back?"

"Calm down, Brindle!" the boy said sharply to the girl. "They'll get back fine! There is no need to frighten anyone. Every Keeper has to learn somehow, just like Catherine and Zelly did years ago."

"What?" I asked overwhelmed. So far, no one had answered any of my questions.

The girl sighed and folded her arms sharply.

"We don't have *time* to train another Keeper," she retorted, ignoring me. Her beautiful, delicate face looked angry as she stared at the boy. He turned from the girl and looked up at me with his dark, little eyes. I was sure he could see the concern on my face, even though I was like a giant to him.

"Don't worry, Timber and Jill," he said. "I will start from the beginning and explain everything to you."

"Yes. Please," I said, somewhat relieved to finally get some answers.

Jill and I crouched down to be closer to the two, small people in front of us. We listened intently.

"First of all, my name is Ayden. My frustrated friend here is Brindle." Brindle huffed as Ayden continued, "We are Noceans and we live here in Mandoria. You both just came through a place called Creshtil Pass." He pointed back to the rocky hillside. "Catherine and Zelly used to call it Mr. Sellers' pond. It had to do with something that happened to them when they were children."

Jill and I looked at each other and smiled.

"We know all about that!" I interrupted.

Ayden smiled and then continued, "Noceans have lived in Mandoria since the beginning of time. We have always had many open passes that lead to the outer world. But since the time of the Drimlor, we now have only two left: Creshtil Pass and Watdoe Pass.

"Who is the Drimlor?" I asked at the same time that Jill blurted, "There's *another* pond?"

Ayden raised his hand to gesture for us to listen.

"The Drimlor are a group of people who invaded Mandoria just a few centuries ago, and they are trying to take over our land and destroy our people.

"And yes, Jill, there is another pond. Watdoe Pass is in the southern part of Mandoria. I have never been there, but others have seen it and they say that many

Noceans live in those parts. But we have heard that *their* pass is now in grave danger."

"Danger?" I asked.

"The passes are especially important to our people. Every century a tree by the outer pond must be dropped into the pass. Aspids grow on the tops of the trees surrounding the passes. Catherine calls them acorn crystals because she says they look like little acorns. We have never seen an acorn, but to us they are Aspids.

"When the tree hits the water, the Aspids release into the pass and fall to the bottom of the pond. All the Noceans in this area venture to the pass for the great gathering.

"Those tiny crystals keep us alive. They keep us from sickness and extend our life span. We call the great gathering 'the year of the Aspid Rain.' Harvesting and storing these crystals is quite a wonderful event for us. It is a time of celebration and thanksgiving!"

"And without Aspids we will die," Brindle added sadly.

Ayden nodded and continued, "Both passes are now at risk. There is only one tree left here at Creshtil Pass with crystals on it. We do not know how many trees are left at the other pass, but we have heard they are dwindling, too. We don't know the reason why the trees have stopped growing crystals."

"I'm sure it's something the Drimlors' have conjured up," Brindle said bitterly.

Suddenly, I remembered Tyler. "We just met some-one who knows a great deal about crystals and rocks," I said hopefully.

Ayden looked at Brindle. "Really?" they both said at the same time.

"Well, Catherine said she spent time studying crys-tals," Brindle pointed out. "But insisted that the answer was in the trees. She believed if we could only find the *right* tree and plant it next to the Pass, the roots of the tree could be nourished by the water. Then the Aspids would multiply on the tips of the branches. She worked so hard on this..." Brindle's voice trailed off regretfully.

"I've wondered if there was something else we could have done. Or someone else we could have talked to," Ayden said.

"The older Noceans greatly dislike any extra hu-mans knowing about us here in Mandoria. But either way, it's too late to look into anything now," Brindle added.

"Why?" I asked.

"Well," Ayden said, sighing. "We're almost out of Aspids."

"We have been on strict rations for close to three years now," Brindle added. "Soon they will be gone."

"Just cut down the tree!" Jill blurted out. "Then you'll have ten years left, right?"

Ayden smiled sadly. "The problem is that the only tree left is the one that the *key* fits into. There have always been other trees around the pond that grew

Aspids. But if the Keeper cuts the last one down it will close Creshtil Pass forever."

"Basically," Brindle said soberly. "We would have to relocate, which is something unheard of in Mandoria. The trip would be too dangerous, and who knows if there would be the same problem at Watdoe Pass in the South! If that didn't work, our people would be destined to perish."

"But Catherine refused to do that!" Ayden chimed in. "She spent most of her life trying to find a lasting answer for our survival."

"This would explain all the books she had on trees," Jill pointed out.

"I can't believe my Grandma was involved in all of this. At least we figured out that the golden eye is the key that fits in the tree," I said.

"Yes. You must have it? How did you get it if Catherine died suddenly?" Ayden asked.

"She wrote my name on some of her things for me to have one day. She wanted me to have her old sewing basket and we found the golden needle in there. Then Zelly told us about Mr. Sellers' Pond on accident. There were other notes, too."

"I think that Catherine wanted her to know about the key and the pond," Jill said.

"She was always planning on telling you, Timber!" Brindle exclaimed. "I thought she already had, but she waited too long!" I could tell Brindle was frustrated as she stood with her arms, still tightly folded. I saw a painful expression in her eyes. I realized her concern was not only for Catherine's death but for the safety of her people as well.

"You depended on her, didn't you?" I asked Brindle.

"We all did—she was the Keeper!"

"So, what exactly is the Keeper?" I asked.

"We depend on the Keeper for our very lives!" Brindle exclaimed. "That is why the news of Catherine's death is so hard for us. The Keeper watches the pass from the outer world and warns us of any dangers. She is a fighter. A warrior. Our trusted protector.

"She is the keeper of the Key. A true Keeper must have a pure and honest heart, or the tree will not accept the Golden Eye from her hand."

Jill and I glanced at each other.

Brindle continued, "She must always be looking for a future Keeper that she can pass it to when she nears the end of her time. She always protects the Key and Golden Eye."

"And would fight to the death to keep it safe!" Ayden joined in. "The Keeper has to continually find new places to hide the Key from the Drimlor, who are relentless hunters. The Keeper must outsmart them. Catherine was brilliant at this!

"One time, it was just after the year of the Aspid Rain and during the third moon. I remember Boden had caught her with his trap. Boden is the Drimlor. He planned to keep her tied up until he found the key. He could tell that the key was close but never could find it. She had him going mad, that was for sure! By the time we got to her it was nightfall, and the beast was exhausted and finally asleep. We untied her only to be completely shocked when she snuck over to the Drimlor and untied the bound key from under his dreadlocks at the back of his head. I never laughed so hard in all my life! She had tied it there as he was binding her up."

"Yes, she was brave," Brindle said. "But Stroder thought she was sometimes careless, Ayden. He always warned her that one swipe of the Drimlors fist and she would have been dead."

"But it *was* funny," Ayden said as he chuckled under his breath.

"Also, the Keeper is completely responsible for getting the tree into Creshtil Pass during the year of the Aspid Rain."

"That's every ten years?" Jill questioned.

"Yes," Brindle said. "The crystals must remain connected to the tree as they fall into the water of the pass. This will cause them to release and descend to the floor of the pond. This is tricky with the Drimlor on full alert.

"The Keeper is more important to us than anyone else! We need her for our very existence. We stay close to her and always seek to keep her safe. Many of our people have died while trying to protect her."

Ayden moved forward and knelt on one knee. He looked back at Brindle as she moved forward and joined him.

"We will forever be in your service, Timber."

SHERRI GRIMAUD

They both lowered their heads as if to honor me.

I pulled my head back and glanced at Jill.

"What are you doing?" I asked.

"Timber," Jill whispered. "You must be the new Keeper."

"Uh. Me?" I asked with a slight uneasy chuckle in my voice. "No," I said, shaking my head. "I am *completely sure* I would not be the best person for that job!"

Ayden and Brindle stood.

"I would love to help take care of you, but I honestly can't move when I get scared or even nervous. I freeze! I could probably keep the Key hidden but never fight that… Drimlor…Boden guy."

Jill laughed out loud, "Yeah, she does freeze up, that's true! But Timber, you don't even have to worry about that. That's what you have me for. I will always be here for you and keep you moving. Together we could defend these little Nocean people and even fight off the Drimlor."

"You have the Key, Timber," Brindle said. "And even though I don't think we have enough time to teach and train a new Keeper, we don't really have another choice. Besides, the tree accepted the Golden Eye from your hand, right?"

I nodded slowly.

"It would not have done that unless your heart was honest and good." She concluded.

"Catherine chose you, Timber," Ayden said. "She wanted *you* to be the Keeper, ever since the day you were born."

"How do you know that?" I asked.

"Catherine longed for a grandchild to be able to take her place one day. And you were the first born," Ayden said.

"I remember the story well," Brindle joined in. "They still tell us about the last time of the Aspid Rain. I was not born yet, and Ayden here was only three at the time. But Catherine had to go to the forest late at night, which is extremely dangerous for a Keeper. It was the tenth day of the fourth moon."

"Hey, that's my birthday!" I exclaimed. "April tenth."

"Catherine chopped on a large tree for many hours, with an old ax," Brindle continued. "It was 12:30 at night, only thirty minutes into the new day, when the tree finally split and dropped on top of the pond. The Noceans talk about how Catherine yelled at the top of her lungs, '*Timber!*'"

I gasped.

"Didn't your Grandmother name you when you were a baby?" Jill said with amazement.

"Yes, she did," I whispered. "But I knew nothing about why or how she came up with the name. She only told me it was her favorite."

There was a moment of silence as my mind processed this news.

"I never would have imagined all of this," I said. "I was named because of a tree falling into a pond to keep these amazing little people alive. My grandmother was their Keeper and one day she wanted me to be their Keeper too."

"Has it been fourteen years since the last tree has fallen?" Jill asked.

Ayden and Brindle nodded.

"We have to figure this out!" Jill exclaimed. "How many Aspids are left?"

"There is probably enough for two weeks for all of our people," Ayden said sadly.

"Oh my gosh!" I exclaimed.

"What about the other pond? I think we should at least try there first," Jill suggested.

"We sent a band of Noceans to southern Mandoria a few different times," Brindle said, looking at Jill. "But they have never returned."

"We do need to make a decision," Ayden said. "But we cannot do this without Stroder and the others of course."

"Who is Stroder again?" I asked.

"He is one of our great leaders. He's the one who took off into the trees when you told him about Catherine's death," Ayden answered.

"I'm sorry. I really upset him."

"He'll be okay. It's just that Catherine and Stroder… they were close," Ayden said, glancing at Brindle.

"Stroder is the leader of our Runners. The Runners are a special band of Noceans that safeguard the northern lands of Mandoria. We defend our people. We are known for running ahead, whenever there is a change or disturbance in our land. And we protect our Keeper at all cost."

"Are you a Runner?" I asked.

Ayden raised his bow and broadened his shoulders.

"I am," he said in a firm voice. "And so is Brindle. The whole group that was here when you and Jill came through the pass are Runners.

"Stroder is the oldest and is the best fighter we have. He is the only Nocean who has ever killed a Watchman."

"To kill a common Drimlor that lives here is not so hard," Brindle joined in. "But a *Watchman* in full Drimlor form is nearly impossible."

"I don't understand," I said.

"A Watchman is like a giant to us as Noceans. He can change forms and look like an old man if he wants to. But he is Drimlor when he is in his true form. This is when he stands on two legs, but his upper-body is an animal," Ayden explained. "He's part beast, with hair that is twisted over his ugly, demented face and green glowing eyes. Oh, and he smells of death."

I nodded. "Yes, he was at the pond and his eyes were glowing."

"He is the Watchman over Creshtil Pass," Ayden said. "He is a Drimlor, and his name is Boden. He is a mighty warrior chosen by his people to be the Watchman."

"He is *not* so mighty!" Brindle snorted under her breath.

"But he was like an old, crippled man at first," I said, remembering. "And then he seemed to change right in front of us."

"I didn't see that like you did, Timber." Jill said. "I was trying to swim away and then got caught in that current."

Ayden and Brindle's eyes were both huge. They looked completely shocked.

"I don't know any people who have seen that before," Ayden said.

"A Watchman is a Drimlor that has been given special gifts," Ayden continued. "When they are chosen, they leave their people and go through the pass to the outer world. This is an excruciating process for them. If they survive it, they change into Human size and must live where the pass is—I think Catherine called it 'Bellen Road.'

"One of the Watchman's gifts is the power to change the way he looks. He gets strength from the pass and must stay in that area or he will lose this power, become disoriented, and eventually die. If he leaves, it can only be for a short amount of time, and then not again for a couple days. But, like I said, he can only do this in the outer world, where you live.

"And Stroder killed a Watchman once when he was out by the pond?" Jill asked in amazement.

"Yes." Ayden said. "Since we are so much smaller than you, the Watchman is a giant to us. But Stroder killed him. He is the only Nocean to ever do that. We were so happy! Many moons passed until they chose another Watchman."

Jill and I sat up and looked over the land of Mandoria. We were so amazed with this place and all that we were learning.

"I don't quite understand something," I said. "What exactly does the Watchman do or even want?

"He wants us to die," Brindle stated matter-of-factly. "But we will fight to the death if we must!"

Ayden continued slowly, "The Watchman's whole purpose is to get the Key and swim back through the pass. If he does this, then his job will be done, and the pass will close forever. Their whole goal is to close all the passes and destroy our people forever. The Drimlors' don't want us here."

"Why didn't he just take the key from the tree and swim into the pond?" I asked.

"First of all, the key cannot be retrieved from the tree except only by the Keeper's hand. And second, when a Drimlor becomes a Watchman, he can never return without the Key," Ayden answered. "The water will burn him if he even touches it—unless he is holding on to the key."

"That's why we saw him being careful to not touch the water," Jill stated.

"The pass and the water are a great protection from that beast!" Brindle added.

I noticed how the sun was making its way across the sky and wondered what time it was back home. Tiny bird sounds were coming from within the cluster of trees near the edge of the small mountains range.

"I can only imagine what it would be like to be your size and have the Watchman shoot darts at you," I said.

"What? Did that happen to you?" Ayden gasped. He raised his bow and Brindle moved her hands sharply out to her sides and stepped back.

"How did you know about the Watchman's darts?" Brindle exclaimed shocked with my words.

"Right before I went under the water, I saw him aim a weapon at me. Then darts flew into the pond just above my head."

"We must tell Stroder and get those out of the pass, Ayden," Brindle said.

He nodded. "I have never heard of a Watchman that has missed a human," Ayden continued. "Especially Boden! You are incredibly lucky, Timber. At the end of the dart, Drimlors' put the dew from a Heriscan Plant that paralyzes their victims for a time. The dew is poisonous and burns through their veins and causes their body to shake. This gives the Drimlor the chance to easily kill their prey. Or slow them down. Or simply take the Key."

"That is, if there isn't anyone around to help remove the dart," Brindle stated. She squared her shoulders and spoke with courage as if she would defend anyone against them.

I had a sick feeling well up in my chest as I realized what almost happened to me. But then something else came to mind. "If I'm the new Keeper," I said slowly, "he'll be coming after me now."

"That's right, Timber," Ayden said, watching me carefully.

"But he might not know that Catherine is dead yet," Brindle added.

"Oh, I'm sure he's already checked out Catherine's house. He only saw you two at the pond, so I know he's curious," Ayden said. "Besides, he now knows one of you was carrying the Key."

"Wait," Jill said quickly. "I don't understand why he can't just get the key out of the tree."

"There are rules and laws that govern Mandoria and the area around Creshtil Pass," Ayden explained. "One of those laws is when the rightful Keeper delivered the Key into the tree, it cannot be retrieved by anyone except the one who put it there."

"Ayden, there will never be enough time to explain everything, or even teach her all that she needs to know," Brindle said. She was obviously getting frustrated. "We should go get Stroder."

"Wait, the Watchman knows where my grandmother lives?"

"Sure, he does," Ayden said ignoring Brindle.

"But I live right next door," I said.

"There's one thing you need to know about the Watchman. He *can* leave the area where the pond appears and disappears, but he begins to lose his strength quickly if he stays away too long."

"If he goes to my grandmother's house, he will find out that the Connelly's live there now. Will he hurt them?" I asked, feeling anxious for my new neighbors.

"No. The Watchman doesn't want any trouble with the humans of the outer-world. His only focus is getting the key away from the Keeper. If he stays away from the area of the pond too long, he could forget what he is doing, or like I said, he could die. The Watchman is most dangerous around the area of the pond."

"How does Timber keep the key safe?" Jill asked.

"Wasn't it wrapped in a golden cloth?" Ayden asked.

"Yes, I think it's still here," I reached into the wet pocket of my shorts and pulled out the crumpled golden cloth. "Here it is."

Ayden nodded approvingly.

"Well, hold on to that! You must keep the needle tightly wrapped in it when it is out of the tree. This cloth is made from Noceans' hair, and the Watchman cannot sense that the needle is in the area if it is in the cloth. You must always remember that when the key is out of the covering or out of the tree, the Drimlor will hunt you down like a wild animal and kill you if he has to, to get the key. They say that the Watchman feels pain if the key is exposed to the air in the outer world, but I am not sure what happens."

I felt sick inside. I couldn't even turn my head to look at Jill.

"Do you think he is waiting out by the pond right now?" I asked anxiously.

Brindle nodded. "I *know* he is!" she said.

Tiny fluttering sounds came from the trees and I recognized the noise as the light pattering of people running. Ayden and Brindle ran forward into the clearing and stopped to listen more closely. They looked poised and alert, yet ready to attack if necessary. Out of the trees came half as many Noceans as before. Ayden and Brindle relaxed their stance.

"Ayden!" one of the boys yelled. "We cannot find Stroder, and soon it will be night fall."

Ayden looked at us.

"Timber, we need to get you and Jill back before evening comes."

"Okay… but why?" I asked. I was not quite ready to leave this beautiful place—mostly because I was not ready to see the Watchman again.

"Because at nightfall the Drimlor awakens," Ayden said. "They rule the darkness here in Mandoria. And we need to find Stroder before we go into hiding."

I took a deep breath. I didn't even want to ask about that one.

Jill grabbed my hand. "Timber, it's going to be okay," she said.

"We'll help you two get through Creshtil Pass," Ayden said. "And get to the pathway. But you will be on your own after that."

"Don't worry about the Watchman," Brindle stated while she took a tiny dart from the side of her leg and loaded it into her small bow. "We'll take care of him!"

Unlike me, I could tell Brindle enjoyed going to battle against the Drimlor. She obviously had no fear. Or maybe she was simply committed to the cause.

Ayden and the others gathered at the small rocky hillside. They began preparing to enter the pond. They covered each other's arrows with a flap of material that tied around the quiver. One boy tied his bootstraps again. Brindle tightened the buckles on her wrist bands and secured her grip on her handheld bow.

"Timber, you will need to get the key out of the tree as quickly as possible and wrap it in the cloth," Ayden said. "Keep it safe!"

"I will," I said.

"Please try to come back tomorrow," Ayden continued, "so we can make a decision with the others on what we are going to do."

"We'll be here," Jill said as she glanced at me. Her green eyes were bright with determination.

"Oh, and Timber, do you know where Catherine's things might be?" asked Ayden.

"Yes. Mother went through all her stuff with Aunt Nell and Uncle Martin. They put some extra things in a shed behind my house."

Ayden looked at Brindle and the others. "I hope they didn't get rid of it," he said to them and with a sigh turned to me. "Look for another golden cloth like the one in your pocket. It will be much bigger and have three large loops on one end. It will fit on your forearm and hang down about to your knee."

"What is it?" I asked.

"It's a shield that Drimlors' darts can't penetrate," Ayden said. "We'll have another one for you when you return, but it might help you tomorrow. Be careful, Timber!"

"Ayden," another boy said, pushing his foot through the rocky hillside and into Creshtil Pass. "We really need to hurry!"

Then he disappeared.

Jill and I watched as the Noceans pressed their way one by one into the tiny hillside. They looked as if they knew exactly what they were doing.

I had a slight feeling of panic come over me when I thought about the water on the other side. Jill looked at me with big, anxious eyes. Brindle glanced at me then turned and pressed quickly into the rock.

The last Nocean left was Ayden. "Are you guys okay?" he asked as he approached the hillside. "Is it the water?"

We both nodded apprehensively.

Ayden looked at us knowingly. "You probably felt like you were drowning. This is what I do," he said as he positioned his hands on the rock. "I take a deep breath then push out all the air in my lungs before I press my face into the water. Then, with only my head in, I take a deep breath of the water. It fills my lungs, and the rest of my body goes easily into the Pass. You will get used to it. Remember, only a Nocean can take you to the top. See you inside." He gave a small grin, exhaled deliberately then pushed his face into the rocks and disappeared.

"Are you ready, *Keeper*?" Jill asked as she motioned me on.

I took a deep breath.

"Sure!" I lied as I exhaled all the air from my lungs then pressed my nose through the rocks of the small hillside.

CHAPTER NINE

BODYGUARD

I did just what Ayden said to do. But panic still filled my body. I waited, then thought of grandma and how she must have done this all the time. Slowly, I took a deep, long breath of water into my lungs. The same feelings rushed through my entire body. Instantly, I felt deeply relaxed. I drew in another deliberate breath of water. It was hard not to notice the intense, wonderful feeling of the water moving in and out of my throat. I opened my eyes.

To my amazement, the Noceans glowed a brilliant color of gold against the darkness of the cave. I smiled. They looked like huge, glowing fireflies. All of them were suspended effortlessly in the water around me. I moved aside as Jill came through the opening. I reached back and took her hand.

The Noceans began to swim swiftly through the water of the cave. They looked like speeding flashes of light and reminded me of fireworks on the Fourth of

July. Ayden slowed down and waved for us to come as Jill and I tried to keep up. We approached the entrance of the cave, and I could see the dark outline of three jagged openings. The turquoise water looked brilliant and inviting through the holes of the cave. A school of shimmering silver fish swam along the rocks beneath us.

The Noceans stopped in the water just outside the entrance. Ayden motioned for me to come. Brindle waved for Jill.

A brilliant display of colors surrounded us as Ayden reached his whole arm around my finger and squeezed tightly. I had not touched one of these little people before and was amazed at the softness of his skin. The other Noceans zipped through the water above us. Ayden tugged once and my arm stretched quickly above me, and then we were off. I was unexpectedly moving upward with exhilarating speed. The pressure was intense and thrilling. I twisted and soared through the silky blue liquid.

Then, we stopped. My head broke gently through the top of the thick water with not even a sound or ripple. The air tickled at the back of my throat, and I cleared it quietly. Jill was instantly at my side. It felt good to see the huge, beautiful trees that surrounded us. We were at the backside of the pond, and I could see the entrance to the pathway at the other end. Ayden still had a grip on my finger. Brindle moved quickly next to Ayden. The others were nowhere in sight.

"Timber," Ayden said as he let go of my finger. "The Watchman is not here. You and Jill swim to the other end and we'll meet you there." Ayden and Brindle sank under the water and were gone.

I looked at Jill and we both began to swim as quickly as we could to the other side. The water was soothing and wrapped itself around me like silk. I worked my way through the thick, soft fluid and my mind could think about nothing but this wonderful place. The pathway. The people. The magic of Mr. Sellers' Pond was the most beautiful thing I had ever known. If only I could have come here with Grandma. No matter what the dangers are or the challenges that lie ahead for me, I would do whatever it takes to help these little people survive.

Jill and I came to the edge of the water. The Noceans were lined up along the edge of the pond. They looked different—less relaxed. They were in a stance that was ready for battle. I thought of how Ayden called themselves Runners. The young men had their bows out in front of them with an arrow pulled back ready to release at a moment's notice. Brindle and two other young women held one arm straight above them, and the other out in front. They were holding tightly to their loaded bows, while moving them slowly back and forth to scan the area. They were ready to fight.

Ayden slightly tilted his head to the right, never taking his eyes off the pathway. "Move quickly, Timber!" he yelled back to me.

I stepped out of the water and noticed how the fluid clumped back together down my legs and under my feet. It moved gently back into the pond. Jill and I walked toward the entrance to the pathway while the Runners crept slowly ahead of us. They moved forward with a steady pace. These little people were our protectors now, and despite their size, I felt perfectly safe.

"I'm not sure where Boden is," Ayden said. "But we got you safely to the pathway. You'll have to take it from here."

I squatted down closer to the Noceans.

"Thank you, Ayden, for your help," I said.

I looked at the others. "I feel so lucky to have met you, and I'm going to do everything in my power to help you."

"Right now, you just need to worry about the Watchman," Brindle said while she scanned the area again. "You are not a trained Keeper yet."

"Go on, Timber. Get the key," Ayden said. He looked as if he didn't want me to leave but had to send me on my way.

Jill grabbed my hand, and we ran to the pathway. I looked back, but the Runners were gone.

When we came to the end, Jill dramatically slowed down and stopped me with her hand. She leaned her head out and looked slowly in both directions.

"Go, quickly," she ordered.

I reached in my pocket as I ran to the base of the tree and pulled out the golden cloth. I quickly climbed, looking carefully in every direction for the Watchman. Nothing seemed different to me in the forest. Jill stood at the base of the tree, waiting. I saw the tip of the needle and gently laid the golden cloth over it. I pulled hard and it turned sharp with a click and then another. It was released with ease. I quickly wrapped up the needle and put it deep in my pocket.

I had forgotten about the wind, but I could hear it coming this time. It sounded like wild horses running through the trees, coming straight for us. I looked at Jill, and she had already grabbed onto a tall, thin tree trunk a few feet away. I leaned over, closed my eyes, and held on tight once again. The wind blew in upon us, but it was different this time. It was warm and strong, yet gentle. The leaves sounded beautiful as they fluttered like little bells through the tops of the trees. Then it stopped.

I climbed down the tree and saw Jill staring with her huge, sad eyes toward the pathway.

"It's gone," she said quietly.

Instantly, an empty, lonely, feeling came over me. It was there a moment ago—the path, the people, the pond. I took a deep breath and put my hand on my pocket.

"Everything is right here, Jill," I said reassuringly.

She looked puzzled.

"As long as we have the key, we can see this whenever we want."

The sorrow cleared from Jill's eyes.

"That is true…for a while, anyway. But we need to figure out how to save the Noceans without having to chop the last tree down. Or it *will* be gone forever.

"Also, be ready, Timber. There is a Drimlor out here somewhere who would kill for something we have. We need to get out of here, fast!"

"Right!" I agreed. "Where do you think he is?"

"I don't know, but the moment we forget about him, he'll get us—I'm sure of it."

Jill and I ran quickly and quietly through the forest. We carefully watched in all directions. We ran up the hill and made our way through the brush. Finally, we made it to our bikes.

"I can't believe we made it!" Jill exclaimed, as she lifted the branches off the bikes.

"I know," I said. "Do you think he forgot about us?"

"I don't know, but I don't feel safe yet! Let's get out of here!" She flung her backpack over her shoulder and moved her bike up to the edge of the dirt road.

"Hurry, Timber," Jill said looking back in the trees.

I felt an urgency come over me as I watched Jill fumble with her bike.

"Come on!" She exclaimed. Her bike was pointed away from town.

"Where are we going?" I asked, moving my bike next to hers.

"We should go a mile over and then head back to town. That way, we can get off Bellen Road."

"Sounds good," I said.

Jill and I peddled quickly on the edge of the dirt road.

The sun was lowering in the sky, and I thought of the Noceans in Mandoria. I hope they found Stroder before they needed to go into hiding.

Finally, Jill and I turned off Bellen and headed safely back to town.

"It won't be long now, and we'll be home," Jill said.

"Do you think it's about dinner time?" I asked, "Because I'm starving!"

"Yeah, me too," Jill said. "Hey, I still have our lunch in my backpack. Shall we stop and eat?"

"Let's wait till we're home, okay?" I said. "I would just feel better!"

"That's probably best," Jill agreed.

I could see a convenience store up ahead and cars driving across the intersection. It felt good to be around people again and away from where the Watchman lived. We passed by Millie's Restaurant and headed over the railroad tracks. We made our way across a busy road, and then another.

Finally, Jill and I turned onto my street and headed under the canopy of trees. A huge sense of relief came over me. The moving van was still parked in Grandma's driveway, but I couldn't see the Connelly's anywhere. Jill and I parked our bikes in front of my house at the edge of the porch.

"It feels good to be home!" I said to Jill.

"You got that right," she said.

I turned around and leaned up against the front of the porch. Jill stretched her arms out wide to the side. Suddenly she stopped and looked right at me. Her face was white as a sheet.

"What is it?" I whispered.

"That smell!"

"What?" I asked.

And then, I smelled it: a thick, sour scent of death.

"He wouldn't," I started to say, but then stopped when I saw a dark figure directly behind Jill, walking up the middle of the road. The air felt motionless around me. *The Watchman was here!* He was hunched over and limping slightly. His forehead was lowered and his eyes glowed green, looking directly at me. Jill saw my face and slowly turned around. Everything seemed to stop except the movement of the angry Drimlor.

"Give it to me!" he roared. The sound of his voice pierced the quietness. His dirty teeth showed through his long angry mouth.

"No!" Jill screamed. "Run, Timber!"

To my surprise, I was able to move. I bolted around the house and busted through the side gate. Panic seared through my body as I headed for the backyard. I could feel Jill right behind me and heard her slam the metal gate.

I stopped just around the back side of the house to listen. Jill's eyes were filled with terror as she ran desperately to my side. Her cold hand clenched the skin on my arm.

The Watchman was breathing hard and groaning as he shook the gate.

Suddenly, I caught Tyler's beautiful, dark brown eyes from over the fence. He was standing on Grandma's back porch, holding a baseball bat and glove. He looked surprised and deeply concerned.

Jill and I must have been a sight to see. Our hair was still somewhat wet from being in the pond and our arms and legs were dusty from the ride home. My skin felt clammy and cold. I must have looked white as a sheet from the terror that consumed my whole being.

"What happened to you two?" Tyler asked. His eyes shifted as he noticed the man trying to break through the fence.

I pointed my finger in the Drimlors' direction, and forced out a panicked whisper, "He's trying to get us!"

Tyler tilted his head as his eyebrows pulled together.

"Is he trying to hurt you?" he asked quickly.

I nodded.

Tyler dropped the glove, leaped off his porch and jumped over the fence with the bat held high.

"Hey, you," I heard Tyler yell alongside the house.

The sound of the gate shaking stopped. There was no reply. I waited.

Would he hurt Tyler?

"I told you once that Catherine doesn't live here anymore. And she doesn't live at this house either," he continued. "Now get off this property!"

Jill looked at me with worried eyes. We listened.

"You tell your friends," Boden said, in a deep scratchy voice. "That I *know* who the Keeper is now."

"Uh…okay," Tyler said in a strange, exaggerated tone. "But you still need to get off this property, or I will call the police."

"She has something I need," Boden's voice was getting louder with frustration. I could hear the metal fence rattling again. "Tell her I'll be waiting for her!"

"Whatever, old man," Tyler sneered. "Now get out of here."

A minute passed. Then I heard Tyler yell, "And don't come back!"

I could hear Tyler's footsteps coming toward us. "So, what's going on?" he asked as he rounded the corner of the house. He held the bat down to his side. "You two look dreadful!"

I took a deep, long breath and exhaled into my hands. "Is he really gone?" I asked as I ran my fingers through my damp hair.

"Yeah," Tyler said. "That guy was creepy. Did you see his weird contacts? I wonder where he got those?"

I peeked around the side of the house, then looked at Jill. She ran quickly to the other end and looked around the corner.

"What was he talking about? He knows who the new Keeper is?" Tyler asked, flipping his brown hair to the side. "And did you take something from him?"

I could not answer. I just stared at Tyler, who was standing in front of me like a bodyguard. At that moment he was my hero, my knight in shining armor! His tall, lanky frame looked gorgeous against the beautiful orange and yellow sunset that was resting in the trees behind him. He stood up to that dreadful creature! I sighed. Okay, so Tyler didn't know who he really was and that the Drimlor could have paralyzed all of us before he killed us—nonetheless, he was still my hero and my gorgeous new bodyguard!

"He's gone, Timber," Jill said, as she walked to the back porch. We both sat down on the steps.

"So, didn't you say he was trying to get you?" Tyler questioned.

"Yes," I said, nodding my head. I couldn't lie to him.

"No!" Jill said in a louder voice, looking at me reprovingly.

Tyler tilted his head to the side and knew she was trying to hide something. "Hey, I just saved you from that creepy old guy. You were obviously scared to death about something. Don't I deserve a small explanation?"

"Jill, I think we might need Tyler."

Jill rolled her eyes at me and shook her head in disapproval.

"Besides, we have to talk to him about the crystals and as *quickly* as possible!"

"What?" Tyler asked. "Crystals?"

Jill sighed. "Maybe... but no one else Timber!"

"Okay," I agreed.

"Tell anyone else what?" Tyler said, raising his eyebrows. "Are you guys in some kind of trouble?"

"No," I said. "Well, maybe. It's just a long story."

"Hey, what did you tell that man about Catherine?" Jill asked.

"He came to our house a while ago. I told him that she doesn't live here anymore. I think my mom might have told him that she died."

"Great!" Jill said sarcastically.

"I hope that was okay?" Tyler asked. "What's going on?"

Jill wiped some dust off her legs. "We are such a mess! And we're both starving!"

"It's okay, Tyler," I said. "He was bound to find out sometime. I will explain everything. But first we are going to eat and get cleaned up. Would you be able to meet us out here later?"

"Timber, I don't feel too safe hanging out here in the backyard while a Drimlor is lurking around," Jill stated.

"Drimlor?" Tyler asked, confused.

"I agree!" I said. "More than you know! But they did make it clear that he can't be away from Bellen Road for too long. *And* he doesn't want to make any trouble in town."

"Yeah, but—" Jill said.

"Can you meet us here, on the porch?" I asked quickly, cutting Jill off and pointing to the enclosed deck on the back of our house. "The screens are awesome! If the light is not on, you can see out, but no one can see in."

"That's fine," Tyler said, looking back at his house.

"And the backdoor locks, right?" Jill asked as she continued to cover all safety measures.

"Yes!"

"What time?" Tyler asked.

"Is eleven alright?"

Tyler paused and looked back at his house.

"I might have to sneak out, but I'll be here," he said.

"But you need to decide something first," I continued, in a firm and steady voice.

Tyler stared at me intently.

"If you want to know what's going on you will have to keep the secret. Forever."

"That's a long time," he said. I saw the corners of his lips raise.

"This is very serious!" I said.

"You guys are kind of scaring me a little. But for you, Timber," he said, winking, "I'll keep the secret till the day I die."

My heart dropped to my stomach. This time it was not from fear, but from the knowledge that this gorgeous boy *must* like me! He had too! I smiled and looked down.

"O-kay," Jill said awkwardly. She knew perfectly well what just happened. "But I get Timber for the next few hours," she continued, grabbing my arm jokingly. "And then you can have her back."

Jill pulled me in the direction of the house.

"We will meet you here later," she said.

"See you, Tyler," I said with a little giggle.

Tyler nodded with the cutest grin as he turned and jumped over the fence.

"What was that all about?" Jill whispered as we walked into the house.

"Jill, I think he likes me!" I said. My voice went high at the end and I giggled again.

"You think," she agreed.

"I forgot to tell you that last night we talked in the backyard. He helped me roll up the sleeping bags. And he even said something about my blue eyes."

Jill put her hand on the doorway and looked at me. "Chad's not going to like this, Timber!"

"I know...But Tyler is so cute!" I said.

The phone rang. I picked it up as I looked at Jill. She rolled her eyes at me, but I knew she totally understood.

"Hello?

"Oh hi, Mom—

"Yeah, we had a good day!

"Yeah, it was long, but really fun!

"Fine!

"Okay.

"Okay.

"Hey, can Jill sleep over again?

"No, probably on the back porch."

"Ok, I promise.

"Sure.

"I love you, too!

"Bye!"

I hung up the phone and sighed.

"What is it?" Jill asked.

"It's just hard not telling Mom what *really* happened today," I said.

"Yeah," Jill agreed. "But Timber, I really don't think she'd believe you, even if you did tell her."

"You're probably right," I laughed.

"Hey, I better put this needle up," I said, laying my hand on my front pocket. "And I should probably get the leather notebook to show Tyler later."

"Okay," Jill responded as she opened the refrigerator door. "And I'll find us something to eat."

After I securely locked the needle in the sewing basket, Jill and I ate dinner. I quickly rinsed the dishes. Then we each took a shower and got cleaned up. It felt good to straighten my hair and put some night clothes on. I let Jill borrow a pair of sweats and a T-shirt. Then we found the sleeping-bags and got them set up in the back porch on two of our long lawn chairs. Mom came home later and checked on us before heading up to bed.

Finally, we propped our heads on our pillows and talked about the day while looking off into the dark night sky. We waited and waited for Tyler.

"I'm getting tired," Jill said. She let out a long yawn and gently shook her head.

"Me too," I said sleepily, my eyelids growing heavy. "It's been a long day!"

"Hey, did you see that?" I said, pointing my finger toward the side screen.

"No, what was it?"

"I saw a light flicker across the sky. I think it was a falling star!"

"You know what they say about falling stars?" Jill said.

"What's that?"

"You get to make a wish!"

"Oh yeah," I said slowly as I gently closed my eyes. I felt myself starting to drift off to sleep, but not before I made my wish to somehow save the little people of Mandoria. And that my "new bodyguard" would be by my side forever!

Suddenly, a loud sound pierced the stillness and my eyes shot open.

CHAPTER TEN

SHARING THE ADVENTURE

Jill and I sat straight up. We watched as a dark figure walked toward us from under the tree branches that hung down over Grandma's fence. I could see that it was not the Watchman, but for a moment I was confused as to who it was.

"Who's there?" Jill whispered loudly.

The moon was not quite full yet, but it was high in the sky and brightened the whole backyard. Shades of black and white illuminated the silhouettes of the bushes that lined the fence.

"It's just me," Tyler whispered back. He stepped out of the shadows and walked up the stairs to the door of the porch. "Sorry it took me so long, but I wanted to make sure my parents were asleep."

Jill unlocked the door, then locked it again behind him after he entered.

"I understand," I said. I was completely awake now. "My Mom got home a little while ago, and I think she is asleep now too."

"Thanks for coming!" Jill said. "We've decided that we could really use your help. That is, if you still want to be a part of this?"

Tyler sat down on the small chair that was right next to me.

"Sure, I'm in," he said, as he exchanged smiles with me and Jill. It was darker inside the porch, but I could still see his face as the moonlight shone through the side windowpanes.

"So, tell me what's going on?" he inquired eagerly.

A train whistle blew three long sounds in the distance.

I pulled my knees next to my body and took a deep breath as Jill crossed her legs, resting her elbows on her knees.

"Well Ty," I started. "What I'm about to tell you might be kind of hard for you to believe."

"I'm still trying to believe it all!" Jill joined in.

Another haunting train whistle echoed far away.

I started at the beginning as Tyler listened carefully. I told him about Zelly and Grandma Catherine and how we learned about Mr. Seller's pond from the leather notebook we found in the granary. I pulled it out from under my pillow and handed it to Tyler. He examined it carefully.

"Wow, this thing looks really old!" he said.

"Yeah, and look at the note grandma wrote in there," I said as I gently turned the old pages.

Tyler read it to himself.

"Looks like she wanted you to know about a pond," Tyler said as he flipped through the pages again from the beginning. "What's this right here?"

"That's in Walter's handwriting," Jill said. "It says to plant something with the trees."

"But the writing is smudged off," I said. "Probably because it's so old."

"There are a lot of little side notes in the margins," Jill said, pointing to parts of the page.

Tyler closed the book and wrapped the leather strap around front.

Then I told him about how we found the golden needle.

"Do you have it?" he asked curiously.

"Yes," I said.

"We do!" Jill quickly added. "It's hidden in her room and we think it is *real* gold."

I could see Tyler's eyes grow wide with amazement and he slightly leaned back.

I continued. I told him about the encounter we had with the man on Bellen Road and about his moving, green eyes.

"That's the guy that was here today," Tyler said.

I nodded.

I explained how we found the tree and how the wind nearly killed us right before the beautiful pathway appeared which led us to the pond.

"It sounds like a tornado might have formed right above you two," Tyler suggested. "That happened to my cousin in Kansas once."

I told Tyler about the wonderful pond, then about the terror we experienced when we were pulled down into it, and how we both had to breathe the water into our lungs.

Tyler's big, brown eyes glanced to Jill, then back to me. "Did that *really* happen?" Tyler asked. He was extremely serious all of a sudden.

"I thought I had drowned!" Jill quickly added.

I nodded in agreement.

"People *die* when that happens," Tyler said. His eyebrows rose high above his eyes.

"Yeah, but we didn't!" Jill retorted.

"This might be hard to believe, at first," I whispered. "But Tyler, we could show you tomorrow, if you want to go back with us?"

"I don't know about the whole drowning thing," he said, tilting his head slightly to the side.

"The water feels very good, Tyler," Jill said. "If you feel scared at all, it somehow seems to take your fear away. It's like magic—it heals."

"Yes. I think it actually *does* heal you," I said. "Remember your scratches, Jill?"

"That was weird!" she nodded, then turned to Tyler. "My whole body got scratched from the wind when I was dragged on the ground. Then, after I had been in the pond for just a little while, the scratches were gone!"

"Wow," Tyler said. "This is all crazy, but why do you have to go back?"

"Well, there's more," I responded, and took a deep breath.

Tyler's legs were propped up in front of him and his elbows rested on his knees. He kept looking at something at his feet.

I carefully watched his response as I told him about the passageway through the hole in the bottom of the cave and about the little people that lived in Mandoria. I explained the situation they were in, with only one tree left. Finally, I told him about the Drimlors, the Keeper, the Watchman, and the crystals. After I finished, I tried to catch the look in his eyes, but they were locked onto the floor. He seemed deep in thought.

I paused for a long moment. I caught Jill's glance and she gave me a funny, concerned look. I wondered if Tyler thought we were making this up. I was sure I'd have a hard time believing it too if someone were telling me about it.

"Well, Ty?" I asked as I lightly tapped his knee. "What do you think?"

He took a long deep breath.

"Why do you have to breathe the water into your lungs?"

I paused. With all the strange and magical things that happened today, his only question was about the water?

Jill looked at me. "Well," she started saying, slowly. I could tell she was as confused as I was. "You don't *actually* have a choice. The water just pulls you down and finally you have to breathe it in."

"The water really does feel good!" I said reassuringly. "Tyler, it's not that bad. And Ayden said that you get used to it after a while."

"It's just that…well, I almost drowned once," Tyler said.

"Oh, you did?" I asked. "Oh my gosh! I am so sorry Tyler. How did it happen?"

"Oh, it was a long time ago," he continued. "I can swim and all. It was just a bad experience."

"What happened?" I asked.

Tyler paused. "Some kids held me under the water once."

"Why would they do something like that?" I asked.

Tyler started to pick at the seam of his jeans. I could tell he didn't want to talk about the situation.

"It was really nothing!" he said. He flipped his long brown hair out of his eyes. He would not look at me.

"Well, don't worry," Jill said, as she reached out and touched his arm. "If Timber and I got through it okay then *you* will too!"

"How do you know it will be okay next time?" Tyler asked.

"Well, that's what I wondered as we had to go back through the pass to come back," I said. "But it worked just fine!"

Tyler's big brown eyes grew even bigger. "Twice?"

I nodded.

"So," I said, pausing for a minute. "What do you think? Will you still come with us?"

"I guess..." he said. Finally, his eyes glanced thoughtfully in my direction. "I want to see for myself if all this is really true. I'm not saying that I don't believe you guys, but I would like to see for myself. But you might have to help me with the whole water thing."

"We will," I said reassuringly.

"I think our first concern shouldn't be about the water, though," Jill said. "But about getting past the Drimlor."

"So, he's trying to get the key from you, right?" Tyler asked.

I nodded.

"Well, that will never happen as long as I have anything to do with it. Even if he does have poisonous darts."

I smiled as I looked at my courageous bodyguard.

"Ayden told us that the poison paralyzes a person for a while," Jill said.

"Well, I have a sling-shot that I'm pretty good with," Tyler said, squaring his shoulders. "I'll use it tomorrow if I have to."

I felt a huge sense of relief to know that Tyler was coming with us.

"We also need to look in the granary for that shield thing that Ayden told us about," I said.

"A shield?" Tyler asked.

"He told us that my Grandma had a golden cloth that the Noceans made of their hair. It is supposed to fit on your forearm, that way you can move it to block the darts of the Drimlor."

Tyler stretched his legs out in front of him and leaned back on the chair. "A cloth made out of hair?" he asked in disbelief.

"They say that it will block the darts!" Jill said. "They acted like it was very important."

Tyler shrugged. "Okay. But I do have another question. You mentioned something about crystals?"

"Well, all they really told us was that the crystals grow on top of the trees around the pond," I said. "Except that now there is only one tree left with crystals on it. They can't figure out why they've stopped growing on the other trees that surround the pound."

"So, the only tree left is the one that the key fits into, right?" Tyler said, trying to keep all the facts straight.

"Yes," I said.

"I've never heard of crystals that grow on top of trees. Of course, they develop inside trees, but only over centuries of time. It's a form of petrified wood. Have you seen these crystals? What do they look like?" he asked.

I shook my head. "No, we didn't see them."

"What kind of tree is growing them?" he asked.

"I don't know," I said shrugging my shoulders. "But my grandmother spent her whole life studying trees."

"She has a *million* books to prove it!" Jill interrupted sarcastically.

"Ayden told us that she insisted that the answer was finding the *correct* tree and then planting it next to the pond. Maybe she felt the magic of Mr. Seller's Pond would make the crystals grow," I concluded.

"Well," Tyler said. "It sounds like we are dealing with a magical tree and a magical pond. So, if all this is true, a lot could affect what is happening there. But you would think that there would still have to be some basic variables in place. If crystals form on top of the tree, then a certain process still must take place for that to happen. Maybe it is as simple as one of those variables not being there anymore. If we could find out what that is, then maybe we could change it.

"Tomorrow, I would like to get a few samples of things so I can take a good look at them under the microscope. Do you think the Noceans will let me do that?" Tyler asked.

"I'm sure they will," I said.

"I think they will try just about anything that could help their situation," Jill added.

"Hey, we need to look in the granary for that shield," I said as I held up the flashlight.

"Let's do this quickly because I should probably get some sleep, before we head out in the morning," Tyler said.

The moon was straight above us as we all crept through the backyard and to the granary. Another train whistle blew in the distance and echoed through the silence of the night. We opened the heavy side door and searched through all of Grandmas' things but found nothing resembling a golden cloth—only endless books about trees. After closing the door of the granary, we walked slowly back to the porch.

"Hey, Timber," Jill said. "Did you see any golden material in that old sewing basket?"

"No," I said. "But I guess I could have missed it."

"You could double-check in the morning," Tyler said. "Before we go."

Jill opened the screen door. "Come on, Timber," she said. "We should probably get some sleep, too!"

I didn't want Tyler to leave. To my surprise, he gently grabbed the tips of my fingers and leaned in next to my face.

"Don't worry about anything, Timber," he whispered as he looked into my eyes. "We'll figure all of this out. And no crazy man will get you, either. I will be right there," he said, pointing to the upstairs corner of Grandma's house. "That is my room. So, if you need anything, I'll be sleeping right by that opened window."

"Thank you," I responded.

"See you in the morning," he said, then jumped the fence and disappeared into his house.

I stood there looking at the fence that separated our homes. Tyler was too good to be true. He was kind. He was smart. And he liked me. *What could a gorgeous boy like that see in a girl like me?* I wondered, shaking my head.

"Timber?" Jill said, as if she could read my thoughts. "Yes, you are *really* lucky! But don't worry, he'll be here tomorrow. Now come on, let's get some sleep!"

"Okay," I said, with a sigh.

Jill locked the back-porch screen door and turned the dead bolt to secure it.

I crawled into my sleeping bag as the cool night air settled in upon me. I stared up at Tyler's room in the corner of Grandma's house and felt safe and protected as Jill and I drifted off to sleep.

***

"Timber!"

"Timber!"

His voice nudged at the corners of my mind like a beautiful church bell ringing from a foggy, distant hillside.

"Timber!"

Where am I?

"Timber! Jill! Wake up!" His voice was much closer.

I heard the screen door shake, and my eyes shot open.

"Oh," I heard Jill yawn beside me. "What time is it, Tyler?" she demanded in a sharp voice.

"It's time you woke up!" he said. "I couldn't sleep all night. Besides, I want to know if this is all true!"

"Oh, Tyler," she groaned. "It is too early!"

"It's only seven."

The morning air was crisp and cool upon my skin. I blinked a few times and gently rubbed my eyes.

"I'm ready to go, you guys," Tyler continued. He was relentless.

"Okay," I said slowly. "Usually, I get up around eight or nine."

"Me too, but I couldn't sleep," Tyler said again.

"Okay, okay!" Jill said sharply.

I sat up and saw Tyler through the screen.

"You'll have to give us some time to get dressed," Jill said.

"Why don't you let me roll up your sleeping bags while you two go get ready?" he suggested, then chuckled to himself.

I felt a little embarrassed. I could tell my hair was a mess as it hung crazy in front of my eyes.

"Sounds like a good Idea," I said. I jumped up and unlocked the screen door and ran into the house. Jill was right behind me.

"Good morning, girls!" It felt good to hear Mom's voice as we entered the kitchen.

"Hi, Mom," I said.

Mom was standing at the counter buttering some toast that had just popped out of the toaster. Her hair was pulled up into a bun, and she was dressed in her work clothes.

I quickly ran and gave her an extra-long hug.

"Hey Timber," she said.

She seemed a little shocked. "So, what's this all about?"

"Oh, nothing," I said. "I just want to say that I love you!" I felt a little silly after I said it, but I was just so glad to see her again after everything that happened the day before.

"Well, I love you, too," she responded, a little apprehensively, as if she could sense something was off.

I longed to tell her everything but gently bit the inside of my lip.

"So, you two sure got up early," she continued.

"Yeah, Tyler woke us up," Jill said. She still had a sharp, annoyed edge to her voice.

"I thought I heard him out there," Mom said.

"We asked him if he wanted to go on a bike ride with us today," Jill said. "And he did not want to waste one minute!"

Mom's eyes were wide with excitement, and she had a slight smile on her face.

"That is nice of you to invite him. He's such a cute kid, isn't he?"

"Yes, he is!" Jill firmly agreed, glancing in my direction.

Besides being tired, Jill was her normal self this morning. She was quick to speak and be the center of conversation.

"And I think they both kind of like each other," Jill said, nudging my side playfully.

"Ah-ha!" Mom said quickly, a gleam in her eye.

"Jill!" I said sharply.

"So, what's Chad going to think about this?"

"Mom!" I whined.

"I tried to warn her about that!" Jill joined in.

"Well then, Jill," Mom continued in a teasing voice. "You're going to have to be their constant chaperone."

"Oh, I will be!" Jill exclaimed, holding her chin up high in the air.

I yawned and tilted my head to the side.

"Are you guys done yet?" I asked, exasperated.

I would be forever teased by Mom now, thanks to Jill.

"Okay," Mom said in a more serious tone. She handed Jill and I each a piece of toast.

"I have to go to work early again. We're finishing up that inventory today."

I nodded as I took a bite of toast.

"Please check in with me, sometime," she continued.

"We will."

Jill tugged at my arm. "We should go get ready!"

"And you wouldn't want to keep him waiting now, would you, Timmy?" Mom jeered.

I glared at Mom as I began to follow Jill out of the kitchen.

"Oh, I'm just kidding, honey!" Mom said. "You two have a good day. And I am glad you are including Tyler. He needs to make new friends here in Springfield."

Jill and I stopped at the restroom and washed up, and then we ran upstairs. The beads clattered against the doorway as we entered my bedroom.

"Can I borrow some shorts?" Jill asked. She was already looking through my things.

"Sure," I said.

We quickly got dressed in shorts and t-shirts and put some make-up on. Jill pulled her blond hair back into a ponytail, and I straightened mine again.

Mom's voice came from the bottom of the stairs. "I'm going to go, girls. See you later!"

"Okay, Mom! Have a good day!"

"You too!" she yelled back.

I opened the sewing basket to look for the golden shield. I examined each piece of material carefully and laid it gently on the bed. Finally, I got to the bottom.

"The shield's not here," I said.

Jill was leaning her face next to the mirror putting on the last touches of mascara.

"I sure hope mom didn't throw it away by accident."

"She might have," Jill sighed. "She wouldn't have known it was a shield. We'll just do our best without it!"

Suddenly, a pebble hit my front window.

Jill and I jumped and moved to the window at the same time.

"What are you doing?" Jill shouted down.

"I'm waiting," Tyler yelled back with his hands propped at his waist. "Are you guys ready yet?"

Tyler looked good in the morning sun. He wore a loose brown t-shirt with some long, dark blue shorts and a pair of white high-tops. His brown hair shined in the gentle sunlight and hung just below his ears. His bangs were off to one side. He sat on a red bike and had a brown backpack over his shoulder. In his left hand was a slingshot that hooked back over his wrist.

"Almost," I yelled back with excitement.

Tyler turned and smiled as mother stopped next to him. I heard them talking, and I took the golden needle out of the locked compartment in the bottom of the sewing basket. I carefully kept it wrapped in the shimmering gold cloth and placed it in the left pocket of my khaki shorts.

"Let's go!" Jill said as she pulled the noisy beads aside at my doorway.

We quickly moved through the sound of rattling beads and headed off down the stairs.

The ride went quick as we rode our bikes North of town. The morning air felt new and fresh. We passed by Bellen Road and went a mile down to Monticello Drive. Our plan was to ride out a mile on Monticello, then backtrack to Bellen, hide our bikes again, and then quietly work our way through the forest to the tree.

During the ride Jill was in front of me and Tyler was at the rear. There was not a soul on the road once we got to Monticello.

"We're almost there aren't we?" Tyler asked as he moved up next to me.

"Yes. Only a mile now," I said.

"I think when we get to Bellen Road we should hide our bikes in a different place than before," Jill said. "You never know if the Watchman saw the broken branches from yesterday."

"That's true," I replied. "But what do we do if we see him?"

"The trick is to notice him before he notices you!" Jill said.

"Don't worry Timber, we'll take it really slow and watch carefully," Tyler said.

A gust of cool air rushed by and filtered through my clothes. My hair blew wildly behind me.

"My parents told me last night that it could get stormy this week," Tyler said.

"Really? That's all we need, to be caught in a rainstorm," I responded.

Jill joined in, "The weatherman isn't always right, you know."

"Hey," Tyler interrupted. "Did you guys ever find that shield thing you were talking about?"

"No," I said. "I hope my mother didn't throw it away."

"Maybe it would help if we could ask the Noceans when she used it last," Tyler suggested.

"Good idea!" I said.

The trees were tall and thick along the side of the road as we approached the end of the mile.

"How 'bout we hide our bikes over there?" Tyler said, pointing to an opening in the trees to the left.

Just overhead, a group of huge, black crows began to caw nervously. The sound sharply penetrated the air, like they were somehow warning the Drimlor about our presence. Fear blew through me like a cold east wind.

"Sure," I quietly agreed. "But I wish those birds would shut up!"

We climbed off our bikes and hid them behind some trees. Tyler was careful to quietly cover them with fallen branches while looking off in different directions in the forest.

"Let's go!" Jill whispered.

We followed her lead and slowly began walking through trees toward Bellen Road.

The crows relentlessly cawed above us.

Tyler reached into his pocket and pulled out a large black marble. He placed it in the leather pouch of his sling shot and held it tightly between his fingertips, ready to fire at a moment's notice. He was suddenly *profoundly* serious and almost stood like one of the Runners from the day before. He looked back at me quickly and motioned me closer with a quick nod of his head. I obeyed and fell in right behind him. It was amazing how Tyler really believed everything we told him without seeing it all.

Jill's hand sharply motioned for us to stop. She leaned her head out of the trees and carefully looked down Bellen Road. Then, waving us forward, we moved quickly to the other side. We walked deeper into the woods than the day before. I could no longer see the road behind us.

Tyler tapped Jill on the back and motioned for her to get down. We all crouched down and crept through the forest like cats sneaking through the brush to catch a mouse. I held on to a strap from Tyler's backpack and concentrated on where to place my feet so they wouldn't make a sound. I carefully followed in Tyler's footsteps, amazed at how quiet we were as we made our way through the trees. Jill carefully led us down the hill.

I looked up and noticed Tyler's hair moving back and forth as he searched in all directions for any sign of trouble.

My foot suddenly caught on something. Without warning, I landed hard on the ground in front of me, whacking my arms on Tyler's shoes. Something had cinched around my ankle and was pulling with great force at my leg. The ground began to move violently underneath me.

"Ty!" I gasped. I grabbed at the brush as I noticed him moving away from me. I tried to claw my fingers around anything I could to slow myself down. I was being dragged away!

A strong hand grabbed me by the wrist.

"Hold on!" Tyler yelled. "Get her other arm!"

Jill landed fast on my hand and we gripped each other frantically. She grabbed my shoulder and all of us began to slow down. Their weight held me from being pulled into the brush.

My ankle was pounding with pain!

"What is it?" I screamed, trying to look down at my foot. It felt like a rope of some kind.

"Hold still!" Tyler demanded.

He grabbed me by my shorts and positioned his leg against the trunk of a nearby tree. He let go of my wrist and pulled out a pocket-knife, flipping the blade out quickly.

"Hold on to her, Jill!" Tyler yelled. We began to move again. Tyler quickly put the knife in his mouth and grabbed on to my arm, stopping our movement abruptly.

I was sick to my stomach! I felt like I was being stretched apart.

At the same time, we all noticed a shiny object in the dirt, out to the side of my head.

I gasped.

The shimmering gold cloth lay open wide and the beautiful golden needle was exposed to the air of the forest.

"The needle!" Jill screamed, gripping tighter at my arm and shoulder.

"Isn't that supposed to be covered up?" Tyler said, his voice muffled by the knife between his teeth.

A loud, painful roar echoed like angry thunder in the distance.

Fear shot through me.

"Great!" Jill exclaimed. "What are we going to do now?"

"When I tell you, Jill," Tyler said quickly, "let go of her and cover that needle!"

I glared at Tyler.

"Don't worry, Timber," he said, behind the knife in his mouth. His face was hot with fear, yet deeply determined.

Another angry roar pierced the air from in the distance.

Suddenly, Tyler grabbed my leg and lunged for my feet.

"Now!" he yelled.

Jill reached for the needle.

Tyler held on to my legs as we began to move vigorously along the ground. He grabbed the knife from out of his mouth and quickly cut the rope just under what was around my ankle. We rolled forward then stopped abruptly. I was on Tyler's lap. I gasped. We both were sitting on the edge of a dark, deep hole in the ground. We watched the rope fly out over the hole, flip back and forth, then drop out of sight. Then we heard a loud thud, like a boulder crashing from deep within the pit. Tyler quickly wrapped me up in his arms and leaned us away from the ledge.

I looked at Tyler and felt the security of his warm arms around me.

Jill was standing behind us like a white, marble sculpture.

Another loud roar thundered through the forest. It was closer this time!

Jill's eyes grew even wider.

"Run!" she whispered desperately, holding the needle out for me to take.

Tyler and I bolted up off the ground. I grabbed the needle and shoved it in my pocket as we followed Jill running deeper into the forest.

Pain throbbed down the front of my legs and deep in my ankle. I kept moving but limped as I tried to run. I carefully dodged branches and fallen limbs that seemed to get thicker. My ankle felt huge and heavy. Tyler noticed me struggling and took hold of my hand.

Fear was pounding through my body as I could hear a heavy, uneven sound of movement in the distance.

"Jill," Tyler called up to her in a loud whisper. "Let's hide over there." He pointed to a thick area of brush.

I looked over my shoulder to see how close the Watchman was but saw nothing. When I turned back, Tyler and Jill were gone.

Tyler's arm reached out for me from under the bushes. I placed my hand in his, ducked down tightly, and crawled quickly under the prickly branches that seemed to grab at me as I entered. I felt dust settle on my skin as I crawled behind Tyler. It was a tight fit, and the ground was bumpy, but I felt safer under the bushes than out in the open forest. We quickly curled up at the base of a tree trunk and listened intently.

The heavy, uneven sound grew louder and louder. Tyler firmly laced his fingers into mine and gently rubbed the side of my hand with his thumb.

Jill glanced at me then back toward the sound.

I held my breath.

An ear-piercing roar resounded around us.

"I know you're here!" the Watchman screamed.

His voice was filled with intense anger as he took deep, labored breaths of air. The brush moved violently just ahead of us. "I *will* find you!" he continued.

I noticed the slingshot on Tyler's wrist. The black marble was gone. Tyler tilted his head slightly to the side as if he noticed something. I stretched my eyes in his direction, not wanting to make a sound, barely moving my head. Tyler pointed to the ground just off to the side of Jill. He looked back at me. I looked at him questioningly.

The Drimlor was moaning and wildly hitting at the brush.

Tyler let go of my hand and quietly reached into his pocket for another marble. He looked like he was moving in slow motion. He placed it securely in the leather pouch in his slingshot and held it tightly. He aimed toward the Watchman. I knew he would wait till the last moment before he would fire at the Drimlor.

Jill reached out slowly and wiped the dust off the edge on something long that was just under the ground beside her. It looked like a piece of wood. She gently started to dig at the dirt underneath it. Like the revealing stamp of a cookie cutter, all the edges showed perfectly through the dirt. It was the shape of a large rectangle on the ground. She looked quickly back at me and Tyler. Her eyes were wide with anticipation.

Tyler nodded his head twice, motioning for Jill to lift it up. She leaned forward and wedged her fingertips under the edge of the long piece of wood. She lifted as the whole rectangular shape moved upward, revealing a door of some kind. Jill turned her head slowly in amazement. Tyler and I leaned over to look inside. It was an opening into the ground.

It sounded like the Drimlor was thrashing right above us now.

Tyler grabbed the edge of the wood, lifted it up and climbed inside. Jill motioned for me to go next. I moved quietly across the ground and crawled in through the opening.

It felt cold as I stepped down into the darkness. Tyler's warm arms gently grabbed my legs and helped me feel my way to the ground next to him. He reached up and guided Jill down too. Carefully, Tyler shut the secret door above us. The darkness closed in tightly around us.

I could barely breathe.

"It's okay," Tyler whispered. "I've got a flashlight here somewhere."

I could hear Tyler unzipping his backpack and rummaging through his things.

"Here it is," he said.

With a click, the light pierced through the darkness revealing the space around us. We were crouched down in a perfectly dug-out hole in the ground. It was about four feet deep, and there was enough room to easily hold all of us.

"It's a hiding place!" I exclaimed with a whisper.

"Probably one that Catherine and Zelly dug out years ago," Jill quietly concluded.

"Look over here," Tyler said. He shined the flashlight into a smaller hole that went farther back into the ground. Twisted little roots hung down from the top. The hole looked jagged and uneven, like someone had dug it out with a small shovel.

"What is it?" I whispered.

"It's a tunnel," Jill said.

Tyler leaned his head in and looked at the ceiling and sides of it. "I think it's an underground passage," he said. The hole seemed to swallow up his voice. "I think we should find out where it goes," he continued, looking back at Jill and me.

I took a deep breath of cold stagnant air. I did *not* want to go crawling through some hole in the ground, even *if* my grandma dug it out.

"Let's hope this place is not the Watchman's hideout!" I said in a weak attempt to try and derail their idea.

"He couldn't even reach the hole through all the bushes, Timber," Jill said sharply. "And the opening didn't look used for a very long time!"

"But we don't know what's at the other end of the passage," I whined. "And what about the Noceans?"

"Ty, I think we should see where this goes!" Jill said, ignoring me.

Tyler looked at me with concern.

"Timber, we're going to be okay. You can follow between me and Jill. And besides, I think we should go, just in case he happens to find *this* opening. If Catherine dug this out, it probably would help us in some way."

Jill looked at me. "The first thing we should do is get safely away from the Drimlor, and then we'll get to Mandoria."

I was outnumbered and I knew it.

"Okay," I sighed.

"Follow right behind me, Timber," Tyler said as he headed off into the opening.

I watched his feet disappear behind the distant light of the flashlight. Then, I reluctantly crawled into the tunnel behind him.

CHAPTER ELEVEN

UNDERGROUND

The staunch, musty, smell of dirt was all around me as I crawled behind Tyler through the hole in the ground. It was hard to take a deep breath, and I wasn't sure if it was because of my own fear or because of the small, confined tunnel. I labored with all my might to place my elbow as far in front of me as I could and push with my feet. Long, cold, wiry roots flipped against my face and moved slowly over my shoulders and legs as I inched along.

"Are you okay back there?" Tyler finally asked. His voice sounded different in such a small, confined area.

Tyler's shoe dug into the dirt in front of me and flipped back at my face.

"I'm not so sure about this," I called up to Tyler. My lungs could not seem to expand very wide. I hated crawling inside this little space!

"Just don't think about it, Timber!" Jill quickly joined in from behind me. "Try to focus on something else."

"Hey, do you think this is what a worm feels like?" Tyler asked, trying to lighten the mood. He chuckled out loud.

"Ty, stop it!" I whined. "I don't even want to think about *that*!"

"Okay, Timber," Tyler said. "Hopefully, it won't be too much further."

The dirt felt cold and rough on my elbows and knees.

I tried to focus on the moving shadows from Tyler's flashlight. Even though I knew Jill was behind me, it was creepy to think about how dark it was back there.

"How much longer?" I asked. To my dismay, no one answered. I could only hear the loud, scratching sounds of movement in the dirt. Maybe my voice was not loud enough or maybe they were trying to manage their own feelings. I guess I didn't *need* an answer; besides, no one really *knew* the answer. Suddenly, it was much harder to breath.

The air was stiff, cold, and stale as I took it into my lungs, but it felt hot and steamy coming out. Thick perspiration gathered around my mouth.

"I can hardly breathe!" I said, louder this time. Once again there was no reply. The scraping sounds seemed like they were all of a sudden digging into my ears. Tightness gripped at my chest. I began to gasp loud and hard for a breath of air.

"Tyler!" I exclaimed. My body stopped moving. I felt Jill hit my shoes. *"I can't do this! I have to go back!"*

"Keep moving!" Jill screamed. I could hear the terror in her voice. The pain suddenly wrenched tighter, at my chest!

"Timber," Tyler said in a calm, clear voice. "I know we're almost to the end. Can you just keep moving, *for me?*"

His voice was soft and smooth like warm, melting butter, and it eased the pain knotted in my chest. I closed my eyes and thought about Tyler's big brown eyes. The tightness in my chest slightly relaxed. Yes, I could probably do just about anything for him! I took a slow, deep breath of rotten, earthy air and began again to move forward.

"That's it, Timber," Tyler said encouragingly. I knew he could hear me scratching my way forward again.

"You can do it!" His voice was like a beacon for me to follow. "Just keep moving forward."

I tried to keep a steady pace behind him.

"We're almost there," Tyler coaxed me on. "Just a little bit—"

The rhythm of his voice stopped.

"Further!" he labored to say.

It sounded like he was pushing on something.

"Hey you guys, another room!" he exclaimed.

Relief flushed through me, and I felt an urgent need to get out of there!

Tears welled up in my eyes as I saw the glassy light that filled the space at the end of the tunnel. The shadow from Tyler's head peered in at me.

"Hurry up, Timber!" Tyler said, with excitement in his voice. "Are you okay back there, Jill?"

"I'll survive," Jill said wearily. I could hear her frantically scratching through the dirt.

I pulled myself through the opening and quickly moved out of the way so Jill could get through.

The flashlight was on the ground directing light to a portion of the dugout. Tyler was sitting back in the shadows. I quickly scooted over next to him and laid my head on his shoulder. Tears streamed silently down my face. Jill moved to the other side. Each of us took some deep breaths and sat, exhausted, against the dirt wall of the small room. I closed my eyes and held on to Tyler's arm.

"Are you alright?" he asked as I wiped the tears from my eyes.

"Hey Timber, don't cry," he whispered. "You did it!"

"I *hated* that tunnel!" I responded sharply. The skin on my legs stung and my ankle was still throbbing.

"Yeah, me too!" Jill quickly agreed.

"You're so dirty," Tyler said. He was talking to me. I opened my eyes and looked at him. "And you have scratches all over you," he continued. His voice was kind and sympathetic.

"I'll be alright!" I said. "Besides, we're all dirty!"

A few minutes passed in silence.

"Just tell me there's an opening in here," Jill said. "I don't want to go back."

"Oh, I'm sure there is," Tyler said.

"What's that?" Jill asked.

I opened my eyes as Jill picked up the flashlight from off the ground. She got on her knees as she directed the light to a cubby-hole in the dirt wall.

"Look!" She exclaimed.

Tyler and I moved closer.

Jill pulled out a long golden cloth that was neatly rolled up. Her eyes grew wide with excitement on her dirty, smudged face.

"Here it is!" she said as she handed the shield to me.

"Well, we know now that your grandma must have dug out this underground passage," Tyler said.

"She could have made the hole a little bigger!" Jill said sarcastically.

"Yeah," I quickly agreed as I took another deep breath of air.

"And the Watchman must not find out about this!" Tyler added.

I held up the corners of the silky, golden material as the bottom of it rolled out underneath my hands. There were three wide loops of silky cloth along the top. I slid my hand through the bands one at a time, then held my arm out in front of me like I would a regular shield.

"So, how do I look?" I asked, modeling my new protective gear.

Tyler let out a slight laugh, "The question is does it really work?"

"We'll have to test it out later," Jill said, as she stuck her arm back in the cubby hole. "Hey, another flashlight!"

Jill handed the flashlight to Tyler and he turned it on, adding a greater burst of light to the small dirt room. Then he turned it off.

"What's this?" she said, pulling out a tube-like thing that had an intricate casing around it. It was connected to a thick string that could fit perfectly around the neck.

"I don't know," Tyler said, taking it from Jill.

I took the flashlight and shined it directly on the item. It was a couple inches long and had a little knob at the top. Tyler gently turned the knob and another vile inside moved up and down. A dark liquid moved back and forth.

"It looks really cool, but until we actually know what it is, we should probably keep it here in the cubby" Tyler said.

"Yeah, you're right," Jill said. She took it and slowly put it back in the hole. "You'd hate for it to blow up or something."

"Hey, another piece of material."

Jill pulled out a small rectangular piece of golden cloth. It was about six inches long with long, golden strings attached to the ends of it.

"I wonder what that does," I said, lifting the long strings out to one side.

"There is one more thing in here," Jill said, pulling out a circular piece. "It looks like an ancient coin that was hand carved or something. Look at the little spindles on top of it."

We looked carefully at our findings.

"These things are so cool! But we should probably get going," I finally said.

"Yeah," Tyler agreed. He took the flashlight and began looking around the ceiling of the little dirt room.

"Should I keep the shield?"

"I would," Jill said. "I think Ayden wanted you to have it, anyway."

I took it off and put it in my back pocket as Jill put the other things away.

A sharp, bright light shot into the little room.

"Here it is!" Tyler whispered.

I squinted and pulled my head away from the blinding stream of light. He waited a minute for our eyes to adjust and then opened the door wide enough to look out.

"What's out there?" I asked, still trying to adjust to the light.

"All I see is bushes," Tyler said.

Jill and I peered out the opening beside Tyler. Bushes were everywhere!

"There it is!" I whispered.

"The tree!" Jill exclaimed, grabbing my arm. "The underground passage is a secret way to get to the tree!"

"Or a quick means to get away!" I added.

Slowly, Tyler lowered the wooden door. The darkness made my eyes ache.

"So, your Grandma dug this tunnel out for safety reasons," Tyler said. "And maybe to hide some things."

"I can't even picture my Grandma doing this," I said in amazement.

"Well, she did," Jill said. "And if it can remain hidden, it will be a great way to escape the Drimlor."

"Do you still have the key?" Tyler asked.

"Yes, it's right here!"

"Well, let's do this then!" Tyler said.

"Why don't you two stay here?" I heard myself say in amazement.

"What do you mean?" Tyler asked.

"I'll run to the tree and put the needle in," I continued, bravely. "You'll be safe in here from the wind. Then you can come out and we'll go to the pond together."

"That's a good idea!" Jill said. "But I think we should *run* to the pond and get in the water as quickly as possible in case the Watchman is anywhere near."

Tyler flinched when Jill talked about the water.

"Are you okay, Tyler?" I asked.

He took a deep breath. "I'll be alright!" he said. "But I'm not too sure about letting you go out to the tree by yourself."

"I think I'll be okay." I said.

I was deeply concerned but didn't want to put all of us in unneeded danger.

"Besides, the Watchman doesn't even know we're here!" Jill joined in. "Who knows where he is even at?"

I was grateful for her reassurance.

I slowly took the ancient needle out of my pocket. Careful to keep it covered, I gripped it tightly in my hand.

"Well, I'm ready," I said. "Will you hold the door for me, Ty?"

"Sure," he responded.

Tyler pushed hard on the thick wooden door. The bright sunlight jabbed at my eyes as I crawled onto the ground under the dense bushes around the opening. I stopped for a moment to let my eyes adjust. A strong waft of fresh air filled my lungs with an invigorating, warm sensation. Birds chirped happily in the trees. Before moving on, I glanced behind me at the two large sets of eyes peering out of the opening in the ground. I smiled and shook my head. This whole situation was hard to believe.

I crawled to the edge of the bushes, scanning the forest for the Drimlor as I did so. Then I locked my eyes on the tree that stood about fifteen feet ahead of me. I felt my body bolt out from under the scratchy bushes. I could hardly believe I was doing this!

I climbed up and over the big, long branches of the tree and placed the golden cloth holding the needle next to the knot. I opened the cloth and hastily put the eye into the hole and pushed. Just like before, it was taken from my hand and sunk halfway into the tree with a click and then another as it made a half turn.

I wrapped my arms and legs around the huge tree branch I was sitting on. Just like before, everything grew perfectly still—the calm before the storm. I could barely see the edge of the underground passage that lay safely beneath the brush. I closed my eyes and waited in the gripping silence.

The wind started with the same violent sound of crashing metal. I clenched the large tree branch even tighter. Although I knew what was coming, fear still shot through me like a bolt of lightning. Sharp drafts of air whipped hard against my skin as the tree seemed to vibrate underneath me. Dirt and twigs lashed wildly around me.

Hold on, Timber! You know it will stop! I told myself. *Only thirty more seconds or so!*

The wind whipped forcefully a bit longer around me, and then it was over. I released my arms and legs. I sat up as I saw Tyler and Jill running over from under the brush.

"Let's hurry!" Jill whispered with excitement as they both approached me.

"Are you okay?" Tyler asked. His eyes were wide with concern.

"I'm fine!" I exclaimed.

Tyler noticed the elegant pathway and froze like a beautiful honey-brown bear.

"Do you like it?" I asked.

"So... this is *real*," he responded slowly.

"Hurry up!" Jill commanded as she glanced in the distance. "He knows we are here, I'm sure."

We followed her through the beautiful, ornate pathway.

"Wow!" Tyler said, as we reached the beautiful, crystal-clear pond. His expression was filled with total amazement.

"Get into the water, now!" Jill demanded.

Jill already had her shoes off. Tyler and I slipped ours off too. I grabbed his hand and we walked slowly into the edge of the pond. I carefully watched his response as the water moved up and around our legs.

"This is amazing!" Tyler responded, holding tightly onto my hand.

The feeling of the warm, silky water was soothing on my aching legs and ankle. I felt pleasantly refreshed and exhilarated.

"The water feels different," Tyler commented as his fingertips examined the silky feeling left on them.

"It does!" I agreed.

Jill lunged out along the top of the water and moved quickly into the middle of the pond.

"Let's go!" Jill called to us impatiently.

I pulled Tyler along with me as we made our way next to Jill. Tyler's eyes looked relaxed as he laid his head back in the thick, clear water.

"This feels so good," he said, in a slow, awestruck voice.

Jill looked at me and smiled.

"It does, Ty! But we need to get going," she said.

"I could stay right here, forever!" he responded.

Jill took Tyler's other hand and he slowly lifted his head out of the thick soothing water. I could tell he was trying to refocus on why we were even here. She grabbed my other hand and looked into our eyes as we made a circle between us.

"On the count of three, blow all the air out of your lungs, then we'll go under the water together," Jill said. "Okay?"

It took Tyler a moment to realize what she said. His expression dramatically changed; his beautiful eyes now filled with worry.

"Uh, why?" he asked.

"Tyler, we have to go under the water *now*," Jill said.

"Please, not yet!" he begged. He glanced quickly in my direction.

"You don't understand, Tyler. The Watchman must know the pond is here. The fact that we can't hear him yet could mean he is aiming his darts at us right now," Jill exclaimed.

"She's right," I said, looking into his troubled eyes. "We have to get *under* the water right now."

"On three," Jill announced again.

"Wait!" he said, sharply.

"You can do this," I said, trying to comfort him. "It really is going to be fine."

"Okay, okay," he said. Tyler closed his eyes and took a deep breath. "I guess I'll never really be ready, so let's just get this over with!"

He took another deep breath and slightly tilted his head back.

"One," Jill said slowly. She quickly scanned the area around the pond.

My eyes were fixed upon Tyler. He almost drowned once, and now he was going to put himself through that same thing for something he didn't even know was true yet. *Who is this boy anyway? And willing to take such a risk?* I wondered.

"Two," Jill said. She closed her eyes to concentrate. "Three," Jill concluded.

At the same time, we all exhaled slowly and dropped into the thick, silky water. Jill pulled down slightly on our hands. The soft, fluid wrapped around us like a thick velvet comforter. I felt the current begin to gently tug at our feet.

I relaxed with it. Quickly, I inhaled the pure, cleansing liquid into my lungs. That was easy! I felt free and invigorated. I opened my eyes and the colors exploded around me, just as before.

Tyler pulled hard on my hand and I suddenly jerked upward. With great strength he pulled his hand from mine. His eyes were frantic, and his strength was *unreal* as he lashed out wildly to swim to the top. The current pulled us downward at a slow and steady pace.

I looked at Jill. I could tell she was relaxed and calm. She must have already taken in the water.

I moved in front of Tyler and tried to get his attention. *I know exactly what you're going through,* I thought. I reached out gently to grab his face. Finally, he noticed me. I could tell he was trying to be brave, but he looked like he was suffocating. He stopped the frantic movement of his arms and reached out with great force, clasping his fingers through mine. Over and over, he squeezed my palms as if he were begging for me to release him. *How can I bear to see this beautiful boy suffer?* His sad eyes burrowed into mine. Finally, I blew water into his face as he opened his mouth and gave up the fight. He inhaled long and hard.

Tyler closed his eyes as if resigned to his fate. But then his expression dramatically changed, and a little smile slowly formed at the corner of his mouth. He took another deep breath and opened his eyes wide. He looked right at me. I could tell he was enjoying the feeling of the water in his lungs as his chest puffed in front of him.

The downward current stopped, just a few feet above the bottom of the pond. We continued to descend the rest of the way and placed our feet on the soft dirt beneath us.

Jill moved in and rested her hand on my arm and gently put her other hand on Tyler's face. She smiled as if to acknowledge how well he did. She motioned her head to the side and slowly waived for us to follow her. I knew exactly where she was going. I smiled at Tyler, let go of his hands and began to swim. He immediately followed and then swam up beside me.

Tyler's brown hair swayed gently in the turquoise water. He was so fascinated with the pond. His eyes were wide with wonder and amazement, and he slowed down many times to enjoy the breathtaking beauty of the moving creatures. As we swam, he gently touched the plants and flowers that grew in colorful clusters along the way. Tyler pointed to some brilliant, shimmering rocks that lined the edge of the boulders nearing the cave. I looked at him and smiled.

Jill stopped in front of the three jagged openings leading into the cave. She turned and motioned forward to us. I grabbed Tyler's hand and pulled him through one of the large openings into the darkness. Quickly we swam to the back of the cavern where golden streams of light escaped from around the large stone. Jill and I gripped the edge of the stone and pulled it over.

I looked at Tyler and pointed to the bright opening through the billowing pillows of dirt that lead to Mandoria. Tyler looked confused. He didn't understand. Jill motioned for me to go ahead. I slowly moved forward and through the soft, sponge-like lining of the opening.

The air in Mandoria felt cool and dry upon my face as I entered. I gently coughed and pulled the rest of my body through and sat next to the rocky hillside.

Tyler's hand came through the rocks next. I gently grabbed his fingertips and helped him through the opening. His wide brown eyes looked at me in amazement as he coughed. Jill followed Tyler.

We sat on the soft grass in the clearing that was surrounded by miniature trees. I could tell Tyler was trying to take it all in as we were yesterday.

"That was the most amazing thing I have ever seen!" Tyler said, rubbing his eyes and pushing his wet hair out of his face.

"The pond is beautiful, isn't it?" I responded.

"Yeah," he said. "I've never seen so many colors at one time before. And we could breathe after all!"

"I'm so sorry, Tyler," I said sympathetically, wincing at the memory of his earlier pained expression. "I wanted to stop the pain for you."

"Thank you for your help, Timber," Tyler said quietly, also remembering.

"It's incredible isn't it?" Jill said. "Ty, you did good taking the water in!" she added.

"That was by far the scariest thing I have ever done!"

"Well, it's over now," I said to Tyler, and raised my hands. "This is Mandoria."

"It's beautiful here!" he said, looking around the valley. "But where are the little people?" he asked.

"The Runners will be here soon!" Jill said.

"Hey, look at your legs," Tyler said. "The scratches are gone."

"Oh, I know," I responded, rubbing the smooth skin on my legs. "I told you that the pond was magical. And my ankle doesn't even hurt now."

"That is so cool!" he exclaimed. "It heals wounds."

A soft, steady fluttering came from the trees.

"Here they come," Jill whispered with excitement.

CHAPTER TWELVE

THE BOY WHO DIED ON BELLEN ROAD

The Noceans began to appear along the edge of the miniature forest. They moved swiftly as they encircled us in the clearing. I recognized Ayden with his long golden braid that hung down beside his face. His eyes were kind, and he looked happy to see me. He smiled quickly, then moved directly in front of me. Brindle was at his side, along with Stroder.

Stroder had left so fast the day before, I didn't get a chance to really meet him. I hated having to tell him about Grandma Catherine. I watched His face carefully as he positioned himself slightly in front of the others. His eyes were fixed upon Tyler.

These people were little compared to us, yet they were still breathtaking in how they carried themselves. They looked disciplined and intensely focused. Stroder's face was slightly fuller than the other Noceans, and his eyes were big but darker and deeper set. He was tall and

205

muscular, and I could tell he was their leader by the way the Runners responded to him. Maybe he earned this rank by killing a Drimlor that was the size of a human.

Stroder looked slowly over to Jill, then back to me.

"Timber," he asked in a firm voice. "Who is the boy?"

I glanced at Tyler, then Jill.

"Um. Well, this is Tyler."

Stroder stared intently at me for a moment. I recognized a familiar coldness in his expression. Pain has a hollow look to it when you lose someone close to you.

"I thought Tyler could help," I said quickly, pulling my knees up to my chest and wrapping my arms around my legs. "Because he knows a lot about rocks and crystals."

"No one else!" he said.

His eyes were blank with emotion, but I could sense he was disappointed in me.

"No one else must know about us!"

"Okay," I answered.

"I promise, I'll *never* tell anyone about you here," Tyler quickly spoke up. "I helped Timber and Jill get away from the Watchman today, and I'll do it again if I have to!"

Brindle stepped forward, moving her small, handheld bow slightly upward.

"Did you see his green eyes?" she asked with deep concern in her voice.

"I did," Tyler said. "And if you let me, I will try to help your people figure out why the crystals have stopped growing. Timber told me about your problem. But first, I have a few questions."

"I appreciate you helping to keep Timber safe from the Drimlor," Stroder spoke calmly to Tyler. "But there are many things here that you know nothing about."

"Stroder," Ayden said. "He might have an idea."

"No!" Stroder cut him off sharply, and then swallowed slowly as he spoke her name. "Catherine spent her *entire* life studying the problem. There is nothing more anyone can do."

"Runners!" Stroder called, in a loud voice. "Retreat to the forest, then ease down, on guard!"

At his command, the Runners moved quickly to the edge of the trees and stood carefully as to guard the perimeter. I assumed he ordered them to move so we could talk more privately.

Brindle and Ayden remained standing next to Stroder. They too must be leaders among the Runners.

"Look," Stroder said.

He spoke directly to me, slightly more relaxed than before.

"We are making a decision about what we need to do. Our people only have a handful of rations left. There are not enough Aspid-crystals for even the Runners to survive another week, let alone the whole village of Noceans who need them as well."

"Only a week left?" I asked. I couldn't believe it. *That's not enough time!*

"We are getting weaker with every passing minute," he continued. "I know what we have to do."

"No!" Ayden said, passionately. "That is not the answer, Stroder!"

"But Ayden," Brindle said. She looked longingly at his face. "That might be the only way for us to survive."

"No one knows exactly how long we will live without Aspids before we start to get sick," Ayden said. "It could be months!"

"We can't risk it, Ayden!" Brindle shot back sharply. "Others died during the last Aspid rain."

"And nobody knows why!" he retorted.

"Ayden," Stroder said calmly. "You know it was because there were not enough Aspids."

"But Timber doesn't even know about everything yet," Ayden glanced desperately at Stroder. "She should have the chance to choose, too!"

"No!" Stroder said sternly. His eyes looked razor-sharp as he held his gaze with Ayden.

Everyone became quiet.

"Wait!" I said. "What do you think the answer is? And what is it that I need to know about?"

Stroder cleared his throat, "I think we should cut the last tree down by the pond." He paused, then continued, "And have you close Creshtil Pass forever. We would then harvest the Aspids and have another ten years to figure out where we will go or what we will do."

"And just plan to die?" Ayden asked sharply. "I want a plan to *live*! Now tell her about what else she deserves to know."

Brindle sighed and rolled her beautiful big eyes. "It really won't matter, Ayden. Besides, you know this is just about your little crush."

I looked at Jill, then to Tyler. They, too, looked confused about what was going on here.

"Crush?" I asked.

Ayden's tiny eyebrows pulled together sharply above his deep dark eyes.

"It's not a crush," he said defensively to Brindle.

"Every time Catherine spoke about you, Timber," Brindle said. "Ayden got all excited and couldn't wait to meet you."

Brindle spoke with sarcasm. "You know you have a crush on her!"

"I just loved hearing Catherine talk about you, Timber," Ayden said sheepishly, looking at me with kind eyes. "I thought it would be nice to know you. Catherine loved you so much and used to tell me that you and I were a lot alike."

Ayden glared at Brindle. His cheeks were slightly pink.

"I just thought one day you would make the choice too, Timber. And then I could live where you live."

I smiled to think this small Nocean boy enjoyed hearing about me before he even met me. *What did Grandma tell him?* I wondered. *And what did he mean "live where I live"?*

Suddenly, I felt Tyler laced his fingers through mine. Then he gave me a funny look. *Was he jealous?* I chuckled to myself.

"Come on," Jill whispered, leaning closer to Tyler. "Look at them…they are little!"

"We may be small," Ayden said, his dark eyes pierced back at Jill. "But every Keeper is allowed the choice."

"What choice?" I asked, confused.

"If she chops down the last tree," Stroder said to Ayden, "it would be easier on her if she knows nothing about it!"

"You're just mad that your Catherine didn't make the choice soon enough!" Ayden said sharply.

Stroder made a fist and clenched his jaw. He turned away and took a long, deliberate breath.

"Ayden," Brindle whispered sharply with disappointment.

"Your Catherine?" I asked.

"Enough," Brindle said as she stepped between the two of them. "Stop this! I do think we should answer any questions Tyler might have about the Aspids."

I could tell that Brindle was trying to change the subject to prevent a fight. But I still wanted to know about what *the choice* was.

"Maybe Tyler somehow has a new idea?" Brindle continued. "Besides, he's already seen the green eyes of Boden."

"This is all a waste of time!" Stroder said sharply. "And time is something we don't have!"

"Please?" she begged.

Stroder tucked his bow down and folded his arms, full of frustration. He stared at the rocky hillside.

"Well, Tyler?" she asked, turning to us again. "What questions do you have?"

"Umm. Okay," Tyler said. "I was wondering what the crystals look like?"

"They are usually dark red," Brindle replied. "But the older Noceans remember a time when they were clear."

"What's their texture like, and how big are they?"

"Well, they're hard and a little bumpy and they're about the size of my hand." She held out her little hand and delicately cupped her long tiny fingers. "Catherine told us that they look like little acorns."

"And so you crush the crystals and mix them in with your food?" Tyler asked. "Are they like vitamins?"

Brindle and Ayden both nodded.

"Do they have a taste?" Tyler asked.

"Sure, they're kind of bitter if you eat them by themselves," Brindle responded, wrinkling her nose. "Well, they just have a strong taste."

Tyler tilted his head to the side and raised his eyebrows. "Hmm. Did Catherine discover what kind of tree they grow on?"

Stroder turned his head sharply and looked at Brindle. "This is a waste of time!" he said.

"They're Oak Trees," Brindle answered, ignoring Stroder.

Tyler leaned back against the hillside. "I've never heard of an Oak tree producing crystals," he said, "But there must be a specific process that takes place inside the tree, maybe like the way petrified wood forms, but that would take hundreds and hundreds of years. I would like to remove a crystal from the tree before we go home and get a sample of the water, that way I can look at them both under the microscope."

"There aren't crystals on the tree right now," Ayden said.

"What do you mean? I thought there is *one* tree left out by the pond."

"There is," he responded. "But they can only be seen after it rains in the outer world. And only by the light of a full moon."

"I bet the chances of *that* happening are pretty slim," Jill joined in, with a quick laugh. "How can it be rainy with clouds in the sky *and* be clear enough to see a full moon?"

"It happens!" Ayden continued.

"More times than you know!" Stroder joined in. "But the crystals cannot be removed, even in the moonlight. They can only be seen that way. They come off only as they mix with the water of the pond after the tree has been cut down."

"Do you think I could have one of your crystals then?" Tyler asked hesitantly.

"No!" Stroder said sharply. "Look, Catherine has asked all these questions and has done all the tests that anyone could even begin to think of."

"Okay then," Tyler said confidently. "Tell me the shape of the crystal molecule that is found in the Aspid. This will tell us if it is a rock or a mineral or possibly that it derives from a plant. And what are the elements present when the process of growing takes place?"

Everyone looked at Stroder.

He glared at Tyler and clenched his jaw.

"I don't know the answer to those questions. But Catherine had the crystals tested once, years ago. She didn't think it was that important. She believed the *type* of tree was the answer. She studied every kind! She even had this old leather book she found from another Keeper."

"We have that, too!" I exclaimed as I glanced over to Jill. "So, Winston was another Keeper?"

"Yes, but he was killed by the Watchman," Stroder continued.

"Hey, that reminds me," I said. "There was a boy who was once killed on Bellen Road. Do you guys know who that was?

Stroder tilted his head to the side in deep thought as Ayden and Brindle glanced at each other.

"No," Stroder said. "I haven't heard anything about that."

"I wondered if the Watchman killed him too," I said.

Stroder looked unconcerned. But something felt off to me as he continued talking.

"But in that notebook," he said. "There was something about how they used to plant things with the trees. Did you see that in there? Catherine tried everything she could think of. She even planted hundreds of different combinations, with different types of trees, but nothing ever grew the crystals. Eventually the other types of trees she planted died off. Now there are mostly young oak trees, but only one has Aspid buds. And that is the one the key fits into that opens up the pass."

"There are two things we know," Tyler interrupted. "We know that the crystals grow on top of the oak trees. And we know that the water in the pond has special changing qualities. It heals. And it speeds up that healing process.

"No disrespect toward Catherine, but I believe before we plant anything with the trees, we should take a closer look at the properties of what we are wanting. We have the crystals, or Aspids. I don't know how Catherine had them tested, but I would like to look at them under my microscope. It's true, I know a lot about rocks and crystals."

Everyone was completely quiet. Tyler sounded reasonable, and I could tell they were interested in what he had to say.

"We know two of the elements: the tree and the water," Tyler counted off. "But something is missing. A third element is needed—possibly a fourth. I need to see the shape of the molecules in the crystal. It could be something simple or extremely complex, but I'll never know until I can look at it."

"What is needed to grow crystals?" Stroder asked.

"Every situation is different. But the process of growing crystals usually involves dissolving, absorbing, evaporating, and crystallizing. In the case of rocks or geodes, this could take thousands of years with the need of dramatic temperature changes, like the heat from a volcano. But I think with this, it is something entirely different because of the simple fact that they can be eaten."

"There is never heat in the pass," Stroder added.

"It's worth a try!" Brindle said with a hint of excitement in her voice.

"Yeah, come on Stroder!" Ayden joined in. "Catherine never thought of this!"

"She thought of everything!" Stroder snapped back defensively. "The elders are not going to be happy with this! We only have a handful of Aspid left."

"Well, a handful will never be enough anyway," Ayden added.

Suddenly, the sound of loud, wild birds came from back within the trees. I looked across the tops of the trees. They reminded me of enlarged broccoli plants that went on forever. The birds fluttered wildly and then took off like tiny black spots filling the distant sky.

The Runner's moved in unison to face the sound of the disturbance and then slowly turned to Stroder.

"A few of you stay here and the rest, follow me," Stroder said as he moved to the edge of the clearing.

"Get a crystal!" Ayden called out.

Stroder's dark, mysterious eyes glanced at Ayden. Reluctantly, he nodded and then took off into the forest with some of the Runners.

"What is it?" I asked.

"It's probably nothing." Ayden said. "He's just taking a few Runners to check out the disturbance."

"If a Drimlor is waking," Brindle said sharply. "They'll just put him out of his misery!" She had a wicked look stir within her beautiful eyes. I wasn't going to ask what that entailed.

"Ayden," Jill said. "The Drimlorians sleep during the day, right?"

"Yes," he responded.

"You told us that the Noceans go into hiding at nighttime. Why is that? And where do you hide?"

"The Drimlorians rule the night around here," Ayden said simply.

"They don't rule anything!" Brindle snorted.

"Well, they awake during the darkness," Ayden said. "And they hunt for food and for Noceans. Their only reason for being in Mandoria is to kill us for the land. They believe this land is theirs and that when the last Nocean falls, darkness will prevail."

"And I guess we don't really hide," he continued. "We just cover our villages carefully before nightfall and remain silent."

"What do you cover them with?" Jill asked.

"Our hair. You see, our hair grows quickly and saves our people in so many ways. Aspids make the growth possible."

"Catherine calls it a miracle!" Brindle said as she pulled her golden hair forward and watched her fingers move through it. It shimmered in the sunlight.

"We have special coverings out of our hair that we pull over our homes," Ayden continued. "We are incredibly careful not to leave even a crumb of evidence for the Drimlorians to sniff out at night. With our homes covered, we remain mostly undetected."

"Then how do they even know you're here at all?" Jill asked.

"Oh, they know we're here!" Ayden said. "Long ago there was a Nocean named Drimel. He was born many millennia ago. He rebelled against his father, who was the leader at that time. He wanted to be the next ruler because he was the oldest child.

"When he was denied, he became furious and even tried to kill his own father. He was then banished from Mandoria. Over time, Drimel's anger took root and grew inside of him. Because of this fury, his body and form began to change. As time passed, he looked more and more like an animal. Some Noceans think that the water of the pass accelerated this process in him. But to me, with or without the water, anger can transform the sweetest person if it goes unchecked."

I smiled at Ayden's gentle perspective. He was strong and obviously willing to fight for his cause, yet he was kind and had a tender understanding.

"Later, Drimel returned to Mandoria and stole away many beautiful Nocean girls. They were never found. From this, a new and evil group of people formed, and they call themselves Drimlorians. Over time they grew taller and even stronger than Noceans."

Brindle snorted with disgust.

"But they can be injured and die just the same!" she huffed.

I shuttered to imagine Brindle wounding or killing anyone, even if it were to defend her people.

"The strongest Drimlorian leaders are the ones that return from closing the passes successfully. They actually receive special gifts when they become a Watchman. And upon coming back to Mandoria, they receive other gifts."

"What is significant about the Drimlor's green eyes?" Tyler asked.

"Only the Watchman's eyes glow," Brindle said. "The Drimlorians who live here do not glow. Boden can read the eye and records the retina permanently. Since Tyler and Jill have seen his green eyes, the Drimlor knows that you're both linked to the new Keeper. If anything should happen to Timber and he still doesn't have his objective, then he will forever hunt them, too. This is one reason Stroder does not want you to tell anyone else about Mandoria. Ultimately, it puts more and more people at risk. This is not 'fun and games,' Timber. The Watchman will kill if he must."

"I didn't think about that," I said guiltily.

Silence filled the air as the weight of Brindle's words fell on me.

I looked at Jill with her big green eyes and the little black mole that was on her lower right cheek. Her hair was beginning to wave as it dried. We had been best friends ever since I moved to Springfield. We had done everything together—*except* die. I hated that word! I shuddered at the thought of going through another funeral, of carrying the guilt and grief of losing my best friend. I couldn't put Jill's family through it, either! What would her mother think about me for allowing her to be a part of this dangerous situation?

Then I looked at Tyler. His long legs were out in front of him and his shoulders slightly slouched. He kept looking at me with those big brown eyes. We had only just met. How could he be so instantly loyal to me? And willing to risk everything to be a part of this situation? I'd thought of him as my bodyguard, but was it fair to label him that way and endanger his life, too?

"So, there's no turning back," Tyler said finally, straightening his posture. "We get it. The Drimlor could kill us."

"He killed that little boy on Bellen Road, didn't he?" Jill asked.

Brindle's eyes widened as she looked at Ayden.

Ayden shook his head. "No," he said.

I smiled and glanced at Jill.

"There's something you're not telling us about that boy," I said.

"We know nothing about any boy!" Brindle said firmly.

Suddenly my stomach rumbled loudly. I grabbed it with both hands.

"You must be hungry," Tyler said.

Everyone laughed.

"Well, it *is* past our lunch time," he admitted, trying to save me a little embarrassment. Maybe he was getting hungry, too?

Ayden reached out for Tyler. "Why don't you come with me and we'll get all of us something to eat?"

"Okay," Tyler said.

Tyler leaned over and whispered to me and Jill. "Do you think they have a McDonald's here?"

Jill and I laughed.

"Catherine used to love these," Ayden said, as he stood out by the edge of the trees, motioning for Tyler to hurry.

Tyler crawled over to where Ayden was. "Do you want me to walk through the trees?"

"No, just lean out into the forest as far as you can. You should be able to reach them."

Tyler followed Ayden as he ran into the trees.

I stood up and stretched high into the air. The warm sun felt good upon my skin as I looked out across the miniature trees. I could see smoke far in the distance along the tiny, beautiful mountain range, and wondered if that was where the Noceans lived. Small, majestic waterfalls caught my attention as they added movement and life to this vast, wide valley.

Jill stood up.

"It's so beautiful here!" she said, with wonder in her voice. "In a tiny sort of way, that is."

"I know!" I laughed.

"I think they do know about that little boy," Jill whispered quietly.

"I know," I responded. "I wonder why they won't tell us."

Tiny little birds fluttered in the trees around our feet.

Tyler turned around and placed a dark red object on the grass in the clearing. He glanced quickly up at me and Jill. "One double cheeseburger!" he said, winking at me. Then he leaned back into the forest.

I laughed out loud as Jill and I quickly knelt back down on the ground. A sweet, gentle, aroma filled the air. I picked up the object with both hands and leaned back against the hillside. It resembled a squash or gourd of some kind and had a little raised tip on it. I lifted the hard, dark-red object up to my nose. All my senses suddenly became more vivid.

"I want to eat this!" I said, with excitement as I felt my mouth begin to water.

"Let me have that!" Jill said, reaching out for it.

I pulled it back and sharply glanced at her.

"No," I whined.

"Here's one for you," Tyler said and handed Jill one.

Tyler turned around, sat down in the clearing, and held another one close to his nose.

Ayden ran back from within the trees.

"What are these?" I asked.

"They're Trelums," Brindle answered. "Catherine and Zelly said they are like a sweet fruit."

"How do we eat them?" Tyler asked. I could tell he was as anxious to eat as I was.

"At the tip, where they were picked from the vine, just peel back the hard-outer shell," Ayden said.

The smell was amazing as I worked at peeling the dark red Trelum. Inside were pockets of plump, yellow spheres.

"Just eat those," Ayden said, pointing to the yellow fruit inside.

I picked one and put it in my mouth.

"Wow! These explode on your tongue!" I said.

"They are *delicious*," Jill exclaimed.

"Yes," Tyler joined in, nodding his head.

"We love them, too!" Brindle said as she held her hand out for one of the soft yellow spheres. It was the size of her small, little hand.

"But they are a little better with Aspid powder," she said as she bit a small whole in the skin and drank the juice slowly.

I handed Ayden one and he motioned to the other Runners in the clearing to come and eat as well.

"Please, Ayden," I said. "I still have some questions."

Ayden looked up at me and then glanced at the others.

"Sure," he said. "Anything, Timber."

"Well, I was just thinking." I said slowly, "If I am your new Keeper and will be risking my life out there with the Watchman, who could kill me at any moment, while I chop down a tree for your people…"

Ayden and Brindle put down their Trelums and stared directly up at me.

"Don't you think it is only fair for me to know everything?" I asked. "You know… before I go ahead and do all that?"

"Timber," Tyler said sharply. "Umm, don't forget about us. We will be there to help you!"

Jill tapped Tyler on his leg, trying to quiet him. She knew exactly what I was attempting to do.

Ayden directed the Runners back to the edge of the trees. They took their Trelum spheres and retreated quickly.

"Timber, we hope that we will not have to chop down the last tree." Ayden said slowly. "And we know it is a big job to be a Keeper. It can be extremely dangerous. Winston was killed trying to protect us. But yes, I believe it is only fair that we answer all of your questions."

Brindle looked at Ayden and then to me.

"I want to know about the boy who died on Bellen Road. And I want to know about *'the choice.'*"

"Timber," Brindle said quickly. "If you know these things, it might make it harder for you to say goodbye to us if the pass has to close. And then…"

Ayden looked at Brindle and raised his hand to stop her.

"If we tell you," he spoke carefully and a little quieter. "You must not say anything until we have solved the Aspid problem.

"Okay," I said. "I promise!"

I looked at Jill and Tyler. They, too, nodded in agreement.

"Alright," Ayden said. "Catherine and Zelly found the tree when they were about twelve years old. It was not long after that that they started bringing a boy with them. His name was Steven. They came regularly and cut down a tree for us whenever we needed it. Back then, there were plenty of trees with Aspid-crystals on them. And they seemed to chop them down more often."

"Every five years, I think," Brindle said.

"Steven fell in love with Catherine," Ayden continued.

I looked at Jill and we both giggled.

"She really liked Steven. For a while they were together. But later she met a boy named William."

"Grandpa Will?" I asked. "He died when I was a baby."

"Yes," Ayden said. "She fell in love with Will and later married him. But you can imagine how hard this was for Steven."

"Wait," Jill said. "Did you guys know Steven?"

Ayden and Brindle nodded at the same time.

"Before Catherine married William, Steven and Zelly still helped her take care of the pond. But when Steven was about sixteen his mother died. He was extremely heartbroken. His father began drinking and leaving for long periods of time. People found him in the outer world and tried taking him."

"Catherine said something about 'the State,'" Brindle said. "If I remember correctly."

"Catherine and Zelly tried to help Steven. After all, they were still really good friends," Ayden said. "Steven wanted to come to Mandoria more and more."

"One night he begged Catherine to bring him here again. But she told him no. Later that night, his father came home late. He was drunk and started hitting him. Steven ended up in the hospital with broken bones."

I gasped. I could hardly believe all of this. My grandmother's life was full of so many things and people I never knew about. This was like discovering a deep ocean of secrets that my grandmother kept carefully locked in the treasure chest of her heart.

I took a deep breath. "So, was this that same boy who died?" I asked.

Ayden raised his hand slightly.

"This is when we told Catherine about the Keepers choice," he said, continuing slowly for us to understand.

"There is a way for a human to become a Nocean. This is '*the choice*' Timber.

"A special drink is carefully put together. It contains water from the pond, crushed Aspids, a drop of Noceans blood, and a drop of the Watchman's blood. This must boil and be hot when swallowed."

"So, I could become one of you guys?" I asked incredulously. "But you are so much smaller than us."

"The Keeper who drinks this will sleep for one full human day," Ayden continued. "When she awakes, she will be the size of a Nocean."

"And," Brindle added, "Ayden will have his wish come true!"

I looked at Ayden and smiled slightly.

"So…you shrink?" Jill quickly interrupted, then chuckled to herself.

"But there's one catch," Brindle said, in a more serious tone. "You can *never* become human again or return to live in the outer-world."

"Timber's not going to do that!" Tyler blurted. "And she's not going to drink some hot, creepy drink!"

"Wow!" Jill exclaimed, looking over the trees and around the landscape. "To live in Mandoria! That would be really cool… except for the whole 'not being able to return' thing!"

"No!" Tyler said louder. "She's not going to leave her family or us!"

"Look Tyler," Ayden acknowledged. "She doesn't have to make the choice right now."

"She's never going to make that choice," Tyler mumbled to himself.

"But I don't understand something," I said, ignoring their remarks. "How did the Keeper's choice affect Steven?"

"Wait!" Jill said. Her green eyes grew larger as if she suddenly understood everything.

"Grandma Catherine," I said slowly, putting everything together. "Grandma Catherine chose for Steven to come to Mandoria, didn't she? The water heals broken bones. So...who exactly is Steven?"

Unexpectedly, Ayden and Brindle sat straight up and turned their heads to the fluttering sound coming from within the forest.

The rest of the Runners returned to the edge of the trees.

There he was, standing in front of the others. He was strong. He was their leader.

"Stroder!" I heard Jill's voice whisper.

CHAPTER THIRTEEN

MUCH TO LEARN

The Runners were in a single file behind Stroder at the edge of the clearing. They were helping each other carry a long rolled up cloth under their arms.

Ayden and Brindle ran to assist them.

"They finished it?" Ayden asked excitedly.

"They did!" Stroder responded as they set the long cloth on the ground and unrolled it.

"I see that Ayden and Brindle have been letting you sample some of our cuisine here in Mandoria."

Stroder was looking at Jill, who was holding a Trelum in her hands.

"Yes," she responded. She still had shock in her voice from what we had just learned about Stroder. To think this little Nocean leader was once big and lived in the outer world like we do.

"These are delicious!" Tyler added, taking his last bite.

"Hey, that cloth looks like one of these," I said as I reached into my back pocket.

Everyone watched as I pulled out another similar cloth and laid it on the ground next to the other one. It was older and less brilliant but looked like it was still in good condition. Stroder reached out and gently touched the edge of it.

"Catherine's shield!" Ayden exclaimed. "I didn't know if you would find it, so I had the Noceans make you another one."

My heart broke for Stroder as he looked longingly at the cloth. He loved Catherine all his life. It seemed so unfair to have lost her twice.

"Thank you," I said. "We can still use it. Maybe Jill could have it."

"So how does it work?" Tyler asked. "They're just made out of your hair, right?"

"We need to show you," Stroder said. "Every Keeper needs one, Timber. Catherine would have wanted you to have hers.

"Can you and Jill put them on and kneel down by the edge of the clearing."

Jill and I moved quickly. We slid our arms into the three thick straps along the top of the soft material and knelt next to the trees.

"Hold the shields out in front of you to block the darts," Stroder called out.

"Runners, take aim," he yelled, loud and strong.

My heart started to pound in my chest as the Runners gathered in the middle of the field. They did just as they were told. They took an arrow from their quivers, placed it in their bows, and pulled back. They were prepared to fire. Brindle and Ayden put one hand straight up into the air and aimed their crossbows directly at us.

"Fire!" Stroder yelled.

Even though the arrows were tiny, I knew they could sink into my skin. I ducked quickly to hide my head behind my arm. They flew as fast as lightning and straight at us. Not one point penetrated the soft material. In fact, the arrows abruptly stopped and fell to the ground.

"Wow. So, how does it do that?" Tyler asked.

Stroder stood tall and broadened his shoulders.

"It's just the strength of our hair!" he proudly stated.

The Runners went quickly to retrieve their arrows.

"Timber, you and Jill must wear these as you come and go through Creshtil Pass and around Bellen Road," Stroder said. "They'll protect you from Boden's darts."

"But his darts are much bigger," I said warily.

"Yes, but you must trust the shield. And remember," he continued, "the shield will not only block darts but even bullets from a human gun.

"Now, where did you find Catharine's old one?"

"In the underground passage we found when we were hiding from the Watchman," I answered.

Stroder slightly smiled as a pleased look fell upon his face.

"Good," he said. I'm glad to hear that the old tunnel is still holding up. It took Catherine and I a long time to dig it out many years ago."

"We found some other things in the passage too," Jill said. "A necklace with some kind of tube connected to it, a thin piece of cloth with strings, and a thick coin with spindles on it."

Stroder nodded, then said, "Catherine must have kept those in the tunnel just in case she needed them. We used to use the necklace as a weapon before we found a better use for it. We used to draw the water into it, pull back the nob, and shoot the Watchman with it."

The Runners laughed.

"That used to be one reliable weapon!" Brindle exclaimed, chuckling to herself.

"Does the water hurt him?" Tyler asked.

"The water from the pond burns the skin of the Watchman," Stroder said. "Unless, of course, he has the Keeper's key in his hand.

"The thin piece of cloth with strings on the end of it is for the Keeper to cover her eyes at night when you're in the woods. This is used mostly when you cut down a tree. It helps the Keeper to see better in the dark."

"Why would I cut down a tree at night, again?" I interrupted.

"Remember, Timber," Stroder said, "a tree can only be cut down in the light of the full moon. And more Aspids are released if they have first been touched by rain from the outer world. That is why it is best to chop down a tree during a full moon and in the rain." Then he added, "And just so you know, a full moon is closely upon us."

I glanced at Tyler. He nodded.

How could I ever chop down a tree? At night, even? And with some creature searching to kill me, no less. How would I remember all of this?

"It will be okay, Timber," Jill said, as if reading my thoughts.

"We'll do this together," Tyler said, gently touching my hand.

"The Watchman has very keen senses at night," Stroder continued. "Especially his sight. But with the cloth covering your eyes, you too will have better vision."

"Is that cloth made from your hair, too?" Tyler asked.

Stroder nodded.

Brindle spoke up, "Yes, but the eyepiece has been dipped in the Spring-Wells of Mandoria and then heated on hot coals for many hours. The wells are the purest form of water that feeds into the pass."

"There was a coin too," Jill said. "It had little spindles on it that moved. It reminded me of a compass, but it was a coin."

"We found that on Winston," Ayden said. "After he had died."

"We don't know what it does. Or what it's even for," Stroder added.

"What about the tube necklace?" Tyler asked. "You said you used to use it for shooting the Watchman. What's in it now? It looked like some kind of black liquid."

"Yes," Stroder said. His voice was deep, and his emotions were controlled. "Now, Timber I strongly advise that you leave the vile alone!"

"Okay," I said.

"The Keeper who uses it must have lots of experience and be able to concentrate perfectly."

"What is it?" I asked.

"The liquid is actually dark red and was molten from rare rocks that are found in the Mountains of Latharus. One drop mixed with a tube full of water from our pond will create anything the Keeper imagines up in her mind."

I tilted my head to the side questioningly. *What?*

"If the Keeper aims the tube out in front of her and imagines a large ferocious lion, then, as she sprays the mixture into the air, the lion will appear."

"Cool!" Jill exclaimed.

"The Keeper has to control her thoughts and focus only on the lion for him to do exactly what she wants," Stroder continued. "This is a great tool to use against the Watchman, but it can also be very problematic. If the Keeper can't maintain concentration, then the thing you think about will become an entity unto itself and you will lose control over it. The only way to make it disappear is to spray it with pure water from the pond.

"We tried it only one time with Catherine."

Ayden and Brindle looked at each other and laughed quietly to themselves.

"Catherine imagined a huge beast that would fight and kill Boden. She did well for about 45 seconds, then her concentration broke, and the beast ran off into the forest."

"I remember chasing down that creature for days!" Brindle laughed.

Ayden joined in, "Yeah, remember what happened when we sprayed him?"

"The splash was a title wave of water... that nearly drowned us!" Brindle said, laughing at the memory.

"Yeah...I am leaving that one alone!" I said.

"Well, you might start practicing something," Ayden suggested. "Try to empty your mind of all thoughts. Then completely relax and think of nothing. When you can do that, then you can begin to practice thinking of only one thing at a time. It really takes time to learn how to not be distracted."

"Ayden," Stroder said, shaking his head. "This is too much information for her. And she'll probably never even get the chance to try it."

"They say that Winston was working hard at it!" Ayden continued, ignoring Stroder's remark. "I'm sure it takes a lot of practice. But it is a great tool against the Watchman if you can learn to *perfectly* focus!"

My mind was racing with thoughts and questions. *How could I ever be able to concentrate on one thing and not get distracted?* If Grandma could not do it then I know there was no way I could. *I'm just a young girl. How could I ever learn to protect these people?*.

The sun was starting to dip in the huge blue sky. I knew it wouldn't be long until it would tuck itself quietly behind the small mountains that lay in the distance. Mandoria was the most beautiful place to me—the sights, the sounds, the amazing little people.

The Runners were valiant, ready to serve and protect at any cost. They had immediately accepted me as their Keeper. *But how can they care about us so quickly and so deeply? Could it be real that Ayden has a silly crush on me? What would it be like to live in this beautiful place and join these little people?* I wondered how long a Noceans life was here in Mandoria.

A warm east wind bounced off the treetops and filtered through my hair, which was now completely dry. I gently rubbed my eyes and thought about my mother and Kate and Ryan. An empty, lonely feeling settled into my heart. *How could I ever make a choice to leave my family behind?*

"Stroder?" Tyler said, his voice interrupting my thoughts. "Did you get me one of your crystals?"

"I did," he answered, reaching under his small little overcoat.

Stroder pulled out a dark red crystal and handed it to Tyler. It was about half the size of a marble, but to the Noceans it was a large handful.

Tyler quickly grabbed his backpack and unzipped the long black zipper. He pulled out a small, plastic container with a rubber lid and opened it.

"I'll put it in here so I can look at it through the microscope later," he said as he dropped it into the plastic tube.

Stroder looked deeply troubled, and I couldn't tell if he was upset about giving Tyler one of their last crystals or if he felt like this was a huge waste of time. Or maybe I had it all wrong; maybe it was just Grandma being gone and having to keep moving in a world without her in it. If that was the case, then I understood perfectly!

"I promise I'll keep it safe, Stroder. And I'll return it as soon as I can," Tyler said.

Stroder nodded.

"We need to get going, Timber," Tyler said. He suddenly sounded anxious to leave. "I have a lot of work to do and not long to do it."

"Is it okay if I get a sample of the water, too, when we are at the pond?"

Stroder nodded once again to Tyler.

I didn't want to leave, and I noticed I wasn't the only one who was feeling this way. Ayden's head hung down over his slightly sunken shoulders and his long braid hung almost to his knees. He glanced up at me.

"Can you stay a *little* longer?" Ayden asked hopefully.

"No. Tyler is right," Stroder insisted. "We need to get them back in case we have to deal with Boden."

"I just want to get back before dark," Tyler said.

"Does the crystal look like something you have seen before?" Jill asked.

"Oh sure!" he answered. "It actually looks and feels just like a rock. But I'm going to have to examine it more closely, maybe even chip a little corner of it to look at under the microscope."

"Well, let's go then," Jill said. She held her shield out in front of her.

I rubbed the shield that was draped over my arm and looked over Mandoria.

"Runners!" Stroder called out, motioning forward with a slight movement of his head.

The Runners moved swiftly to the rocky hillside and prepared to enter. One by one they began to push their way through.

"Tyler," Ayden said. "You should fill your water bottle now, before we leave."

Tyler did as Ayden suggested. He took the lid off and pushed his water bottle into the pass. He smiled and glanced at me.

I could tell he was fascinated with the water just on the other side of the rocks. When he pulled the bottle out, it was full of water from the pond.

"That should do!" he said, as he held up the dripping water-bottle in front of him. Tyler quickly screwed the lid back on and tucked it into his backpack.

All the Runners had gone through except Brindle, Ayden, and Stroder.

"Let's go!" Stroder said, as he put a leg into the rocky hillside. "We will get you to the pathway, and then you'll be on your own!"

"We'll be fine!" Jill said. She suddenly looked at Tyler. "Do you think we'll have to use the underground passage?"

"I hope not!" I quickly interrupted, vividly remembering the feeling of suffocation.

"We might," he said, sending me a sympathetic look.

"You should probably use it to stay hidden from Boden," Stroder added as he turned and entered the pass.

I noticed that when Stroder talked about the Watchman, he often used the Drimlors' actual name, calling him Boden. I wondered why but realized that it wasn't the time to ask any more questions.

Ayden looked at me. I could tell he longed to say something but didn't.

"Don't forget to *always* watch for the Drimlor," Brindle said in a firm voice. "The moment you get side-tracked, he'll be right there!"

Ayden followed Brindle through the hillside.

"Ready?" Jill asked, as she put her head next the rocks. "Tyler, we have to get this Keeper back safely!"

"Yes!" he responded as he put his backpack on and positioned his sling shot on his wrist.

Jill exhaled long and hard, and then moved through the softened rock.

Tyler looked back at me and quickly took my hand. He pulled me close and looked deep into my eyes as if he were searching for something. He let his sling-shot dangle to the side of his wrist as he gently grabbed my shoulders. My heart jumped, and then suddenly felt like it was melting into my chest.

"Timber don't worry. I won't let anything happen to you," he said in a reassuring voice.

"Stay close to me, Okay?"

"Okay," I whispered in response to the words of my bodyguard. I barely nodded my head. At that moment, I felt as safe as anyone ever could.

Tyler exhaled and then pushed his head and shoulders into the rock. Then, he stopped and with intense strength squeezed my hand. I knew exactly what was happening. This was only the second time for him to take the water in. I watched his knuckles turn white around my fingers, then his grip released slightly. *That was quick!* I thought. Gently, he pulled my hand into the rock by my fingers. I looked back at Mandoria one last time and then moved through the hillside.

The soothing, warm water wrapped around me as I entered Creshtil Pass. I took a deep breath. Tyler kept a hold of my hand as we swam out of the darkness of the cave, joining Jill and the others.

Ayden wrapped his arms around my finger, and we took off together through the glistening, turquoise fluid of the pond. Soaring upward. The speed was intense. The rush was exhilarating!

And then, just as quickly as it had started, it ended. I felt the cool air upon my face as I gently broke through the surface of the pond.

Before I could even take a breath, I was yanked with great force back down into the water. *What's happening?* Ayden no longer had a hold of my finger. I started to panic. Tiny white bubbles danced wildly around me. I felt like the back of my shirt was caught on a tree branch as the powerful downward thrust of the current pulled at me. I looked up and could tell I was just a few feet from the surface. I noticed Jill was right next to me. Ayden had us suspended. His head was tilted upward as his little arms were outstretched to his sides holding on to the back of our shirts. He was desperately using all his strength to keep us from being pulled back down.

Suddenly, like the muffled sound of popping balloons, darts punctured the water around us.

The watchman was there! I thought with sickening realization.

Panic gripped at my chest.

I turned to look at Tyler and noticed a silver marble was secure in the leather strap of his slingshot. He had a tight grip and was ready to fire. Ayden must have known this too as he pushed Tyler up to the top.

I could see Tyler's legs fighting hard to keep him suspended through the wild motion of bubbles. Darts penetrated the water around him, again and again. I closed my eyes in horror. He was sure to be hit. I could not bear another funeral! Not another death!

Minutes passed like hours. There was no sound. Tyler was nowhere.

Finally, Brindle appeared at Ayden's side and grabbed Jill's shirt. We both were pulled to the surface. I coughed quietly and took a breath of air. Jill did the same.

I scanned the area quickly. The Watchman was not there.

Tyler stood at the edge of the pond. How he was not hit, I will never know. He was holding his slingshot in front of him. The Runners were at his feet.

"Swim!" Ayden said, with great anxiety in his voice.

Brindle and Ayden disappeared under the water.

Jill and I pulled our way through the thick, soft liquid across the top of the pond. Fear had drained my strength. I felt like I was slowly trudging through the water.

Jill reached the edge of the pond before me and held out her hand to help me out of the water.

A small group of Runners were positioned perfectly where I was getting out.

Tyler was guarding the pathway, just a few feet away.

My mind kicked into high gear, cycling through what I needed to do next. *Okay, run through the path! Climb the tree! Retrieve the golden needle! And sprint for the tunnel!*

Suddenly, from within the trees, a dart whizzed past my head.

"Get down!" Jill screamed as she held her shield out in front of her and huddled over me.

Tyler pulled back his slingshot and fired a marble through the air. The Runners released arrows at the same time.

The Drimlor let out a gut-wrenching sound that flooded the empty space around us.

"Ahh! You all will die!" he screamed in a wild, scratchy voice from within the forest.

"Go now, Keeper," Stroder yelled, looking right at me. "We'll hold him off!"

Jill and I stood up holding our shields out in front of us. We ran for the pathway.

Two darts hit the golden, glistening cloth that hung from Jill's arm while more hissed past my head.

I felt a hot pinch at my neck, and I stumbled to the ground. I rolled onto my back and frantically clawed at the pain at my throat. I felt a hard, metal piece that was stuck in my skin and yanked it out with one quick jerk. I looked down at my hand that was holding a black metal dart. *But I am the Keeper. How could this be happening to me?* Slowly I turned my head and looked directly into Tyler's big brown eyes.

"No!" he screamed.

I felt like I was watching a movie scene. Tyler's arms were trying to reach out and grab me, but he seemed to be moving in the opposite direction. He was mouthing words over and over, but I could hear nothing. Terror filled his eyes.

Something was terribly wrong.

I dropped to the ground and could feel the dirt press against my face. The burning sensation from my neck moved through my veins with each beat of my heart. I gasped for one last breath of air as I saw the Runners begin to move, bouncing back and forth, through my violently twitching eyes.

Dirt scraped across my body.
Water enveloped my skin.
Everything went dark.

CHAPTER FOURTEEN

BLACK DOTS

Immediately I recognized the scent of Mandoria. I could smell the strong fragrance of fresh green grass and the sharp essence of wildflowers. I was lying on the ground and gently resting my head on my arm. Birds were busy chirping in the distance. The sounds began to come and go in a swelling motion. My head started spinning and my stomach felt twisted and nauseous.

"Oh," I moaned slowly as I squinted into the glaring sunlight. "I think I'm going to be sick!"

"You'll be okay, Timber!" a quiet, familiar voice said.

"No! I am going to be *sick!*"

I strained to lift my head, but it felt as heavy as a bowling ball. My whole body ached. I quit trying to get up and just laid still.

"This is normal, Timber."

Slowly my eyes focused upon Ayden, who was leaning against my arm.

"Just relax and these feelings will pass," he said as if he knew exactly what I was experiencing.

"What happened?" I whispered.

"You got shot by the Watchman," Ayden said.

"By his dart?" I gasped trying to reach for my neck. My arm felt tight and slow.

"Relax, Timber!" Ayden scolded. "Please—just for a few more minutes. I promise this will pass!"

"Okay. Okay," I moaned. "Where is everyone?"

"They're still in the Pass," Ayden said. "They're securing the perimeter. We'll go as soon as you feel better."

Ayden stood up and walked over to look at my hand. He gently lifted my pinky finger to examine it.

"What is it?" I asked.

"Lay still," Ayden said, ignoring my question. "I've got something for you to drink that will help."

I watched Ayden walk to the edge of the clearing and drag a heavy, large wooden cup over to my head. It reminded me of an old-fashioned goblet found in an antique store.

"Take a sip!"

Slowly, I lifted my head and drank from the rim. The taste was bland, like watered down tea, but it was warm and soothing on my throat.

I watched Ayden as he helped to hold the bowl out in front of me. His eyes were full of great concern.

"That's it, now rest a bit," he said gently.

"Didn't you say that if I were ever hit by a Drimlors dart, the effect would last for an hour? Have I been out that long?

"No. Only a few minutes," Ayden said. "But you were lucky, Timber. We got you into the water as fast as we could. It speeds up the healing and helps lessen the pain. If you were not by the water or with us to help you, it would not have been good."

Ayden walked over to my hand and lifted my pinky finger up again.

"What is it?" I asked. "Why do you keep doing that?"

He gently rubbed the tip of my finger and then set it softly on the grass. "If a person survives a Drimlor's dart, a tiny black dot appears on the outside tip of both little fingers."

I quickly raised my fingers to look for myself. There they were. One small black dot on the outside of both pinkies. I quickly rolled over to my stomach and tried rubbing them off.

"They won't come off," Ayden said. "The dots are permanent. In fact, every time a person is shot, new ones appear. If their fingers get a full line of dots... well... They will die."

"What?" I gasped.

"I know it sounds bad, but I only knew one Nocean that it has actually happened to. Over time, you get better at dodging those darts."

"Do you have any?" I asked.

Ayden brought his hands together and gently rubbed one of his own little fingers. He lifted both fingers and held them out for me to see. The row of tiny dots filled half of each finger.

I gulped. "You've been shot many times!" I exclaimed.

"Yeah, but not for over two years now," he said, puffing his chest. "You should see Stroder's."

"Why?"

"His are down to the third knuckle."

"So, he could die soon?" I asked.

"It's been fifteen years since his last one," Ayden smirked. "I doubt he'll be leaving us any time soon.

"Timber, usually when the dot appears, the symptoms start to go away. How are you feeling?"

"Better," I said, tilting my head to the side.

It was amazing how quickly the pain had faded.

"Should we go?" I asked.

Ayden broadened his shoulders and moved his bow out to the side. The look in his eyes changed slightly, and I could tell he didn't want to leave just yet.

"Well…Yes," he said, in a softer tone. He paused for a moment.

"Before we go, Timber, I really want to talk to you about coming to live here in Mandoria. I was so worried when you got hit by the dart. I thought something would go wrong and I wouldn't get to see you or hear your voice ever again. I know this may sound funny, but I want to get to know you better. I want you to come live with us here in Mandoria. You would love it!

"I never dreamed Catherine would die, and I don't want something to happen to you the way it did to her. She used to tell me that you and I were so similar. She knew that I would like you. And I do! Please tell me that you will make the choice to live in Mandoria."

I smiled. Ayden's honesty was sweet and to the point. I could tell Brindle was right about the crush thing, but it felt weird to me because I was staring at a boy the size of a Barbie doll. Even though he would be an extremely *good-looking* Barbie doll, it still felt strange.

"Ayden, the truth is I love it here! This is such a magical and wonderful place. But everything is so new to me. I have a family back home—and friends and school. And if I could never go back again..."

Ayden's large blue eyes blinked as his head looked downward. I didn't want to conquer all his hopes.

"But Ayden, one day I would love to live here," I said. "I have some questions, though. Do I have to make the choice now?"

"Well, normally no," Ayden responded. "Normally the Keeper can make that choice whenever she wants to. But if we must cut the last tree down and close the pass forever, then now would be your only opportunity."

"Okay," I nodded. "But there's another thing I don't understand. If Stroder is the boy who died all those years ago, why wouldn't he be an old man now? And I thought the boy's name was Steven."

"Stroder changed his name when he came to Mandoria," Ayden said. "He's not an old man because our life span is much different. This is the appealing part to becoming a Nocean. The hours and minutes are the same as in the outer world, but we live to be much older here."

"How much older?"

"We grow quickly until we become of age. This is about twenty years old. Then we stay that age for five hundred years, sometimes even up to six hundred."

"Whoa!" I exclaimed. "Actual years?"

"Yes," Aden said. "Time passes the same here as for you. But the Aspids nourish us in such a way that a Noceans lifespan is lengthened. Then, as we reach those older years, we go through a change and enter the *Year of the Wise*. This is when we age quickly and prepare to move to the higher Mountains of Mandoria."

"Oh my gosh! Do you live longer when you go there?"

"No one really knows," Ayden shrugged. "They must take the path alone. But the Elders who are preparing for the journey tell us they believe that they live there too with those who have gone before."

"Wait," I exclaimed. "This means Grandma Catherine would still be alive."

"Yes, if she had only made the choice sooner," Ayden said sadly.

"And she would have lived five hundred more years?" I asked in desperation.

"Yes."

Pangs of despair filled my chest again like a wrecking ball.

"But why didn't she do it?"

"Well, Timber, she was fine with just being a Keeper at first," Ayden explained. "She enjoyed the excitement of finding new ways to defeat the Watchman and the thrill of providing the Aspid rain for our people.

"Catherine married William and had two girls. For years she came to the pond, never telling her husband or children because she didn't want to put them in any kind of danger. She loved the secret of Mandoria. Only her and Zelly ever knew. Their pact to never tell a soul was their bond-unto-death! And Catherine liked it that way.

"It wasn't until William died that Catherine started to change her mind."

"About wanting to make the choice and live here?" I asked.

"Yes," Ayden nodded. "She started spending more and more time in Mandoria. And with Stroder. Then they fell in love. That may sound strange, but they knew each other from before and they couldn't wait for the day that they would be the same size again. Stroder begged and begged her to change!"

Ayden looked sad as he rubbed his eyes then shook his head back and forth.

"But she would not do it until she could solve the problem of the Aspids. Her plan was to fix that first and then tell *you* about us. She said you were destined to be the next Keeper and that you had all the qualities needed. She planned to bring you here and teach you everything she knew before she made the choice. After that, she would change and wake up to her new, twenty-year-old Nocean self and live hundreds of years with Stroder."

"Why didn't she just do it!" I said, exasperated.

I felt a well of anger fill up inside of me.

"She could have told me and then changed. Then we could have worked on the problem together. She would have still been alive!"

I took a deep breath and exhaled slowly.

"One thing is for sure; I will not make the same mistake my grandmother made! I will make the choice before it's too late."

"So, you do want to live here?" Ayden asked excitedly.

"I do," I said, firm and matter of fact.

As I spoke those two words it reminded of a marriage ceremony. *Do you take this man…?* I chuckled to myself. *Was I with Tyler in the outer world? Or was I with Ayden here in Mandoria?* I blinked my eyes tightly shut and shook my head as if to get rid of the strange thoughts!

"I can tell that Tyler doesn't want you to come here, though," Ayden said attentively. "He likes you, doesn't he? I saw him hold your hand once."

"But it's not *his* choice, is it?" I retorted.

A spark of anger flipped through my mind as I remembered how adamant Tyler was about me *never* making *the choice*.

Wait. Why am I angry? I really like Tyler! He is so gorgeous! And he is my bodyguard through all of this. I shook the confused thoughts from my mind. Maybe this was what Mom was talking about when she said that girls my age should not have a steady boyfriend because we were just not mature enough to deal with it all. And this situation was even more complicated than your average teenage romance's predicament. I laughed to myself, *Mother would probably not even know the answer to this one!*

"Is something wrong?" Ayden asked.

He must have noticed my confusion.

"Oh nothing," I responded, smiling at him. "First of all, we need to figure out a way to save your people. And Tyler just might be the key to finding out the answer. We should focus on that first."

"You're right," Ayden agreed.

Although I didn't say anything else, I knew in my heart this would be a hard decision to make. I loved my life. And I really liked Tyler! But I liked Mandoria, too. It would be so amazing getting to know Ayden and living another five hundred years where my grandmother was hoping to live.

"Well, let's go!" Ayden said, interrupting my thoughts. I could tell he knew it was time for us to get back.

"Okay, but one last thing," I said as I sat up. "I was going to ask you how old you are, because Stroder looks a little older than you and some of the others."

Ayden's head lilted to the side and he grinned. "I'm sixteen, Timber. Brindle is fifteen. She and I were the youngest to ever become Runners. I was called forth at age fourteen, and a year later she was called at fourteen too. Most are called forth at age eighteen. It's been a great honor for Brindle and I."

"Wow," I said. "There's so much to learn here, isn't there?"

"But you will learn it, and all of this will bring you joy."

"Now, Timber," Ayden said, changing the subject and moving quickly to the hillside. "Please be careful."

I followed Ayden through the rocky hillside and into the pond. I hardly recognized the change from breathing air to water. Ayden wrapped his arm around my finger and swiftly we moved through the beautiful pond.

Something was different.

I felt like I belonged here.

I felt…at home.

At the surface I breathed the air with ease.

"There you are!"

Tyler's voice was anxious and penetrating. He was in the water just beside us.

"I was just coming to find you," Tyler said. "Are you okay?"

"I'm fine now," I replied.

Ayden looked at me. His small eyes were sad. He let go of my finger and disappeared slowly under the water.

"Good!" Tyler exclaimed. "They told me you would be okay, so I stayed up here with the Runners and helped to secure the area."

"Is he gone?" I asked, looking around.

"Yes," Tyler said.

He motioned for me to swim forward as he took off slowly in the water.

"That ugly Drimlor finally ran off after getting burned over and over," Tyler continued. "Timber, I was terrified, but the Runners—they were amazing! They had no fear! When they saw the Watchman, they ran from the pond, like flashes of golden light, and jumped onto his legs."

"What?" I asked, trying to keep up with Tyler's long arms as he swam easily through the pond.

"I was so shocked. The water that was on them burned through his clothes and into his skin. There was a hissing sound and then steam rolling off from under the Runners. He freaked out like a wild animal and tried to get them off. Finally, they all jumped as he ran screaming into the forest."

"Wow," I said, in amazement. "What about Jill?"

"She went with Brindle and Stroder to stand guard at the tree," Tyler replied. "They told me to find you and hurry to the tree!"

Tyler and I reached the edge of the pond and stood up. He gently took my hand. The pillars of light bounced playfully upon our skin as we ran through the elegant pathway. I looked back and thought I saw Ayden standing by the edge of the water. Then he was out of sight as we turned and made our way to the end of the path. I felt torn between two different worlds. *What am I going to do?* I wondered.

Jill looked different as she stood by the tree with Stroder and Brindle at her feet. She almost looked like a Runner herself. Her legs were bent, and her arms were up and ready for any sudden movements within the forest. The beautiful, golden shield hung down elegantly from her forearm. Her loose, blond hair hung over her shoulders as she fiercely searched the trees that surrounded us. Jill locked eyes with mine, and I saw a thin twisted headband that lay across her forehead and went back under her hair.

"Keeper!" Jill demanded. "Get the key!!"

The transformation left me dumbfounded. *She was one of them!*

Tyler gently lifted my arm out in front of me and straightened my shield. He placed his other hand on my back.

"Go ahead, Keeper!" he said, nudging me forward.

I looked at Jill and then the Runners. This was suddenly very real to me. *I am the Keeper of the key*, I thought. *I am the protector of the pond and these little people are my new family.*

A surge of energy burst through me, and I swiftly climbed the tree and retrieved the key.

The wind began to gain strength in the distance, and I leaned down to wrap my arms once again around the tree.

The Runners darted for the pathway.

"Tomorrow, Timber!" Stroder yelled as the wind blew harder.

He wrapped his arms around Brindle's waist and lifted her up over his shoulders. Her yellowish skin looked suddenly white as snow. She couldn't stand up. *Was she okay?* I watched as they ran through the disappearing pathway.

The violent gusts of wind soon stopped.

"Follow me!" Jill blurted out as she ran off into the forest.

Tyler grabbed my hand and practically pulled me out of the tree. We started running. Neither of them seemed too concerned about the noise we were making. Finally, we made our way back to the bikes.

The ride into town was happily uneventful.

I felt exhausted and somewhat anxious as we came upon the dome of trees that formed over our street.

"Do you think the Watchman will be here like he was last time?" I asked.

"I doubt it," Jill said. "He's probably off planning something else."

I could see Mom's car in the driveway.

"Are we getting together later?" I asked.

"I'm sure it's dinner time," Tyler said. "I need to check in with my parents. Maybe later tonight you guys can come over and look at the crystal with me."

"That would be great!" I said as I leaned my bike up to the side of the porch. Jill and Tyler did the same.

"Where have you guys been?" Mom asked as we pushed through the front door. Her eyes were big and full of concern.

"Mom," I said. "We just got back from our bike ride."

"Where did you go, to another world and back?" she asked, sarcastically.

My mouth dropped slightly open and my feet froze to the ground. I could see Jill and Tyler out of the corner of my eye. They were stiff as well.

Mother's eyes grew wide.

"I was joking!" she said in an animated voice. "But we have been worried about you. It's eight o'clock, and you missed dinner."

"What?" I said in disbelief. "Is it that late already?

"I better get going then," Tyler said. "I'll see you two tomorrow."

Suddenly, I realized that our plans had changed.

"Okay," Jill and I said at the same time.

"And Jill, your mom just called again. She said when you get back you need to come straight home!"

"Okay, Mrs. Rhoads," Jill said as she reached for her bike.

"I'll call you later!" I said.

Jill jumped on her bike and I watched her blond wavy hair bounce behind her as she took off down the street.

"Timber, I got off work early today so I could take you and Jill out for dinner," Mom said as she held open the screen door.

"Well, I didn't know. Besides, you wanted us to show Tyler around," I said.

"You've been gone since seven-thirty this morning," Mother whined.

"I'm sorry!" I snapped. I could tell by the sound of my voice I was getting tired.

The screen door slammed behind me as I headed up the stairs. I heard my mother close the big wooden door and lock the deadbolt.

"If you want some dinner, there's some Chinese food in the fridge," Mom called up to me.

"Okay. I'll be down in a minute!" I said.

It felt different to be home as I moved up the winding staircase and headed to my room. Why did it feel like I was here, but only for a visit?

I quickly pushed the noisy beads out of my way and went through the doorway. Everything was just as Jill and I had left it this morning. A few clothes were piled on the floor next to the closet, and make-up was scattered next to the mirror by my stereo.

I touched the front pocket of my shorts and felt the golden needle. Then I closed my eyes and dropped onto the mattress of my unmade bed. I thought of Mandoria. The sun must be setting there by now. I could see the beautiful small mountain range and rushing waterfalls in my mind and wondered what Ayden was doing. And if Brindle was okay. *Are they home with their families? Or are they desperately preparing for nightfall?*

I turned over and pulled the pile of sheets up to my chest.

I wished I were there!

I felt like I was drifting on an old piece of wood in the middle of a wavy ocean current.

Darkness gently settled in upon me.

****

A noise startled me awake.

I must have fallen asleep, I thought wearily.

I opened my eyes and peered into the blackness from which erupted the startling sounds.

Rain pounded wildly on the roof of the porch, and I noticed a strong smell of wet pavement but slightly soured. The curtains were flipping hard against the wall next to my window as the wind blew gusts of cold, moist air throughout my room. Thunder rumbled angrily in the distance like an old man mumbling under his breath. The storm was restless outside in the darkness of the night.

Why was it so dark? The streetlight at the end of the road must be out again. I slowly moved my hand in front of me to feel where I was on my bed, but I bumped the wall with the back side of my hand. I couldn't even see the wall!

The sound of a heavy, hollow thud came from within my bedroom.

Instantly I was wide awake.

What would mother be doing here? And in the dark?

Something bumped the wall and a picture fell to the floor with a clank.

I stared blindly into the darkness and shuddered at the thought, *Maybe it's not my mother.*

Heavy breathing from across the room penetrated the rhythm of the tapping rain and swelling wind. Deep huffing sounds came from within my closet. Whoever it was, they were looking for something.

The blood in my veins ran cold as I realized who the intruder was. I froze, stiff with fear. *It was him!*

Somehow, the rain must have put a damper on his rotten smell.

But still, I could barely breathe. *He was in my room!*

I saw Tyler in my mind with his slingshot cocked and ready in front of him. *Where was my bodyguard when I needed him?* I thought desperately. *Fast asleep, I was sure, and twenty feet away!*

My throat was clenched so tight with fear, I almost felt like I was going to choke. I realized I couldn't scream for help even if I wanted too.

If you cannot scream, Timber, then at least take a breath! I reminded myself.

A sharp burst of light from the hallway filled the room and I could see the outline of swirly designs in the old wallpaper just in front of my frozen head. A loud crash of thunder cracked like an angry whip and then rumbled off in the distance.

The sounds in the closet stopped. Quick, uneven thuds made their way across the floor, and a heavy creak came from the front windowsill.

The knob turned and my bedroom door opened. The beads clanged against the wall as a bright light gently filled the space around me. Mom tripped on something and mumbled as she sleepily staggered over to the window and shut it sharply. Then she made her way over to the other one and shut it too.

"There!" she whispered as she walked out sleepily.

I wanted to say something, but fear held me by the throat. Besides, I knew I couldn't. Mother must never know about any of this. And especially not the Watchman!

After what felt like forever, I took some deep breaths and turned over to stare into the darkness. I listened carefully through the rain for any strange sounds, then quickly got up and locked the windows. I sat down on the floor to peer out into the night. No one was there, or at least, I couldn't *see* anyone. I made my way back to my bed.

I tried to sleep but could only think about how everything had changed. I pulled the sheets up closer to my face and remembered the permanent marks that would forever be with me. Gently, I rubbed the black dots on the outside of my little fingers and listened intently to the rhythm of the rain.

CHAPTER FIFTEEN

THE MISSING ELEMENT

"What happened here?"

Every inch of my body jerked. I gasped, sat straight up in bed and I opened my eyes.

My room was filled with light. It was morning, and the storm had obviously passed.

"I didn't mean to startle you, Timmy," Mom said.

She stood directly at the end of my bed with her hands firm on her hips. "But I cannot believe the mess in here!"

Slowly, I looked around my room in complete amazement. Each drawer to my dresser was open, and clothes were strewn everywhere. Shoes were tossed in the middle of the room. A box from my closet was lying on its side by the mirror with books and papers pulled from it. Grandma's antique sewing basket was also tipped over and strewn through.

Without really thinking, I reached for the front pocket of my shorts and felt the golden needle still safely there. I sighed.

"Gees, Timber," Mom said sarcastically. "Were you looking for something? Last night you didn't come downstairs to eat, but when I came to check on you, your room did not look like this. What happened?"

I could tell she was upset as she kept looking in wonder around my room.

Think fast, Timber!

"Umm. Well," I said, while I scratched the back of my head. My voice didn't sound too convincing. After all, I was in shock too.

"Last night, it was raining so hard," I said slowly, trying to figure out what to say. *How ironic*, I thought, *I'm trying to cover for a Drimlor.*

"I know," Mother interrupted. I could tell she was in a hurry for me to answer. "I came in and shut your windows because the wind and rain were blowing in."

Her eyes were big as they stared right at me, anxious for me to reply.

"Well, sometime last night, I felt kind of scared and tried to find the doll that Grandma left for me," I lied, slightly whining as I tried to sound convincing. "I looked for it in the dark, but I didn't know I was making such a mess."

"Timmy," she said in a softer tone. The look on her face suddenly changed as she sat on the edge of the bed next to me. "I miss Momma too," she said. Her head hung sadly.

In so many ways, Mother was my closest friend. I only wished I could tell her the truth.

"But, if you ever get scared, all you need to do is come into my room or just yell for me. I'll be right there!"

"I know, Mom" I said.

Like I ever could have done that last night, I thought to myself.

"That was a bad storm, wasn't it?"

I nodded.

"Well, you need to get this mess cleaned up," she said. "And honey, I want you home before dinner time tonight, okay?"

"Alright, Mom," I replied, hoping we would make it back from Mandoria by then.

"Tyler knocked on the front door about an hour ago," Mom said as she stood to make her way through my room. "He asked if you could come over when you woke up. He said that he wanted to show you something."

"Really?" I asked.

"I said you could, but now I think you should probably clean your room first."

"*Mom,*" I whined.

"Well, then at least before you take off for the day!"

"Alright!" I agreed. My mother was really a softy on the inside.

She moved the noisy beads out of her way and let them slap hard against the wall as she walked out of my room.

"I'm going to work, Timmy," she yelled. "You be good. See you later!"

"See you, Mom!" I said.

I quickly got out of bed and stepped carefully through my messy room like I was dodging buried landmines. I picked up a new pair of shorts, a white tank top, and some make-up to put on after I washed my face.

I hurried down the stairs and went into the kitchen. I was starving! I quickly set my things on the table and decided to fix a bowl of Cheerios while I watched something on television. It felt good on my throat to swallow the cold milk and cereal. I flipped through the channels on the remote, but nothing was worth watching.

I thought about Jill while I took a few more bites of cold cereal. I wondered where she was. Usually, she was here to wake me up. I worried the Watchman might have visited her house, too, and quickly picked up the phone.

I whispered each number as I dialed. Eight. Three. Five. Two. Four. Eight. One.

I could hear the phone ringing in the receiver.

"Hello?"

Jill's mother answered.

"Hey, is Jill there?" I asked.

"Hi, Timber!" she said, "Jill had to go over to her grandma's this morning and mow her lawn.

"Oh. Okay," I responded.

"But she tried to leave early enough so she could be back before you woke up. But I guess she didn't quite make it."

"That's okay," I said, glancing at the clock above the sink. It was 9:15 a.m. "I still have to get ready. Can you tell her that I will probably be over at Tyler's? She can meet us there."

"All right dear," she said. "Timber, I told Jill she has to be home this evening before it gets too late."

"I know. Mom told me the same thing!" I said as I chuckled to myself. "We'll be back before dinner."

"Okay, Timber. Goodbye now!"

"Goodbye."

As I hung up the phone, I noticed a roll of un-opened Life Savers on the counter. Quickly, I opened them and ate a red one.

Well, at least I know that the Drimlor didn't hurt Jill, I thought. *Maybe he doesn't even know where she lives.* I planned to keep it that way,

I rinsed the dishes and went to get dressed in the bathroom. After I was ready, I headed over to Tyler's. It felt strange walking up the sidewalk to grandma's home and then to her front porch, knowing she wouldn't be there to greet me. I could still see her sweet, happy smile as she would hold open the front door for me to come in. Only now, even *she* felt different to me. I had known a completely different Grandma Catherine. But now I loved her in a deeper, new, and exciting way.

I could hear running from behind the heavy door and a shuffling noise.

"Timber, you're finally up!" Tyler said as he peered around the door. He had a broad smile across his beautiful face and his brown eyes looked right into mine.

"You've got to come see this!" he announced with excitement.

"What is it?" I asked as I stepped through the doorway.

"Well, I couldn't sleep last night, so I stayed up and worked on the crystal."

"Yeah, *I* couldn't sleep either," I said sarcastically.

Tyler had been safely studying rocks while *I* was being terrorized by a Drimlor.

"Good morning, Timber!" Dave hollered, from the kitchen. He was sitting at the table with a coffee in one hand and a newspaper in the other.

"Good morning, Mr. Connelly!" I responded happily.

As Tyler and I began walking up the familiar staircase, I noticed how odd it felt to have the Connelly's things in grandma's house.

"You're not going to believe who was in my bedroom last night," I whispered as I leaned closer to Tyler.

"What?" he asked. Tyler stopped abruptly and turned to me. "Who?"

"I'm sure it was Boden, the Watchman."

"What?" Tyler asked again, but this time with great alarm. His eyebrows pulled sharply together, and his honey-brown skin suddenly looked sunburn. He gently grabbed my arm. "That Drimlor could have *killed* you!"

"I know! But he was not after me," I responded. "Remember how they told us he loses strength the longer he is away from the area where the pond is. The last thing he wants to do is cause a scene. I guess if he were to get held up too long, his life would be threatened."

"Didn't they say he's more likely to get violent when he is around the pond or on Bellen Road," Tyler suggested. "Where was the key?"

"I accidently left it in my pocket," I said, tapping on the front of my shorts. "But I'm glad I did."

Tyler slightly grabbed my arm and looked right into my eyes. "Timber, this can never happen again!"

"Yeah. Well, my *bodyguard* was next-door doing experiments all night long," I said in jest. I realized I had never said that word out loud.

"Yeah, well, that will never happen again," Tyler repeated himself as he lightly pushed me toward his bedroom.

He was much too serious!

"And what are you going to do about it?" I asked playfully. "You can't sleep in my room at night." Although, the sound of that had a secure feel to it.

"I will think of something," Tyler said as he slowly turned the silver knob to his door.

He stopped unexpectedly and I almost ran into him. His face was right next to mine. Suddenly, my heart began to pound in my chest. Tyler's big brown eyes looked right at me.

"If I am going to be your *bodyguard,* then I'm going to have to do a much better job of it, wouldn't you say, Timber?"

All I could do was look into his captivating eyes and nod in agreement. He was the most gorgeous creature God had ever made. And he accepted his new role, almost like he had chosen it for himself already. His lips slightly curved upward as he smiled a quick playful grin and pushed open the door to his bedroom.

I used to love this room in grandma's house. It was the upper corner room that faced the backyard and my home. Two of the walls were nothing but windows. The afternoon sun shined brilliantly on the hardwood floors. Grandma kept all sorts of plants placed around and a few comfortable chairs. This was her 'escape' room. I loved to join her in here to read a good book and drink ice-cold lemonade.

"I love this room!" Tyler said, as if he knew I was thinking through memories.

"Yeah, it was always my favorite too!"

Even though Tyler's things filled the room, it still looked cool! His large, unmade bed was right in the corner between all the windows. Directly above it was an amazing mobile of the planets. *He must love watching the stars as well,* I thought.

Opposite his bed, was a thin desk that was the length of the whole wall. It was obviously homemade but authentic. The whole area reminded me of a science lab. On one end of the desk was a computer that was still on, and beside it was a notebook with drawings and words on it. A pen was resting on top, as if Tyler were abruptly interrupted. There was an opened card-file box setting next to the computer.

Leaning against the wall were instruments of all kinds; things I clearly knew nothing about. There was a funny-looking plastic bottle with a straw-like thing coming out of it and a bunch of small glass jars with black rubber droppers on the tops. Other things that looked more familiar were meticulously organized in a plastic container with little compartments. It was filled with Q-tips, toothbrushes, tweezers, paint brushes of all sizes, sharp instruments that the dentist might have used, and one of those 'baby-nose-sucker' things.

"Wow, you have a lot of really cool stuff," I said as I stepped closer to a large, black microscope on the desk. The light was on and there was apparently something left inside that Tyler must have been looking at.

"Here, this is what I wanted you to see," Tyler said, pointing to the microscope. "Take a look."

I quickly looked through the long black eyepiece of the microscope and tried to focus on the light. Tiny pink shapes that looked like little toy building-blocks came into view. They were all over the glass slide that Tyler had prepared.

"What are those?" I asked.

"Last night I chipped off a few pieces of the crystal that Stroder gave me."

I noticed the red crystal nestled in a crumpled piece of tissue paper next to the microscope. There was a wood-handled instrument with a sharp point at the end lying on the table beside it.

"What you see in there are different shapes of crystals. Most scientists think there are seven types. It's kind of neat," Tyler said, as he lifted up a file card and showed me a picture of the seven different shapes.

They looked like something you'd see in a geometry book.

"See the cube in the middle? That's salt. There is the diamond shape. And that long rectangular tube is sugar."

"So, what kind of crystals are these?" I asked, looking into the microscope again.

"Well, that's what is really interesting to me. See, a crystal is just a solid form of something, like a substance of some kind. Most minerals or rocks are made up of crystals, and the molecules are arranged in an orderly pattern that is repeated over and over throughout the whole crystal. But with *this* one, there's clearly more than one type or more than one substance."

"What does that mean?" I asked, looking at Tyler and folding my arms in front of me. Suddenly, I felt like I was in Mrs. Grey's confusing science class—the one in which I had barely squeezed by with a C.

"Well, I figured out one of the crystal shapes. It's a trigonal shape. See, look at this."

Tyler lifted an opened book that was on the desk in front of us. I took it from his hands. It was worn and old, like it had been used many times. The page was filled with different colored rocks. One rock looked like it had a seashell in it.

"What is that?" I asked, pointing to the first one that caught my interest.

"Those are called Chalcedony. They are just different forms of quartz. But this one here matches the crystal that Stroder gave to us."

Tyler pointed to the picture of the bumpy red rock at the top corner of the page.

"Jasper," I said slowly, as I read the word printed right below the picture.

Then Tyler pointed to a little shape in the corner of the page.

"Right here, the book tells what shape the crystals are that make up each kind of rock or mineral. Look," he said, pointing back to the microscope. "They are an exact match with most of the shapes on the slide. Especially those on the right side."

I peered into the microscope again. Then looked back to the picture on the page in his book. Most of the shapes were the same.

"That is *so* cool!" I said.

Tyler walked to the end of the long desk. There was a large plastic container full of skinny drawers. He pulled one out and revealed a tray full of many different types of rocks, all of which were labeled and organized like you would see in a museum. I realized that every drawer was full of rocks by the shapes and colors that showed through the milky plastic. Tyler had a huge collection! He reached for the compartment that had the word JASPER on it and pulled out a handful of small red rocks.

"I got on the internet last night and found out that Jasper is quite common in Missouri. It is a semi-precious stone. By the way, I also found out that Oak Trees are also common in this area, too."

"So, we know two things now about the crystals: they are made up of Jasper and, of course, they grow on the top of the Oak trees," I said. "But what about those other shapes on the glass slide?"

"I think when we find that out, we'll know what element is missing in this whole equation. And maybe we can somehow replace it, so the crystals can grow again."

"Why can't you just match those shapes to something in this book?" I said as I flipped through the pages looking at all the different rocks; it sounded simple enough.

"Timber, I've been trying to do that all night!" Tyler said curtly. "Some of the shapes kind of look like alum. Most of them remind me of salt. They look so chopped up that they are hard to know exactly. A few even reminded me of sugar. But the weird thing is these elements don't combine with rocks and something *is* mixed with this Jasper stone. Maybe the magic of the pond made that happen."

"I'm sure!" I agreed. "So, what do we do now?"

"Well, I want to do an experiment."

"That sounds great!" I said with excitement. I felt like an eager assistant to a great scientist.

"I think we should start with those things I thought I saw. Like alum, salt, and sugar."

"It's probably salts or alum," I interrupted. "They said it tasted strong and kind of bitter. And isn't salt, like, the 'stuff of life'?"

"Yeah, most of the shapes resemble a cube, which *would* be salt, but alum has a stronger, bitter taste. But the funny thing is I think either one of those would kill a plant, let alone grow from it."

"But we're dealing with a magic pond," I reminded Tyler.

"I know. That's why I decided to try the experiment anyway," Tyler said as he picked up his bulky backpack and unzipped the front pocket. He held it open for me to see the little zip lock bags with white powder in them that had black letters written on the side with a marker.

"I have bags of alum, salt, and sugar and another bag of Jasper rocks." He continued, "What I want to do is dig a small hole at the base of different Oak Trees by the edge of the pond and put a rock into each one, then I will pour some alum, salt, or sugar in the different holes."

"Tell me that process again, for growing crystals," I said as I tilted my head to the side.

"There are four steps: dissolving, absorbing, evaporating, and crystallizing," Tyler said.

"Maybe we could pour water from the pond in each of the holes too," I added. "To might help with the first step."

"That is a great idea, Timber! I never thought about that. Since the pond is right there, I just thought the magic water would do its thing but that might actually speed up the whole process."

"So how long will this experiment take?" I asked enthusiastically.

"Well, that's the thing. I have done experiments like this before, but it was in a controlled environment. Some took hours to go through the evaporation process, others took days, and the sugar one took up to six weeks."

"Tyler, we don't have that much time!"

"I know. But we will just have to trust that Mr. Seller's Pond and the magic within it will work quickly."

I held up my hand and counted on my fingers as I went through the four steps again. "Dissolving shouldn't take too much time. Absorbing will probably take even less. Evaporating, so how exactly does that happen?"

"I'm not too sure unless it's just simply through the air like regular evaporation." Tyler said. "But I wonder if it might have something to do with how the pond comes and goes, each time we go to Mandoria."

"I bet it does," I whispered, thinking of the tornado-like wind. It sounded like a perfect fit to this scientific puzzle. "We will have to go back often then! And crystallizing, how will this happen?"

"I don't know, Timber," Tyler said. "Maybe we will simply know it is done when we see it. Didn't Ayden say something about being able to see the crystals in the rain and by moonlight?"

"Well, it poured rain last night," I said. "I wonder if it's going to rain again tonight?"

"I heard it might last through the weekend," Tyler stated. His voice sounded elevated with excitement. "And Timber, remember the moon? It's full tonight."

Everything stopped. Our eyes locked, and without speaking, we knew exactly what needed to be done.

"Let's find Jill," I blurted out.

"And get to the pond so we can do the experiment," Tyler added, finishing the sentence for me.

The four chimes of Grandma's doorbell rang loud and long throughout the entire house.

CHAPTER SIXTEEN

THE EXPERIMENT

"It's Jill!" I exclaimed when the doorbell chimed.

"Let me get my backpack," Tyler said. He quickly threw his bag over his shoulder and followed me out the bedroom door.

I could hear Tyler's mother talking at the bottom of the stairs as we walked through the darkened hallway.

"So, you can go on up if you'd like," she said.

Jill stood at the bottom of the stairs. She had on brown shorts and a yellow sleeveless shirt. Colorful beads hung around her neck, and like the Runners she had a green twisted headband under her wavy blond hair. She, too, had a backpack over her shoulders. The golden shield was tucked into her back pocket and hung down just below her shorts.

"Hey Jill!" I called out.

Her head slanted upward as she caught my gaze and flashed a beautiful smile.

Tyler and I quickly moved down the old squeaky staircase.

"Hey," Jill said.

"So, what are you kids planning to do today?" Tyler's mother asked. She looked directly at me as she continued to dry her hands on a white kitchen towel.

"I'm not sure," I responded, shrugging my shoulders.

"I was thinking we could show Tyler where Fantastic Caverns are downtown," Jill said, eyeing me.

"That sounds fun!" Maria said.

"Then we'll probably just ride our bikes on the bike path around Tautphaus Park," Jill continued with our imaginary plans. "And there's a live band that plays down at Rumsfield Park at 1:00 on Friday afternoons. We could check that out too!"

"Well, it sounds like you have a fun day ahead of you," Maria said. She looked at Tyler, who was still standing on the first step of the stairway. "Do you need any money?" she asked, grabbing her front pocket.

"No, I'll be fine," he responded, glancing at me.

Tyler's mother noticed something in her pocket and then smiled as she pulled out an unopened roll of Life Savers.

"This is all I have anyways," she laughed and held them up in front of her. "You can have these if you want."

"Uh, that's okay mom," Tyler said.

"Wait just a minute," I said.

Everyone looked at me.

I saw Jill roll her eyes.

"I *love* Life-Savers!"

Maria's bushy eyebrows rose.

"She really does!" Jill said emphatically. "For some reason they are her favorite candy."

"Well then, here you go!" Maria said and handed me the whole roll.

I smiled. "Thank you!"

"Now, it's kind of overcast out there. If it starts to rain on you, just head back here and maybe you could find a good video to watch."

"Okay," Jill and I said at the same time, then laughed together.

"Thanks mom," Tyler added as he headed for the front door. "We'll be back later!"

We followed Tyler out the front door, quickly got on our bikes, and headed down the street.

The trees looked darker and a grayness hung in the air as I noticed the sun was hiding behind the clouds. It was cooler than usual for summertime. I tried to ignore the chill that nipped at my arms.

We talked as we headed north of town. I told Jill about how the Watchman came to my room in the middle of the night. Then Tyler explained what he learned about the crystal and how part of it was Jasper and the other part unknown.

Tyler explained our plans for the experiment, which would hopefully help us figure out the other missing element of the crystal. My job was to poke the holes and plant the rocks safely in the ground at different trees. Tyler would then dump one of the components on top of the rock, soak it with water from the pond, and cover it with dirt. Jill would be the one on lookout for the Drimlor.

I noticed the gray clouds clumped together like overstuffed pillows in the sky. They looked as if they could burst at any moment. The change of weather did not, however, put a damper on our excitement. In fact, it seemed to elevate the anticipated adventure that lay in front of us for the day. We were on a mission!

As we crossed Bellen Road, we discussed strategies for hiding our bikes and making our way to the tree. Since we decided that we should probably have the eyewear with us, we planned to get it from the underground passage before heading to the pond. I was hoping we didn't have to crawl through the tunnel to get it!

"So, what's in your backpack, Jill?" I asked as we turned on to Monticello Drive.

"Oh, I just made us a few sandwiches and threw in a couple of water bottles for us to have if we get hungry," she said. "The question is what's in Tyler's backpack? It looks stuffed."

The sandy dirt was suddenly harder to move through as Jill and I leaned closer to the handlebars. We had to push harder to keep up with Tyler, who didn't seem fazed at all by the changes on the road.

"Oh yeah, I forgot to tell you what else I did last night when I couldn't sleep," Tyler said.

"My paintball gun is in my backpack."

"To fight the Drimlor with?" Jill said sarcastically. I could tell by the sound of her voice that she thought that was a stupid idea.

"Well, get this," Tyler said, unaffected by the look on Jill's face. "I took a syringe and sucked the paint out of the balls. Then I filled them back up with water I got from the pond yesterday."

"No way!" I exclaimed. "So, when the ball hits the Watchman, the water will burn his skin?"

"Yep," Tyler said. "That was the whole idea! And I am much better with a paintball gun than I am with a sling-shot."

"Dang. That's a great idea," Jill said.

"Jill, I even have a little handheld gun for you. But it only shoots one ball at a time."

"I don't care," she said, shrugging her shoulders. "I'll still carry it as long as I have some extra ammo."

Everyone got quiet. We had made our way back around to the other end of Bellen Road. Not another word would be spoken. It was the rule out here, and we all knew it. The only sounds were the normal ones that surrounded us in the trees. Birds chirped freely above us while a steady breeze shook the leaves at a constant pace. But this time there was also the sound of a low flying propeller plane in the distance.

The trees were tall and thick as usual, but they were darker and casted deep shadows that resembled black trench coats around each trunk in the forest. It felt eerie to be here without the bright, comforting blaze from the sun overhead.

Tyler got off his bike and motioned for us to follow him to the opposite side of the road. We had planned to hide our bikes in a different place each time we came out here. Jill and I covered them up while Tyler crouched down over his backpack. He apparently didn't want to take it with him because he was stuffing his pockets with the little zip-lock packets labeled A, S, and SG, which stood for alum, salt, and sugar. He tossed me the bag of Jasper rocks. I knew exactly what to do with them, so I caught the bag and quickly pushed it deep into my pocket next to the golden needle.

Each of us got prepared in case we were to run into the Watchman. Jill slid her arm into her golden shield. Tyler finished screwing the CO_2 tank onto the backside of the black paintball gun. He opened the lid on the top to show us the silver balls in the round container holding the ammo. It was full and ready to fire! He showed Jill how to hold the weapon and how to shoot it. Then he handed her the small gun and did the same thing with it. I secured my golden shield on my arm as Tyler stuffed a few extra silver balls into Jill's front pocket.

Tyler reminded me of a soldier I saw in a movie as he motioned us forward with the long black barrel of his gun. I kept close behind him, and Jill was at the rear. We held our shields in front of us as we walked carefully up to the edge of Bellen Road. Tyler motioned for us to get down as he moved forward to assess the area. He jerked the tip of his gun with one sharp movement and we ran quickly across the dusty road.

I was startled as I felt a cool wet droplet land on my cheek. Then another one hit my nose. Tyler stopped and looked back at us. We didn't move, trying to listen carefully. A slow, soft tapping began to hit the leaves in the trees around us. I deliberately turned my head to look at Jill, and a few drops sunk through my hair onto my scalp and one on my forearm. A chill went down my spine. It was beginning to rain. The gentle rhythm of sounds began to accelerate as Tyler motioned us onward. The rain is a good thing. It helped to cover the crunching sound of our feet as we worked our way through the brush.

I could tell Tyler was trying to find the underground passage as he led us further and further from the road. Then he stopped abruptly, like his feet were stuck in hard cement. I almost ran into him. Jill's paintball gun hit the back of my shoulder and she quickly gained her balance after almost tripping over my feet. Tyler pointed the tip of his gun down to the ground.

Jill and I both looked bewildered at what he was trying to show us. He tapped the earth just in front of him. The sound was hollow and unnatural for solid ground. What could it be? Jill must have felt as concerned as I was. We both took a step back. Tyler looked around the forest and saw a large broken tree branch half buried in the brush. It had clearly been lying there for some time as he tried to lift it out of the earth that was built up around the edges. He handed me his gun and used both arms to pick up the heavy, twisted branch. I looked at Jill and she shrugged her shoulders. She didn't understand what he was doing either.

Tyler stepped closer to the ground where the hollow sound came from and leaned the branch out in front of him. He held his breath and strained to balance the log as he banged it on the hollow earth. Realizing what he was doing, Jill and I ducked half expecting something crazy to take place, but nothing happened. Tyler stretched out farther and did it again. But still, nothing. He looked back at us, shrugged his shoulders, and heaved the heavy log off to the side of the hollow sounding earth. Maybe this was another tunnel Stroder and Grandma had dug out together.

Quickly the large branch sunk deep under the ground as dirt and sand followed it like water going down a drain. Tyler stepped back and spread his arms as if to protect me and Jill. The earth in front of us abruptly opened like a door that swung down into the earth. There was the branch that had sunk only moments before. Without warning and with extreme force, the heavy tree branch was hurled in front of us like a bolder in a huge slingshot. It flew into the air, just missing the trees. A loud, hard smack echoed throughout the forest. We watched it stick unexpectedly to the side of a huge tree trunk in the distance. I stared in horror at the long protruding points that pierced all the way through the log.

I gasped.

It quickly registered in my mind the severity of this situation. Out here in the forest, away from town, the Drimlor wanted us dead! If one of us would have stepped into that trap we would have been killed on the spot.

Tyler crouched down and hastily motioned for us to do the same.

Emptiness resonated through the trees after the loud, stuck branch. The Watchman was probably waiting for that sound. Tyler moved ahead through the forest looking desperately for the entrance to the passageway. Each of us searched frantically. To be hidden was our only desire.

The rain continued to plummet from the sky and onto my skin. I was wet and cold as I followed in Tyler's footsteps. We were in single file again, waddling like ducks through the wet brush.

Tyler pointed to a huge, bushy area and moved rapidly toward it. It looked familiar enough to me. One by one we crawled under the brush. The rain no longer hit my skin, but I could still hear the pattering rhythm loud and clear.

"This is not the place," Tyler whispered quietly, mouthing most of the words. He looked frustrated and worried.

"What do we do?" Jill responded in the same tone.

Tyler moved his hand up in the air as if to say stop and tilted his head like he was listening more closely.

We jumped as an angry crack of thunder burst throughout the sky, then rumbled fiercely off into the distance.

"Let's quit looking for the passage and just find the tree!" I said in a desperate whisper.

Then we heard it. The horrible familiar sound of limbs breaking in the distance.

We watched through the twisted branches of the brush as Boden, the Drimlor, limped over to the tree with the log stuck to it. His ugly face turned slowly to the side, revealing his hunch-back silhouette more perfectly. He scanned the area with his glowing green eyes to see what might have tripped his deadly trap. It seemed like he looked straight at us a couple of times, but the brush must have hidden us better than I thought. He turned and worked the log back and forth, wedging it off the thin long spears until he got it loose. Effortlessly, he tossed it aside.

The Watchman continued to look around the forest as he limped off like a crippled old man. The distance steadily grew between us. I softly squeezed a bit of air into my lungs like I was taking a quick breath through a long straw. Gradually, the seconds formed into minutes as we watched the Drimlor disappear the way he had come.

"Let's get out of here!" Tyler said quietly.

"Okay," Jill and I whispered at the same time.

We crawled out from under the soggy brush and began to run swiftly through the trees, getting blasted by the rain once again. Tyler looked back a couple of times to see if anyone was following us.

"The tree!" I said, pointing back to the left.

Jill circled around me and Tyler, facing backward. She crouched down and held her golden shield out in front of her with the gun directly over the top of it. She reminded me of Brindle, ready and eager to fight if she needed to. Jill moved back and forth anxiously looking for any unwanted movement.

"I'll look after you two," Jill said. "Now get on with the experiment!" I looked at Tyler as I quickly reached into my pocket and pulled out the wrapped needle. I ran to the tree and climbed as fast as I could, then inserted the golden eye into the knot on the branch just in front of me.

The rain suddenly slowed down, and an eerie silence penetrated the air.

"The wind," I whispered as I looked out into the forest. I forgot about the wind, our wild friend who always welcomed us to Mandoria.

I saw movement out of the corner of my eye and turned to see Jill and Tyler cutting through the silence as they ran toward the underground passage. The air was still for another few seconds and then it hit. The breeze gathered strength and seemed to shift gears as wind blew ferociously around me. I closed my eyes for a good long minute and waited for our untamed welcome to be over.

Finally, the wind slowed and then was gone.

I looked over and saw the beautiful entrance to the path that led to the pond.

The magic of this place was breathtaking! I loved everything about it. I wanted to live here forever!

Tyler and Jill met me at the bottom of the tree.

Jill handed me the golden eyewear she must have gotten from the underground room.

"Oh, Thanks." I said quietly, pushing it deep in my pocket.

"Are you ready?" Tyler whispered.

I nodded.

Tyler lifted his black paintball gun up toward Jill. She quickly tucked her handheld weapon under the top of her brown shorts and took the big gun from Tyler. With a smudge of dirt on both cheeks, she reminded me of an Indian brave ready to defend her tribe.

Tree branches snapped in the distance.

"Run!" Jill said in a quick, urgent tone.

Tyler and I bolted into the beautiful pathway as Jill followed close behind us. I reached for the rocks in my pocket. I knew what I needed to do.

The pond and the majestic trees were the same as before.

Instantly, I longed to be in the safety of the water. I longed for Mandoria—to see the people, smell the sweet scents, and to inhale the crisp, cool air. *But first, get the job done,* I reminded myself.

I tore across the sand that was next to the pond and stopped abruptly at the first huge Oak Tree. I dropped to my knees and I stuck my thumb deep into the ground, forming a perfect hole. I fumbled a minute with the plastic bag then took a jasper stone and dropped it down into the dirt. I didn't look at Tyler, who I could feel by my side, but ran on to the next tree. I did the same thing over and over, preparing the rocks at the base of the trees just like Tyler told me to.

Jill stood behind us holding the paintball gun tight in her arms.

Tyler and I worked as quickly as we could.

Jill screamed, "He's here!"

I looked back toward the pathway and saw the Watchman standing beside it. He dropped to his knees, holding his weapon out in front of him and took aim directly at me.

"Get behind the tree, Keeper!" Jill yelled, pointing the gun at Boden.

A black dart flew right next to my head as Tyler lunged at me. His body hit me, and I went down with the force of what felt like an oncoming semi-truck. He rolled me behind a tree.

I gasped for air.

"Plant the jasper!" he ordered, as he peaked around the side of the tree.

I tried to set up as two darts hurled right next to me.

"We need to get in—" I started to say but Tyler interrupted me.

"I know! I know! But first we must finish this! I have a few more alum to do, then the sugar," he said as he reached into his front pocket.

Even though I was flustered, I did as he told me. I poked my thumb deep into the earth then dropped another stone into it. I could hear sharp bursts of wind blasting from the paintball gun. Jill was firing over and over at Boden.

A loud roar suddenly echoed through the trees. The Drimlor's voice was angry and violent.

"Yes! She hit him!" Tyler exclaimed, not even looking up as he anxiously watered the hole then covered it with dirt.

I saw Jill standing alone next to the water. *Was he gone?* I wondered hopefully. I ran quickly to the next tree that was a little farther off.

"Help!" Jill screamed. "Tyler?"

Tyler and I looked around the tree in horror. Jill was kicking and screaming while the Watchman drug her by her leg into the trees.

"Stay put, Timber!" Tyler ordered. He bolted up from my side and ran to grab the gun that had dropped by the edge of the pathway. Then he disappeared into the forest. I knelt and listened.

Jill stopped screaming in the distance.

My heart pounded in my chest as questions swirled in my mind.

What was happening?

Was Jill okay?

What would I do if the Watchman came for me?

A piercing roar screeched from within the forest. I heard muffled noises and moaning, then another roar rumbled off in the distance.

Everything was silent except for my own labored breaths.

Jill and Tyler suddenly came leaping over the brush like wild antelope running from an angry lion. They stopped right next to me and struggled for a breath.

"What happened?"

Tyler gasped for another breath of air as he sat the paintball gun on the ground.

"Is he gone?" I asked.

"Let's just say he's held up for a while," Tyler said through gasps. "But I got out in front of him and tripped him. Then I shot him right in the eye."

"He's burning, at least!" Jill laughed smugly with her hands placed hard on her hips. Her shield hung loosely at her side.

"He's probably getting angrier as we speak!" I said.

"Most likely you're right," Tyler agreed, handing the gun to Jill. "Let's get this experiment done and go to Mandoria."

Jill turned around and aimed the paintball gun into the trees.

I moved ahead to the next tree and pushed my thumb deep into the ground at the base of the trunk. Then I moved on to the next one.

"Timber," Tyler said with a worried voice.

I looked up.

"I don't have the sugar packets," he exclaimed.

"What?" I asked, standing up next to the tree.

"I don't have any sugar," Tyler said as he looked wildly on the ground around his feet. "I must have lost the packets when I was running to help Jill."

SHERRI GRIMAUD

"What are you going to do now?" Jill asked.

"I don't know," he said.

"Well, you really didn't think it was sugar anyways because the Noceans told us the Aspids taste were bitter," I said. "At least we got the other two in the ground."

"No!" Tyler called out sharply. His brown eyes were huge and looked longingly at me. "We have to finish this experiment the way we planned. I chose the three elements that had some similar properties and those are the ones we're going to use!"

"But… we don't have the sugar anymore," I said slowly, feeling my pockets as if for some reason I might find them there. The tips of my fingers moved along my shorts and I felt a long hard role in the front lower right corner.

"The Lifesavers!" I whispered excitedly. "They are sugar! Aren't they?"

"Well, yes..." Tyler slowly said.

"Will they work?" I asked.

"They're going to have to work!" Jill added. "Get on with it before the crippled Drimlor returns."

I quickly retrieved the roll of candies and opened one end. I handed Tyler a green and yellow Lifesaver.

"This is not pure sugar granules," Tyler mumbled while he tucked a green one into the ground. "But I guess it is better than nothing!"

I moved on to the next tree.

"Hurry up!" Jill whispered.

I shoved my thumb into the ground and dropped in another stone. Tyler followed behind me.

"I only have one rock left," I announced.

"Well, get it planted!" Jill insisted. She bravely moved out farther into the forest and aimed her gun toward sounds of branches breaking in the forest.

"That's all we need!" Tyler whispered desperately as he held his hand out in front of him. "Give me another one."

I quickly unwrapped another Life Saver.

"Red Raspberry," I whispered, tossing it to Tyler. "That's my favorite one! It is our good luck, one!"

"Red Raspberry," I said again. "Remember how I told you what Uncle Martin said about Grandma Catherine and Zelly. They used to eat Red Raspberries in the trees by Mr. Sellers Pond. I wonder if that has something to do with the Crystals."

"Who knows, Timber, just hurry up," Tyler said impatiently. His voice was tight with worry as he looked back at Jill.

"I don't see anything yet!" Jill exclaimed.

The sounds were getting louder as I pushed my thumb into the ground at the base of the next tree and dropped the last Jasper stone inside.

"There he is!" Jill screamed.

A sudden powerful burst of air shot from the paintball gun as Jill began to fire. She took a few steps back toward us.

"Run to the pond, Timber!" Tyler yelled as he dove to the ground at my feet, almost knocking me over. "I'll finish this, just get to the water!"

I bolted off running. The sand was hard to move through with my sandals on. I felt like I was leaping forward in slow motion.

A loud, scratchy roar filled the air. I knew the Watchman had been hit.

"Get her, Rotty!" He screamed with an angry, powerful voice that seemed to penetrate the very core of my being. "Go on, boy!"

The water was only a few feet away. *Who is he yelling at?* I wondered.

"Get in the water, now!" Jill screamed in complete terror. Her voice was suddenly just behind me. Then she leaped passed me and splashed into the water of the pond.

I slammed my feet into the sand to slow down then turned around. I was consumed with fear as I saw Tyler running with all his might from a huge, gray beastly animal with long husky legs that were lunging forward with great strength. The creature's head and mouth were not in proportion to the rest of its body—they were gigantic! His enormous teeth were seething with lathering, foamy drool. He looked like a huge, distorted form of a Rottweiler.

Tyler crashed into me with great force. He wrapped his arms around me as he landed squarely on top of me in the water. He was heavy, but the cool, soothing safety of the water instantly enveloped my head and upper body. Exactly at the same time, however, I felt the sharp, crushing grip of a powerful jaw, clamp down on my foot.

"Ow!" I screamed a muffled, painful, cry into the water. It sounded like my voice didn't even leave the walls of my own head.

The back of my skull was suddenly being scrapped along the dirt and rocks that were at the edge of the pond. Although I was wedged under Tyler, I was still being pulled by the creature that gripped on to my foot.

"No!" I screamed with everything inside of me. But no one heard me under the thick, muted water.

Tyler pushed me loose and swam off.

What is he doing? He was my bodyguard. *Was he so scared of this beast that he would feed me to him so he could get away?*

I gasped for a breath of air as I realized I was out of the water now. Dirt and sand were digging into my backside.

"Ugh!" I grunted as I arched my back and twisted my body. I placed my other foot on the snout of the creature that had me caught in his jaw and tried to push him off. But his teeth sunk deeper into my foot.

"Ow. Ow," I moaned reaching down toward the pain.

The Watchman was standing directly over me with the tall trees reaching up to the sky behind him. His green, glowing eyes pierced down at me from under his huge eyebrows as I squirmed in pain.

"That's it, Rotty!" he said. The Drimlor's voice was scratchy as he talked to his obedient 'dog' creature.

The animal released his jaws and I felt warm fluid cover my foot. The pain was unbearable.

"Ow! Oh! Oh!" I screamed. My voice sounded hysterical and out of control. I couldn't tell if it was from the pain, the fact that I was caught by the Watchman, or from the abandonment of my friends. *What am I going to do?* I panicked, of course. I turned over and began to crawl frantically for the pond. My wounded foot obviously did not work correctly so I scratched and clawed with my fingers and tried to push off with my good leg.

"Stupid Keeper!" Boden huffed mercilessly, as a heavy, crushing weight slammed down hard on my good leg. "Now let's go back and get that key!"

I screamed out in pain again and again. I looked desperately at the motionless pond. *Where are my friends?*

To my surprise, two watery heads protruded out of the pond just in front of me and slowly began to take form. Tyler and Jill stood up, boldly holding their weapons out in front of them like angry Marines on a mission to rescue their captured teammate. They didn't waste any time. Quick, hard bursts of air exploded from the paintball guns as silver balls zipped rapidly over my head.

Boden and his creature began to scream and howl at the same time. Jill grabbed my arms with great force and dragged me back into the water of the pond.

The cool softness rapidly encased my whole being. Bubbles danced wildly next to me as Tyler plunged into the water. We swam as hard as we could to stay low and get farther out into the pond.

I quickly inhaled an extensive breath of water into my lungs. I longed for the feeling in my lungs! Immediately, the pain eased, and I felt a sense of safety and relief fill my chest. Tyler grabbed my hand as I eagerly took another breath, and we allowed the water to pull us down into the safety of the pond.

I had to take a few seconds and adjust to the vivid brilliant colors that encircled us. I could tell that Jill and Tyler had to do the same.

I looked down to check on my foot that was in severe pain only moments ago. Large red and purple teeth marks remained along each side of my ankle. The water was already healing the wounds.

Jill got my attention and motioned for me and Tyler to follow her. We swam quickly to the cave, enjoying the colors and friendly creatures that seemed to be different each time we came to this place. Then we swam back into the darkness of the cavern. The stone was covering the opening to Mandoria. Tyler pulled it out of the way and motioned for me to enter.

The warm air of Mandoria was a welcomed feeling upon my skin and I smiled as the sun brightly shining in the sky overhead. I moved quickly out of the way for Tyler and Jill to enter.

I thought I saw the Runners standing by the edge of the trees. I wiped the water out of my eyes and tried to focus.

"You're here!" I said with excitement.

Ayden moved quickly out into the clearing in front of the others.

"That was a close one!" Jill exclaimed, as she also noticed the Runners. "We were almost *killed!*"

Ayden's expression was full of great concern. He looked back at Stroder, who didn't even look up. He was leaning against a stone in a relaxed kind of way, stroking a long piece of grass that he was holding on to.

"What happened?" Ayden asked, looking up at me.

"I'll tell you what happened," Tyler said, in frustration. I could tell he was trying to catch his breath from what we had just gone through. "We went to the pond to do some experiments and we barely escaped the Drimlor and a giant dog-thing!"

"Yeah! And he shot darts at us!" Jill joined in.

Stroder turned his head at the sound of Jills voice.

"I had to guard them while they planted the rocks," she continued, speaking as fast as she could. "Then Boden drug me through the forest! Tyler tripped him. Timber found the Lifesavers and almost got her foot bit off by that creature! I had to grab her while she was bleeding all over the place and drag her into the pond."

I rubbed my ankle as she spoke and some of the Runners moved in to listen more closely.

"What?" Ayden exclaimed in horror. His tiny eyebrows were drawn close together.

Stroder was still leaning against a rock but finally looked at me with a blank, cold expression.

"Are those teeth marks?" Ayden exclaimed. "What experiment? What creature? And what are Lifesavers?"

"Wait a minute," I said slowly, raising my hands slightly out in front of me. Something was wrong. I could feel it. I looked quickly around the clearing and then back at Stroder.

"Where's Brindle? I asked. "And why were you all here, just waiting for us?"

Stroder slowly stood up keeping his dark, icy eyes fixed upon me.

I knew something was terribly wrong.

CHAPTER SEVENTEEN

LEDGE OF CRESTHIL PASS

Stroder moved next to Ayden.

Everyone was silent.

Ayden shook his head with a troubled expression on his face.

"You remind me a lot of Catherine," Stroder said looking directly into my eyes.

I could tell it was still hard for him to speak her name.

"She was smart, alert, and learned quickly what a Keeper had to do. She was also brave and unselfish. She would have done whatever she had to do to save our people." Stroder took a deep breath, then said, "And you are going to have to do the same."

"What are you talking about?" I asked. I could feel my eyebrows pulling together.

"Stroder," Ayden mumbled, as he hung his head and looked at him.

Stroder responded sharply to Ayden. "And you're going to do it, too!" he commanded.

"First of all," Stroder continued, looking back at us. "I'm sorry about the close call you had with the Watchman and whatever animal he has with him now. Each one of you has put your life on the line for us and we are grateful. Timber even carries the marks of the Drimlor's dart. You will have those forever. You are already a survivor, and I know you have the makings of a great Keeper!"

I looked at the two black dots on the sides of my little fingers, and gently rubbed one of them.

"And Tyler, you are a *true* protector. I can tell you understand the role of the Keeper and that you have given yourself the task of defending Timber. From where we come from this is the most honorable position a Nocean could take upon himself. You have got Timber's back, and I think you would die for her if you had to."

Tyler nodded.

"Thank you," Stroder said.

Then he looked at Jill.

I realized I had never heard Stroder speak this much or even seen this side of him, for that matter. He was kind and deeply gentle. Yet I could sense that under his cool and controlled expressions lay a fixed determination to something that might be unsettling.

His face slightly changed as he looked at Jill. A hint of sorrow melted through his eyes.

"All I want to say about you, Jill, is you were born to be a Runner! I can tell it in everything you do! Would there have been a day that you could have become one of us, I would have been honored to 'Run' with you."

Jill smiled at Stroder.

"Wait!" I interrupted. "You sound like this is over or something."

"Look. This is hard for me, too!" Stroder said sharply. "But this is the way it has to be."

Stroder's face looked fixed with determination.

"What?" I asked. I looked to Ayden for an explanation, but he wouldn't lift his head.

"Brindle is very sick, Timber," Stroder said quietly.

"I saw you two in the wind yesterday as we left." I said. "Brindle looked pale and white."

"She fainted," Stroder said. "When we went through the pass, the water did nothing for her. And when we got her home, there were others down too. They are going to die, Timber, unless you chop that last tree down. We have got to have Aspids—tonight!"

"They have all the signs of death," Ayden said. His eyes looked heavy and full of sadness.

"We hate to see these signs," Stroder continued. "Death is soon upon a Nocean when our skin turns white, our body chills, and our eyes twitch with red. Also, when the water from the pass no longer helps us, this means we will die very soon without Aspids."

"I feel so terrible for Brindle and the others. But we're doing an experiment by the pond," I said, with a slight whine in my voice. I looked back at Tyler and then Jill. They both were quiet. *Say something, please!* I thought to myself.

"Tyler. Jill. Tell them!" I said. I could feel hot tears begin to well up in my eyes. I didn't want this to be over. I loved Mandoria! I wanted to spend *my* five-hundred years here someday with these people.

"It's okay," Jill said as she put her arm around me.

"Whatever experiment you are doing," Stroder said calmly. "I am sure Catherine has already tried it. She spent years doing every experiment she could imagine. But we simply do not have that kind of time anymore."

"Stroder," Ayden finally spoke.

Stroder flipped a hard glare at Ayden like he did not even want him to speak.

"I think Brindle will be okay for a day or two," Ayden said.

"I will not take that chance!" he responded adamantly.

"When I came here many years ago," Stroder said, looking back at me. "I was taken in by Brindle's family. She has been like a sister to me. And I will not take a chance with her life! I will chop down that tree by myself if I have to."

"No. We will do it, Stroder. But I still wanted to be able to make the choice," I said. Tears began to stream down my face. "I am the Keeper and I wanted to be able to live here someday."

"Timber," Tyler said. His voice was full of great concern. "You cannot do that! You are the Keeper, but you have a family and Jill and me. Your place is with us."

He gently put his hand on top of mine, something I would have loved for him to do at any other time. But I looked at him and quickly pulled my hand away.

"It is her choice, not yours!" Ayden piped up.

"Look, there is no choice!" Stroder called out in frustration. "You should have never even told her about it!"

"Please let me tell her my plan," Ayden begged.

"No!" Stroder demanded. "That is just a death trap, Ayden, and you know it!"

"I don't think so," Ayden retorted, then turned to me. "I want you to live here with us too, Timber, no matter what Tyler says. If you chop down the tree tonight and we harvest the Aspids, I promise you that I will take off in the morning with a few of the others and go to southern Mandoria. There is another Keeper down there. The Keeper of Watdoe Pass. I will ask him to find you in the outer world, and let you come visit us. And then, whenever you decide to come and stay, we can have their Keeper change you."

I wiped the tears from my cheeks. "I thought I could just change myself whenever I wanted to?" I said.

"You won't be the Keeper anymore, after this pass closes," Ayden said with sad, huge eyes. "And remember, only the Keeper can make that choice."

"But I still want to be the Keeper," I said.

"I know you do, Timber," Jill said softly. "But when the pass is closed, they won't need us anymore."

"Ayden thinks he can just go on down to southern Mandoria with no problems at all." Stroder joined in. "But the truth is the Drimlor's have possession of the land between the north and south. Other Noceans have tried to make it down there to get Aspids, but they have never returned."

"I can do it, Stroder. I know I can!" Ayden said boldly.

I took a deep breath and sighed. Everyone was silent.

"Would you consider going with him, Stroder?" I asked.

"I think it's a stupid, death trap!" he said. "For anyone to go."

I took another deep breath.

"Stroder, If I promise to cut down the tree, would you go with him then?" I asked.

He put his hand on his hip and lowered his bow down to his side. I knew Stroder would not give his word unless he really meant it.

"I am not sure when I want to come and live with your people, but I do know one thing," I said. "I really want to be a Nocean like my grandmother did. I feel like I am still connected to her through you guys, and I love that! I love your people, and I love Mandoria!"

"Timber!" Tyler whined. "Please don't."

"I want to be a Nocean too!" Jill blurted out. She was so quiet I had almost forgotten about her.

Stroder looked up at her. His total expression changed.

"What?" I said in disbelief.

"You do, too?" Stroder asked.

"I know I haven't told you, Timber, but I want to live here, too. I want to become a Nocean and run with the Runners."

"Oh brother!" Tyler moaned and flipped his long brown hair to the side.

"Would you allow that, Timber?" Stroder asked.

"Sure, I would!"

For some reason Jill's desire to become a Nocean seemed to make all the difference to Stroder.

"Well, okay then," Stroder said. "Timber, if you chop down the tree, I promise I'll go with Ayden to southern Mandoria."

I gasped with excitement. "You will?"

"But you both have to know the truth," he continued. "Even if by some chance we make it through the Drimlor's land, the Keeper may not agree to any of this, and it's ultimately his choice."

"But at least there will still be a chance," I exclaimed.

"Yes, for me too!" Jill added.

"That is the plan then," Ayden said.

"I think you two should carefully consider the decision to become a Nocean," Tyler spoke up. "Because you'll *never* be able to be human again.

"I know," I said to Tyler. "We will have plenty of time to make that choice. Maybe even years… But first, we have a job to do."

"She's right!" Stroder said. "Nothing is happening before we chop the tree down. Tonight! No matter what!"

"Why does this have to be done at night?" Tyler asked.

"Over the years we have learned that more Aspids seem to fall at nighttime. We really don't know why. The harvest is just greater by the light of a full moon."

"It's even rainy out there," I said.

"That's even better," Stroder acknowledged. "More Aspids release if they are rained on first in the outer world."

"I don't mean to put a damper on anything," Tyler said, his voice sounded somewhat defeated. "But we should probably get going. We have a lot to prepare for."

"But we just got here," I whined, looking at Tyler. I knew this would be our last moments together without being taunted by a Drimlor and his beast.

"I know," Jill said. "But Timber, remember how hard it was to get here. I am sure the Watchman is ready and waiting. And we need to get back so we can get ready for tonight."

"They are right," Stroder said. "We'll secure the area by the pond for you, so you won't have to worry about that. But you will need to be careful going home.

"Now, has anyone told you what you'll need to do after you chop down the tree?"

"No," I said.

"First, you have to put the key into the tree so that the pathway and pass are there in the outer world. Then use an ax or hatchet and chop the tree down. This could take a while. But…because you will be cutting down the last tree, you must retrieve the needle right after the tree hits the water, then get the key into the pass as soon as possible. It takes the pond a few minutes or so to dry up, then it will be gone. You need to throw the key as far out as you can. We will watch for it while we are harvesting the Aspids."

"So, the pond *actually does* dry up?" Tyler asked.

"Yes," Stroder answered. "But only at the top, in the outer-world."

Tyler's face looked discouraged.

"You know, that is an important part to my experiment. It is called evaporation. I was wondering what the water did each time we came and went through Creshtil Pass."

"It evaporates!" I said in amazement. "Tyler your experiment would have probably worked if we would have only had more time."

"We will never know," Tyler shrugged.

"So, will the pond still be here for you guys?" Jill asked, looking at Ayden.

"Yes. It is always here," Ayden said.

Stroder knelt and tightened his leather strap around his boots. I knew what he was doing, but I didn't want to leave yet. The other Runners began to prepare to swim the pass too.

"Are you ready?" Stroder asked as he stood and looked over the Runners, then to me, Jill, and Tyler.

"Stroder," Ayden said. "Would you mind if I took Timber for a few minutes and showed her the ledge? We won't be long. Then we will meet you up at the top."

"That is fine. It will give us a chance to secure the area."

Stroder looked at Jill. "Let's go then!" he said.

Jill quickly moved with Stroder through the rocky hillside and into the pass. The Runners quickly followed.

Tyler tenderly took my hand. His big brown eyes flashed up at me and my heart fluttered like a butterfly in my chest. I knew I had hurt him earlier. He looked at me intently.

"Timber, I'm sorry if I upset you. My feelings are different than yours. I know you really love this place. And honestly, I'm going to miss it, too. But I just want you to know that you will always have me and Jill. This place and this adventure will be our secret forever. And when the Keeper of Watdoe Pass finds us, I promise I will help you get back. Timber, I will be your bodyguard until the day you tell me not to be."

I smiled as he spoke.

"Thank you, Tyler," I said. His hand felt warm and secure as it held onto mine. "I am sorry if I said anything that hurt you."

Tyler shook his head as if to say everything was okay.

Ayden looked up at Tyler. His hand was firm on his hip.

"Let's go, Timber," he said.

"Where is this place that you are taking her?" Tyler asked, looking over at Ayden.

"It's just a place in the pond. You have nothing to worry about, *bodyguard*!" Ayden responded flippantly.

"Thank you, Ayden. I know the Runners need me at the top of the pond," Tyler said, looking deep into my eyes again. "So, I will see you in a few minutes."

"Okay," I said.

Ayden and I watched as Tyler moved his way through the rocky hillside.

"You are going to love this place, Timber!" Ayden said. He looked up at me with excitement in his eyes.

"So, what is the ledge?"

"The ledge of the pond is a special place that I wanted you to see before you close the Pass."

"I hate it when you say that because I don't want to close the pass. I don't want this to end," I said. "And I still want to be the Keeper."

"I know, but Timber, we'll find you through the other Pass. I promise we will! And you will always be known as the Keeper of Creshtil Pass. You are doing a very unselfish thing for us, to close the pass and save our people. You're putting our lives before yours."

I nodded, swallowing the lump in my throat.

"Let's go!" Ayden continued as he put his leg into the hillside. "I have something that might help."

Ayden went through the rocks, and I stopped for a moment and looked back over the beauty of Mandoria, the small mountains outlining the huge valley and the tiny waterfalls glistening in the distance.

I may never see this place again, I thought sadly. I took a deep, long breath and tried to memorize the sights and smells one last time. My heart was heavy as I closed my eyes and pushed my way through the rocks on the small hill.

The water gently wrapped itself around my body, and I eagerly took a deep cleansing breath into my lungs. Ayden motioned for me to follow him. We made our way to the turquoise water that filled the opening of the cave. As we swam through, the colors of the pond captured my attention one final time. I would miss this—the creatures, the plants, the feelings in this magical place— most of all.

Ayden reached out for my finger. He wrapped his small arms tightly around my index finger and began to pull me through the water. We moved with great speed throughout the pond. The colors were almost a blur to me as we swiftly swam around a huge boulder and up and over a small forest of plants that looked like young trees. Then we slowed down and stopped. I raised my other hand to move my hair out of the way since it had wrapped completely around my face. We were clearly in a different place in the pond.

Then, I saw it. Brilliant shimmering prisms were dropping like thousands of little raindrops from the top of the pond all the way down to the bottom. They formed what looked like an underwater waterfall of

some kind. The tiny prisms fell like small bright rain-
bows that seemed to land in a circle of whiteness which
gathered on the floor of the pond. I stared in amazement. *How could drops of water fall* inside *the pond?* This
was a question for Tyler.

Ayden gently pulled me toward the brilliant waterfall. The droplets of colorful prisms bounced playfully
on my skin as I cautiously moved through and whiteness that encircled my legs until I got through to the
other side. It felt heavier than the water I was swimming in. A huge grey cliff was directly in front of us.
We swam quickly to the top. Ayden entered a small
crevice at the top of a large precipice. I could barely
squeeze through but finally pulled myself between the
rocks and onto a small ledge in an open-faced cave. The
walls were lined with clear bubbles about the size of
a golf ball. I moved out to the edge of the cavern and
looked out over the entire pond. The scene was magnificent and breathtaking. I could see everything— a
brilliant display of organized color and beauty!

Ayden handed me a bubble that he carried with
both of his hands from the wall of the cave. I touched
it softly with my finger and noticed that it didn't pop.
He motioned for me to take it from him. I gently took
it with both hands and looked at Ayden in amazement.

"Don't let me startle you!" Ayden said without moving his mouth.

I quickly tilted my head to the side. I was confused.
He spoke to me in my mind.

"I know I did," he said again.

What is happening? I wondered.

"Timber, the bubbles on the crest are magical bubbles. If you hold one in your hands, we can talk to each other in our minds."

"Wow," I said in my mind. "That is so cool!"

"I know," Ayden said.

I could hardly believe it. I was communicating with Ayden in my mind. We didn't have to use our voices or move our lips.

"This is where Catherine and I would come when she would tell me about you. We would swim up here and talk for hours while looking out over the pond. We were good friends, you know. She couldn't wait to introduce me to you. She always thought we would make a good match, and I secretly hoped you would come live here one day."

"Really?" I said. "I wish she could be here now. You know, Ayden, I really miss her."

"I know you do!" Ayden said. "If you want to see her in your mind, all you have to do is think really hard about her."

"What do you mean, like close my eyes and try to think of a memory of her? I do that all the time."

"No, I mean *really* see her," he said as he looked out over the pond. "Timber, hold the bubble out in front of your face and think of Catherine."

I did as he told me.

Suddenly, I could see my grandmother as clear as if I were standing right next to her. I was not trying to think of a specific memory, but I could see her standing at her sink in her house singing a tune while she washed her dishes. Her voice was crystal clear and echoed through my mind.

"Wow! How did that happen?" I asked Ayden in my mind, looking over to him.

"I told you, it's a magical bubble."

"But—"

"Timber, you can look at your grandma's life and view anything you want through that bubble. And if you can't think of anything, then it will show you whatever it shows you."

"Like doing dishes in her house," I said. "I love this!"

"I want you to take this bubble with you," Ayden said. "That way you can see Mandoria whenever you want to."

"This works in the outer-world?" I asked.

"It sure does," Ayden said, smiling.

He pulled out a few pieces of his golden hair, tied the ends together and threaded it through one end of the bubble. He tied the other ends together and lifted the bubble over my head like a necklace.

"We call these Creshtil-Balls. They are squishy but they will never burst. Just remember one thing, Timber," Ayden continued. "It is not good to spend too much time looking into it. A Nocean could waste away every moment of the day looking through the windows of their mind."

Ayden paused in his thoughts.

"It is meant to be a way to comfort the heart. Especially when there has been a great loss or separation between two people. We often find Stroder up here."

"Timber, I think you'll like this for another reason," Ayden continued. "Even after you close Creshtil Pass, we will be able to communicate with each other through our thoughts."

"Oh my gosh!" I thought. "So, it's kind of like talking on a telephone?"

"Catherine used to say that, too," Ayden smiled. "I don't know what a telephone is, but the Creshtil-Ball works more off feelings and thoughts. And only if the person holding the bubble focuses on the Nocean she wants to communicate with. I hope that for you, that Nocean will be me!"

"Of course, it will be you!" I said. "Ayden, I can't wait to come live with you here in Mandoria."

"I'm sure Tyler will try everything he can think of to stop you," Ayden said with a frustrated look on his face.

"Oh, don't worry about Tyler," I said. "Maybe I can talk him into coming, too."

"Do you think he will want to come here too?" he asked warily.

"Well, not now, that's for sure," I responded. "Thank you for the Creshtil-Ball, Ayden. I will keep it safe and try to keep in touch with you often."

"Oh yeah, and just know that it takes some practice focusing and getting in touch with your feelings, okay?" he said.

"What do you mean?" I asked.

"Well, here in the Pass, surrounded by the water, our thoughts flow easily back and forth to one another. But when you are in the outer world, there is a greater distance between us, and it is harder to connect. But as you practice concentrating and thinking about me here, you will begin to feel my words. And I will feel yours."

"Okay," I replied.

"Well Timber, I need to get you back," Ayden said through his thoughts, then wrapped his arm around my finger. "Are you ready to go?"

"Yeah," I said to Ayden. "Thank you for all that you have done for me. I really do like you, Ayden, and I will forever cherish our friendship."

"Same here!" Ayden responded.

With a smile on his little face, Ayden gently pulled me from the ledge of Creshtil-Pass just above the waterfall of tiny prisms. We plummeted with the energy of a falling star, over the beautiful colors along the floor of the pond. Then, with great speed, Ayden darted upward. We twisted and turned through the silky, smooth water. I closed my eyes and tried to enjoy the last exhilarating rush toward the top.

Cool, dry air moved across my face.

I took a small breath and opened my eyes.

Dark clouds hung heavy over Mr. Seller's Pond.

CHAPTER EIGHTEEN

TIME CREPT BY

Humid air emanated from an overcast sky. Not even a ripple was in the in the water that wrapped like a comforter around my body. I searched the area for movement, but all was still.

Ayden quickly pulled me toward the other end of the pond.

Gradually, the Runners came into view. They were lined up in perfect silence, standing ready to defend. I climbed out of the water and quickly ran to the pathway while the Runners moved like shadows beneath my feet.

Tyler was just inside the pathway, crouched and holding his black paintball gun. He signaled for me to put on the shield. Quickly, I pulled the cloth from my pocket and secured it on my arm. I noticed Jill standing at the tree with Stroder directly at her feet.

Tyler motioned me forward, but I couldn't leave just yet. I turned around and found Ayden following on the ground behind me.

"I wanted to say goodbye!" I whispered as I bent down closer to him.

"It's not 'goodbye' Timber," Ayden responded. "We will all be together one day. We may even see you tonight."

"Timber, you need to go now!" A small voice came from within the group of Runners.

I turned and ran to where Jill was standing as the Runners disappeared into the pathway.

Everything continued smoothly after that. The Watchman and his dog were nowhere in sight. I retrieved the needle, and we held on to the base of the tree while the wind whirled around us, taking with it the beautiful pathway and magical pond.

Without discussion, Jill started to run into the forest. She held the gun in front of her while her shield moved gently at her side. We trusted her instincts and followed as if she was already a Runner leading us to safety. We moved swiftly over the ground and around the brush, jumping fallen logs and broken twigs. Then she dodged a strange group of branches tied up with twine, as if the Drimlor had planned a snare to hedge up our way. Every move Jill made was deliberate and exact as she led us carefully to our bikes.

Not a word was spoken as we headed home. Even though we had not seen the Watchman, we could not divert our attention. We had to remain alert. The wind began to grow stronger and a few sprinkles fell upon us as we worked our way back into town.

We stopped only once, just before we came to the first convenient store. Jill and I took off our shields while Tyler packed his gun away.

We made our way through the streets of town and then safely home.

"Let's go up to my room," Tyler said as we laid our bikes against the side of the wooden porch in front of my house. We needed to make the plans for tonight.

"Yes," Jill said, as if he suggested what she was already thinking.

"I wonder what time it is," I asked.

"It's one o'clock," a deep voice came from just around the corner of Grandma's house.

"Hey dad!" Tyler said as we climbed the front steps to the porch.

"So, what have you kids been up to?" Dave said. His tall broad shoulders poked up from behind the bushes. He had dirty overalls on, a wide-brimmed straw hat and work gloves covering his hands.

"There's farmer Joe!" Tyler mumbled sarcastically under his breath.

We all chuckled.

"We've just been riding our bikes," Jill blurted out. "But thought we better head back because we kept getting rained on."

"Did you get caught in that down-pour an hour ago?" he asked.

"Yeah, but we just hung out under the pavilion until it stopped," Jill quickly responded.

"I don't know about this weather here in Missouri. Is it always like this?"

"It can get crazy sometimes," Jill said.

"But we don't usually have too many storms during the summertime," I added.

"I don't know about you guys," Tyler said. "But I am getting hungry. Can we get something to eat dad?"

"Sure, help yourselves," Dave responded cheerfully. "Mom ran to pick up more plants for the flower-bed. She wanted to finish it as soon as possible.

"I start my new job on Monday, so I thought I better help with this project."

"Okay, Dad," Tyler hollered as we followed him up the stairs.

"I thought you were hungry," I whispered as we went down the hallway to his room.

"I am, but I just wanted to put this away first," Tyler said tossing his backpack on the end of his unmade bed.

"Wow, this is cool in here!" Jill said looking around the room. She gently touched his microscope, then squinted one eye and looked through the eyepiece.

"I know, it's like a small science lab in here," I added.

"Hey, if you are hungry, I still have these sandwiches," Jill said. She pulled her backpack off and unzipped the front pocket. "Mother made these hoagies for us this morning."

"Those look good," Tyler said. He grabbed a sandwich and started to unwrap it. "I'm going to go get us some chips and a few sodas."

Tyler left the room.

"Jill, I wish we didn't have to cut down the tree tonight," I said as I flipped Tyler's covers over his bed and sat down on the edge.

"I know," she responded. "It would have been nice to see if his experiment worked."

"Do you think that Ayden and Stroder will make it through to Southern Mandoria?" I asked.

"It sounds like it will be a challenge, but they are both smart and strong," Jill said. "I have a feeling they won't stop until they get there."

"That's what scares me about Ayden—he seems like he'd rather die than ever give up."

"I think Ayden likes you, Timber," Jill said.

"I know. This may sound dumb, Jill, but the truth is if I were small, I would probably like him too. He is a good-looking little guy."

We both laughed out loud.

"What I like most about him is he is kind," I said. "But at the same time, he would fight to the death for his people.

"Actually, that doesn't sound dumb at all," she said. "Well, it probably would have, but after we learned how your grandma changed Stroder, we know now that it can really happen. And it makes it easier to understand. You know, Timber, I would give anything to be a Nocean so I could live in Mandoria and become a Runner with Stroder."

"Do you *like* Stroder?" I asked.

Jill puckered her lips to the side. "I don't know. There's just this funny connection there. I know I *admire* him. I mean, he's just so *mysterious* and *different*, but in a good way." She laughed to herself, then continued, "I don't know why I like that, but I think he'd be fun to get to know.

"He's also an amazing Runner. I would give anything to be small so I could learn and fight alongside him, like he said…and to spend hundreds of years being a Runner." Jill smiled excitedly at the idea.

"Do you think there could ever be something more between you two?" I prodded. A thoughtful expression crossed her face, but then she shrugged. "Maybe, when I get older. But I don't know if he will ever get past grandma Catherine. I think he admires me though, but only as a kid sister…for now."

I nodded thoughtfully, then said, "I think it's so neat when you become a Nocean, you grow to the age of a twenty-year-old and then you stop aging. Stroder only *looks* like he is a few years older than us."

"I know," Jill agreed. "And a few years down the road, I will look exactly his age. Then we all could live for hundreds of more years together. Except Stroder would live a little less than that."

"I saw him looking at you a few times."

"What do you mean?" Jill asked.

"Well, whenever we discussed things that the Runners do, he would look at you like he was thinking something. Maybe it was just that you would be a good Runner," I shrugged. "All I know is that he was not going to go to Southern Mandoria with Ayden until he heard that you wanted to become a Nocean too. And then, before we all left, he wouldn't leave your side."

"That's true," Jill agreed. She smiled and then took a deep breath. "With our luck something will go wrong, and we'll never see them again."

"Don't say that!" I said. "I hope with all my heart that's not true!"

"What about Tyler?" Jill asked. "You can't have all the guys, Timber."

"I know," I said flipping my eyes.

"And it's obvious that he likes you too, as well as Ayden!" Jill said pointedly.

"I really like Ayden," I whispered. "But I like Tyler too."

"Who wouldn't?" Jill said. "He is gorgeous!"

We giggled.

"Is it so bad to 'like' *two guys* at one time?" I asked.

"I guess not," she said. "Especially if one of those guys is only twelve inches tall."

We laughed louder at the sound of that.

Tyler entered the room with a large bag of Doritos, three Pepsis, and a half-eaten sandwich.

"What's so funny?" he asked.

"Oh nothing," Jill said. "I'll take those, though!" She grabbed the bag of chips quickly from Tyler's hand and plopped down on the chair next to the desk.

"Sure," he responded and sat down on the bed next to me. He took another big bite of his sandwich and handed me a soda.

"Eat up," he said with food in his mouth.

Jill tossed me a Hoagie and we sat quietly, devouring our food.

"I didn't realize how hungry I was," I said as I laid back on Tyler's bed and looked out the window into my own backyard.

"Me neither," Jill added.

"I'm always hungry!" Tyler said through a mouth full of food.

"So, how are we going to do this tonight?" I asked.

"Well first of all, you are not going to bed alone, Timber," Tyler said.

My heart fluttered at the thought of being wrapped in the arms of my bodyguard.

"I don't want that crazy Drimlor sneaking into your room and messing things up for us."

"That's true!" Jill agreed.

"Umm, that reminds me," I said as I pictured the disaster in my bedroom. "My room is still kind of a mess from last night, and I promised Mom I'd clean it up before I did anything today."

"Do you think I will be able to spend the night?" Jill asked.

"I don't see why not, especially if I get my room cleaned. But why are we going to bed? I asked, confused. "I thought we were sneaking out."

"We need to *pretend* to go to bed," Tyler said. His large eyes almost made me feel embarrassed for asking. "Then about twelve-thirty or one, we could meet down by our bikes and take off together. Do you think that will give your mom enough time to fall asleep?"

"Oh sure," I responded. "But I don't think she works an evening shift tonight because she left early this morning. And she said something about taking Jill and I out for dinner. But Tyler, you don't have to worry about my mom. When her head finally hits the pillow, she's out!"

"What are we going to chop the tree down with?" Jill asked, changing the subject.

I got a sick feeling in my stomach at the thought.

"My dad has an ax that's around here somewhere," Tyler said. "I'll find it and bring it tonight."

"Doesn't it take a long time to chop a tree down with an ax?" I asked. "And how are we going to do that without the Watchman hearing or seeing us?"

"We will just have to be ready!" Jill said. "I'm sure we will see him tonight."

"Yeah, and it might take a while for the tree, but we'll get the job done," Tyler said reassuringly. "Even if I have to help you."

"Well, I really need to clean my room, or mom will *never* let Jill spend the night," I said as I sat up on the edge of Tyler's bed.

"Okay," Tyler said. "Jill, will you be with Timber all day, then?"

"I won't leave her side!" Jill exclaimed.

He nodded and then continued, "If any plans change and Jill can't stay the night with you then you have to let me know because I don't want you to be alone tonight."

"I will," I said.

"I can always rig up a line that goes from your bedroom to mine and put a bell on the end of it or something," Tyler said. "Or if worse comes to worst, I'll hide out on top of your porch or even in your closet."

We all stood and walked out the door of Tyler's bedroom.

"Okay then," Tyler said slowly. I felt his warm fingers lace through mine. My heart skipped a beat and I turned to look into his big, brown eyes. "Let me know if you need anything."

"Okay Ty," I said.

Jill and I left and went to my house and spent a few hours cleaning my bedroom. She called her mother and made sure she could spend the night. Then I called the drug store to confirm the plans with mom. She told me she was sorry but would be home late again. Mr. Walter asked her to cover another employee shift. But that Jill could spend the night. Everything was set.

The evening passed slowly but we tried to stay busy. We each took a shower. I gave Jill some clothes because she wouldn't dare leave my side and to go to her house. We watched a little T.V., had a quick snack then decided to hang out in my room while we anxiously waited for the night to pass.

I laid my head against the pillows on my bed while Jill sat down on the floor looking out the window in front of the house.

"Why does time seem to creep by while you're waiting for something?" Jill asked as she turned around, letting the curtains fall from her hand.

"I don't know," I said. "But this is taking forever! I am so worried about everything we need to get done tonight. Do you think we'll be able to do it all without getting hurt by the Watchman or his dog?"

"Timber, you're still the Keeper. But you need to focus on chopping the tree down and leave everything else up to me and Tyler. We will keep you safe.

"And the Drimlor may be smart, but he's still an old guy. And since he burns from the water, we have a rather good weapon to use against him. We just need to stay a step ahead of him."

I held up the bubble that hung around my neck and started to look at it.

"What is that?" Jill asked.

"This is a Creshtil-Ball," I said. "Ayden took me to this place in the pond. It was called the ledge of Creshtil-Pass and he gave me one of these."

"Like a *crystal-ball?*" Jill asked skeptically.

"Well, I never thought of it like that," I said chuckling. "But actually, it is kind of like a crystal-ball."

"Why? What does it do?" she asked.

"It's so neat! While we were on the ledge, Ayden and I could talk to each other through our minds."

Jill leaned up against the bed. Her green eyes were huge in amazement. "Wow! Would it work now?" she asked.

"Ayden said it could, but it would take a lot of practice. All I have to do is concentrate on my feelings and thoughts."

"Have you tried it yet?" Jill asked.

"I looked at it earlier today when you were in the shower, but nothing happened. But it does another thing, too."

"What's that?"

"You can see back in someone's life if you want to. I saw my grandma today."

"What do you mean," Jill said. "Like, you saw a memory?"

"Here, let's try it. I will think about Ayden and you touch the bubble with your finger and see if you can see what I'm seeing."

I closed my eyes and held the sphere out in front of me and concentrated on Ayden when he was a little boy.

Jill touched the bubble.

Suddenly, like someone flipped on a movie within my head, I saw a small, stout child running through the trees of Mandoria. All he wore was a short golden cloth around his waist, but I recognized his younger face with his distinct, deep-set eyes and long flowing hair. Ayden adorably bounced like an anxious little puppy through the trees, eager to run and play.

"Wow!" I faintly heard Jill exclaim. She sounded as if she was standing behind me in a long tunnel.

The place looked different to me, too. The trees were like towers over Ayden's head. I watched as he ran to a huge, beautiful waterfall that seemed to descend down from the sky and land in a large pool of clear water. He jumped in and began laughing.

I let go of the ball.

"Don't stop, Timber," Jill exclaimed. "That was so cool! And look, the ball is squishy."

"Oh my gosh! That was amazing!" I said. "Ayden was so cute when he was little!"

"Yeah, and Mandoria looked completely different!"

"But Ayden warned me about spending too much time looking into the ball. He said if I did, I could lose all sense of time and become consumed with it, if I wasn't careful. We should probably only do that for short periods of time."

"I wonder if it would work for me," Jill said.

I knew exactly who she wanted to look at.

"I'm sure it will!" I responded, "Here, you can try it."

I took the ball from around my neck and handed it to Jill. She eagerly wrapped her fingers around it and laid next to the bed on her stomach. I was sure she began to see something because she was suddenly very quiet.

It was fine with me that she looked at the Creshtil-Ball. I was more worried about the night ahead of us. I turned over on my pillows and stared at the wall in my room, my mind racing with worry.

Was Tyler ready?

Did he find an ax for us to use?

Would I be able to cut down the tree?

What about Brindle—was she still alive? Would they get the crystals to her in time?

Everything dimmed as I drifted off to Mandoria in my mind.

CHAPTER NINETEEN

THE PITCH-BLACK FOREST

I jumped awake. There was a loud clunk against the window. My eyes opened into the darkness that filled my room.

"Jill?" I whispered.

I scanned the room for any large shadows that might be lurking. The only light came from a slight illumination on the floor next to me. Jill was still fixed on the ball that she held in front of her.

Another loud clunk rattled the window.

What time is it? I wondered. I sat up quickly and read the numbers on the clock.

Twelve fifty-five.

"Tyler!" I whispered frantically as I jumped from the bed and peered out the side window. I could barely make out the shape of his tall, lanky body that caught a dim light from the distance.

Quickly, I unlocked the window and pushed it open.

"What are you doing?" Tyler yelled in a loud whisper.

"Sorry, we fell asleep. Give us a few minutes."

I turned around and groped in the darkness for my shoes.

"Jill!" I whispered, careful not to wake mom.

"Jill!" I said a little louder.

She was still frozen to the ball in front of her.

"Jill!" I said again, gently shaking her shoulder.

She gasped and dropped the ball on the floor in front of her.

"Sorry!" I said.

"What...Where am I?" she replied as she turned over and sat up.

Jill looked completely disoriented. I took the bubble from her hands, unwound the strands of Ayden's hair, and replaced it around my neck. Then gently held her cheeks with both of my hands. "Jill, Tyler's out front. We are going to cut the tree down, remember?" I said.

"What happened? Where are we?"

"Get a grip Jill!" I said as I grabbed her shoulders. "You were looking through the Creshtil-Ball." I sighed, quickly grabbing Jill's shoes and jacket at the end of the bed.

"Ayden warned me about that thing," I mumbled as I tossed her things at her feet.

Jill rubbed her eyes, then started to put on her shoes and jacket.

"Are you okay?"

"Yeah, I'll be fine," she said, shaking her head back and forth. "It's just, I can't believe Stroder and all that he has been through."

"Ayden told me to be careful with that ball," I said again.

"I can understand why!" Jill acknowledged. "I feel like I've spent a *life-time* with him." Her voice trailed off, seemingly lost in a memory.

"Jill, we don't have time to talk about this," I said. "We have to climb out the window. Tyler's out there right now, waiting for us."

"But Timber," she whined. "I don't want to chop the tree down. I just want to go live there, right now, with him and the Runners!"

"Jill, there's no time for this," I demanded as I unlocked the window over the front porch. "Stroder will never agree to any of that. Remember, he said he'd cut the tree down himself if *we* didn't."

"Okay. Okay," Jill replied sadly. She finally got control of herself and followed me out the creaky windowsill.

Drops of rain fell from the dark sky and hit lightly against the old tin roof. I felt cold spots form on my face and hands like tiny freckles on my skin. The scent of wet pavement and damp grass filled the air. We slid carefully under the tree branches that hung over the porch, as if to not make any unwanted noise. I lay down on my stomach and inched my way along the edge, feeling with my feet for the wooden slats that lined the end of the overhang. My shoe finally caught hold and I climbed down the side of the porch with ease. Jill followed quickly behind me.

"We're late!" Tyler complained. He was already straddling his bike and had his bulky backpack hung over one shoulder. He flipped his long brown hair out of his face. "We have a lot to do before daylight!"

"Sorry!" I said quietly. A chill went through me as more drops of rain melted onto my skin. I pulled the hood of my jacket up over my head.

Jill and I jumped on our bikes and followed Tyler down the road.

Even though the big light was on at the end of the street, the drastic contrast between dark and light shadows made everything feel strange. As we made our way forward, the darkness seemed to make its way too, as if we were being followed or watched somehow. But the haunting truth was that we actually *might* have been.

Tyler led our expedition as he peddled quickly through town. I followed, desperately trying to keep up, and Jill moved quietly at the rear. She was noticeably quiet. I thought about how she looked after viewing the Creshtil-Ball and her reluctance to chop down the tree. I could sympathize—I didn't want to either! But the things she had seen in the ball had a hold on her and completely changed her feelings about our plans. I wonder if it would have the same effect on me if I looked at Ayden for too long. I already felt like I could love him one day if I made the choice and went to Mandoria. He probably would like me to get lost in the Creshtil-Ball for a while. I laughed to myself.

"Are you two okay back there?" Tyler asked, interrupting my thoughts.

"Yeah, we're fine!" I said as we slowed to a stop. We had made our way to a busier part of town and it felt good to be around lights again. A few cars passed by as we waited for the red traffic light to change in front of Millie's Restaurant. A man in an old green Volkswagen stared at us as he passed by.

"We should probably be careful," Tyler said looking around. "I'm sure this town has a curfew. We might get in trouble if a cop sees us."

"Really?" I asked.

"Yeah, that's true," Jill finally spoke. "My brother said the curfew is at midnight here in Springfield."

"Maybe we should have taken the back roads," I mumbled.

The light changed as Tyler bolted out in front of us. "It's too late now, Timber," he hollered back. "Just hurry!"

We raced as fast as we could through the few streets that lay between us and Bellen Road. Rain hit softly against my face as adrenalin pushed through my veins. *What would I tell Mom if a policeman brought me home? We were on our way to chop down a tree in the forest.* I chuckled to myself. *I'm sure that would go over well!*

There it was. Bellen Road. I wasn't sure if I was happy to have made it there unnoticed or frightened for what lay ahead, but my heart pounded in my chest like a rumbling drum.

That's when I saw it: the biggest, golden moon I had ever seen. *It was definitely a full moon!* It peeked from behind the dark gray clouds that hung just out over the hills in the distance. I gasped and shivered at its appearance.

Tyler was leading the way as we passed over Bellen and took off into the dark rainy night. His backpack was loaded with paintball guns and ammo. And a long wooden handle was sticking out to the side of his head. I knew it was the ax.

This must be easier for him than for Jill and me; he didn't have a connection to anyone in Mandoria, and if he did, I didn't know about it. Maybe he wanted to hurry this whole thing along so he could have the chance to be with someone. I thought of Brindle and her beautiful little face and strong body. I felt a twinge of jealousy, twisted with a pang of guilt that worked its way around my stomach. I took a deep breath and sighed. *No, I am sure that was not it*, I told myself.

The moon had gone behind the clouds again, but I could still make out the road sign in front of us: Monticello Drive. I looked back and saw Jill's silhouette against the fading lights of Springfield. It was amazing how far away from town it felt when it was nighttime.

"Well, here goes!" Tyler said as he turned the corner.

We were met with a brick wall of blackness and we instinctively skidded to a stop.

"It's so dark out here," he said anxiously. "I better get out the flashlight."

I was grateful for the bouncing beam of light that Tyler held from his handlebar. It helped. It cut a tunnel through the darkness for us to ride through. We quickly made our way to the end of Monticello and then the other end of Bellen and hid our bikes near the edge of the trees.

Tyler deliberately turned off the flashlight, I was sure to keep the Watchman from seeing us and for our eyes to somehow adjust to the darkness. But mine never did. I couldn't even see the lights of the city anymore, only deep, subtle shades of black and grey surrounded us. The dark, swaying trees soared above us and blended in with the dreariness of the dark ebony sky.

Pellets of rain continued to pulse upon my skin and shook the leaves like a thousand angry rattlesnakes in every direction. I could not handle this! Panic started to grip at my chest. I reached out in the darkness for Tyler, for Jill, for *anything!* Then, like a warm, soothing blanket, his strong arms steadied my hand movements as he pulled me to his chest. I clenched my eyes shut and concentrated on calming my trembling body. I cradled my head into his chest as he fully wrapped his arms around me.

"It's okay, Timber," he whispered, stroking one hand gently over my head.

"It's so dark!" I said.

"Calm down," he comforted.

My heartbeat blended with the strong pounding cadence that came from Tyler's chest. Then, I felt something different than fear, and I knew my bodyguard felt it too. A sweet sensation moved through our embrace. I desperately wanted to kiss him.

"Get ready!" Jill interrupted with a loud whisper.

I froze against Tyler's chest. Could she see us in the darkness? She must have sensed what was happening.

"Get your shield on, *Keeper*!" she said sharply, reminding me of my duty.

The feelings in my chest disappeared. I released my arms from Tyler and stood up. Faintly, I saw the outline of Jill moving forward. Tyler quickly shuffled through his backpack. I could hear him getting his gun put together.

"Here Timber," he said quietly, in a much more serious tone. "Can you carry the ax?"

"Sure!" I whispered as I pulled my shield into place and gripped the heavy ax in my hands.

We made our way through the forest in single file. I felt disoriented, but I figured it must have something to do with the suffocating darkness. I held on to Tyler's shirt and moved as close to his body as I could. Jill was somewhere in front of us.

Tyler stopped. I leaned my head warily out to the side of him and saw a shadow move up a little ditch. *Was Jill climbing?* I didn't understand. We never came this way before. Maybe she was mixed up too!

A dark gray light crept up from behind me and flooded over us. Then blackness engulfed us again.

What was that? I wondered. Tyler's head was looking upward through the trees. I looked up and saw the moon behind a cloud. Gently, the light flooded us again as it peaked a second time. I remembered Ayden telling us about the best time for an Aspid rain. It was when the moon was full, and rain was falling from an overcast sky. *Well, by that definition it couldn't be a more perfect night,* I thought to myself. *Except for one thing of course—I wasn't ready for it to end this way. I didn't want it to end at all!*

Jill ran across the road. Tyler grabbed my hand and pulled me across too.

It was clear to me now: we were crossing Bellen in a different place. Jill was just taking a detour around the Watchman's traps.

I realized we must be closer to the tree than I thought.

"It's over there, Keeper," Jill whispered.

"What?" I asked. The shadows all looked the same to me.

"The tree," Tyler said. He still had a hold of my hand and began to pull me toward a large, dark silhouette that I could barely make out.

"Quickly," Tyler said to Jill. "Take this gun and keep a lookout for the Watchman."

"Timber," he continued, putting both hands on my shoulders. "We need to get this done as fast as we can." He took the ax from my hand and held it out to the side of him. "Now hold it like this," he said.

"Ty, I can't even see what you're doing."

"Turn on your flashlight, Tyler," Jill suggested. Her voice sounded a little frustrated.

Tyler fumbled around in his pockets.

"Wait. Maybe the eyepiece will help," I said, suddenly remembering.

"Of course! Did you bring it?" Jill asked.

I hastily pulled the thin strip of silky material out of my pocket, threw the hood of my jacket back, and tied the eyepiece around my eyes. To my amazement, I could see everything around me.

"Wow! I can see you!" I gasped. "Everything is perfectly clear."

"Night vision. That's even better!" Tyler said. "Now, hold the ax like this."

"Wait! We are forgetting something," Jill interrupted sarcastically. "Shouldn't the pond be here first before we go chopping the tree down?"

"Oh my gosh!" I said. "That's right! Sorry—it's scary out here at night, and I'm not thinking clearly. You two better hold on to something."

I put my hands on the big tree and quickly climbed over the rough bumps and knots. A wave of sadness seemed to wash over me. I loved this old tree. It led me to Mr. Seller's Pond. And now we had to chop it down. There never actually was a Mr. Seller, and now there wouldn't even be a tree—all of it, gone forever. Grandma would be devastated. It felt like I was eternally betraying her.

I pulled the needle from my pocket, put it in the knot, then held on to the large branch once again. The wind billowed in upon us like a violent, angry storm. Maybe it was the rain or the darkness that made it feel different, but the wind was stronger to me and more powerful than normal. Rain pelted against my body like tiny, cold whips striking at my clothes. A gust of wind shoved me upward, almost knocking me off the wide branch I was desperately clinging to. I wondered if the pond knew it was being visited one last time. I held my breath and waited for it to stop.

Slowly the wind died down, then everything was quiet. Only a few drops of rain fell here and there, like they were dripping from the leaves instead of falling from the sky. I opened my eyes and began to search the darkness for my friends.

I could see movement a little way off, and I climbed down the branches of the tree, found the ax, and waited.

"Are you okay, Timber?" Tyler whispered.

"Yeah," I responded as the moon peaked again from behind the clouds.

I saw Jill holding the paintball gun out in front of her with her shield to her side. Tyler was standing just in front of the pathway.

"Well, here it is!" he said pointing to the entrance. Tyler looked back at me with his big brown eyes. "Let's get this done."

I took a deep breath and held the ax out to the side of me.

I lifted it back and then swung as hard as I could.
Whack!

The sound startled me. It was so loud! I was sure that every creature in the forest heard it.

I looked back at Tyler. "Go on, Keeper!" he whispered. "Get this done as fast as you can. We'll watch for the Drimlor."

The light from the moon vanished behind another dark cloud as I lifted the ax and concentrated on the tree.
Whack!
Whack!

Jill was now circling the area and Tyler was anxiously scanning the darkness.
Whack!

How could a Keeper do this? I asked myself.

I dropped the end of the heavy ax and dragged it back out to the side. Grandma wanted me to find this tree. And Mandoria. She chose me to be the new Keeper. I couldn't help but think about her disappointment.
Whack!

How could I betray her like this?

I thought of Ayden and Stroder.
Whack!

I can't let this end!

My eyes began to burn. Even the darkness went blurry.

"What am I doing?" I gasped. I threw the ax to the ground and dropped to my knees, staring at the palms of my hands.

"Timber!" Tyler exclaimed.

Tears stream down my face from under the golden eyewear.

"I can't do this!" I cried, pulling the material from my eyes, and throwing it on the ground. "No! This isn't right!"

Tyler dropped to his knees just in front of me and grabbed my shoulders firmly. "Timber," he said in a slightly panicked voice. "We don't have a choice anymore! And I'm sure the Watchman knows we are here by now. He is probably on his way."

As he spoke, the moon moved from behind a dark cloud and at the same time we noticed a beautiful red shimmer in the tree over our heads.

"Whoa!" we all said in amazement.

Tyler and I stood up.

The light of the moon touched on every crystal in the tree above us. And the wind gently shook the limbs of the tree, causing tiny red sparkles to dance wildly upon the ground around us.

Something suddenly caught my attention in the distance. I wiped the tears from my eyes and looked intently through the trees.

I gasped as I tried to wrap my head around what I saw.

I grabbed Tyler's arm and looked at his golden-brown face, which was flickering with dancing, crimson lights.

"Climb!" I demanded with excitement. I quickly climbed through the tree. My heart was racing in my chest.

"Why?" he mumbled as he followed me.

SHERRI GRIMAUD

"What is it?" Jill asked from below.

I climbed as high as I could through the branches and positioned myself on the tallest limb that would hold my weight. It felt magical to be at the top of the tree overlooking Mr. Seller's Pond as the glistening red Aspids shimmered around us.

"Look, Tyler!" I exclaimed, pointing over the pond.

Tyler pulled himself up next to me. His eyes were huge and full of wonder.

There, gleaming in the misty moonlight, were three beautiful trees with different colors of crystals: green, yellow, and red—each one shimmering as brilliant as the one we were standing in.

"The Lifesavers worked!" I said as I grabbed his arm and looked into his eyes. "Your experiment. It worked!"

"The trees need... *sugar*!" he exclaimed. Tyler stared intently at the three radiant trees in the distance.

"Remember the leather book?" Tyler said. "Winston wrote in there about planting something next to the trees. I'm sure he didn't mean to plant Lifesavers, but maybe he knew to use sugar, or plant sugar cane even."

"Sugar," I said slowly. "But Stroder said the Aspids were kind of bitter."

Tyler turned and looked into my eyes. "They're probably bitter now, but the whole time Catherine was the Keeper, she didn't know about using sugar.

"Timber, I bet if we just add one cup of sugar to the water every time we come to Mandoria, the trees around the pond would be thriving with crystals."

"They would!" I exclaimed. "I know they would! And the Aspids would probably taste sweet!"

"Maybe we can plant actual sugar cane later," Tyler said. "We figured it out, Timber!"

Suddenly, I realized Tyler's face was right next to mine. There was no place to look but straight into his beautiful brown eyes. Crimson crystals glowed like a thousand fireflies around us. Something in my chest felt unexpectedly like the rushing of an enormous waterfall. Tyler pulled me to his chest and pressed his warm, soft lips upon mine. My bodyguard kissed me. My eyes melted shut as moments seemed suspended in the world around us. Then he slowly released me and lifted his lips gradually off mine. I couldn't move. I felt different. Warm. Weak.

As I opened my eyes, I saw the edge of Tyler's mouth curve slightly upward, and he smiled at me.

"We should go, Timber," he whispered, smiling again.

Slowly, everything came into focus. I took a deep breath, exhaled, then smiled back.

"Wow! I will never forget this night, Timber," Tyler said.

"Me neither," I whispered.

I have never been kissed before! What a wonderful night! In a magical place!

"We need to chop down one of the other trees instead of this one," Tyler said. "I'm glad you stopped when you did, Timber. This tree is the one that turns the key to Mandoria and must never be chopped down."

"Yeah!" I agreed, hoping that my knees would not buckle as I followed Tyler down the tree.

"So, what was it?" Jill whispered anxiously, still aiming her gun into the forest.

"The experiment worked!" I squealed with excitement.

"What?" Jill asked.

"We don't have to chop down the tree! There are three other trees with glowing crystals on them out by the pond." I could hardly understand my words because of how fast I was speaking.

"The Lifesavers worked!" Tyler exclaimed.

Jill's face was filled with such excitement, I thought her beautiful green eyes were going to pop right out of her head.

The moon suddenly went behind the clouds and the glowing lights from the crystals disappeared.

Jill dropped the paintball gun and grabbed my hands. "So, I can still live in Mandoria one day?" she asked in a high-pitched voice.

"And I can still be the Keeper!" I exclaimed.

Thunder rumbled in the distance and rain began to fall harder upon us. But this only seemed to fuel our enthusiasm. Jill and I began to jump with joy as Tyler joined in the circle, holding one of our hands in each of his. For the first time, we felt sure and confident! We knew the answer to Creshtil Pass! We could save the Noceans and we could visit Mandoria whenever we wanted!

"We did it!" we called out at the same time.

We smiled and danced around in the obscure shadows as rain fell from the night sky.

Jill's hand yanked abruptly away from mine.

There was a heavy *Thud!*

"Jill?" I asked in a whisper.

Tyler squeezed my other hand with great force.

A loud, heavy scratching sound pulled through the brush just in front of us.

"Jill," I said again, slightly louder.

Tyler pulled back on my hand as if to quiet me in the darkness.

I froze stiff as I smelled the strong, offensive odor that I knew came from only one source. My heart felt like it dropped six inches and shattered like broken glass in my chest. I couldn't breathe. The Watchman was here, and he had Jill.

The moon peaked again from behind a cloud. I watched with cold anticipation as the light crept slowly across the brush on the floor of the forest. It moved directly in front of us and toward the entrance of the pathway. Suddenly, I saw the foot and legs of a huge, muscular man. One thing was for sure, that was someone new! It could not be the Watchman!

The light revealed an enormous creature standing in the opening of the pathway. He was at least eight feet high. The muscles on his broad back and gigantic shoulders were covered with a thin layer of dingy fur. The sides of his head were shaved except for his protruding Mohawk that shot up high above his skull. Thick strands of hair were twisted like black, fuzzy snakes that hung down upon his colossal shoulders.

The moonlight continued to expose the frightening creature. His massive, hairy arm was cocked back by his shoulder holding an intricate, mammoth-sized bow that resembled the one Boden had, only larger. The light continued to move along his other arm that was extended out in front of him. Then I saw her. Jill's lifeless body was hanging, limp from the grip of his fingers that wrapped tightly around her neck. Her eyes had rolled back into her head and her skin was pale white from the reflection of the moon against the contrast of the pitch-black forest. She almost glowed like a beautiful dying firefly in the night.

"Keeper!" a scratchy voice growled throughout the forest.

I was so frightened that it took me a moment to recognize that this creature was the one yelling. It took another, to figure out he was yelling at *me*.

"Give me the key, and I'll give this one back!" he groaned with a familiar wrenching sound that came from deep within his gut.

His huge, ugly head began to turn slowly in our direction. His chin was lowered under his wide, distorted mouth, full of canine-looking teeth. And a green glow pierced the darkness from under his eyebrows, which abruptly stopped as it met my frightened stare.

Realization wormed its way through my frozen head. I couldn't believe it—*it was Boden!* He was in pure Drimlor form and was the most dreadful creature I had ever seen!

"Give me the key!" he roared as he lifted Jill higher in the air. Her skin looked powder-white and her plump, round lips took on a subtle purple shade.

"Then she must die!" he announced menacingly.

The huge, hideous Drimlor turned his head back to look at his victim, cocked his elbow, and steadily took aim.

"Wait!"

CHAPTER TWENTY

DEATH UNDER THE PASSING MOON

Terror, twisted with anger, consumed every inch of my frame as I stared at the enormous Drimlor that held Jill up by the neck. They nearly filled the opening in front of the pathway.

"What did you say?" the Drimlor snarled again as his head turned slowly in my direction, looking straight into my eyes.

There was nothing left to do but give him what he wanted. I would not stand by and let Jill die! Stroder would have to figure out another way to save his people.

"I said, wait!" My voice hissed forth like steam out of my icy throat. "You can have the stupid key! Just don't hurt her!"

"Then get it, Keeper!" he roared, spit flying wildly from his mouth.

Tyler gripped my hand, but I pushed it away. I was not interested in any of his ideas. I would not allow Jill to die!

As I turned and started to make my way to the tree, Tyler crouched low to the ground. *Was he trying to hide?* I wondered. I ignored him and moved as quickly as I could to climb the tree. I had to get the golden eye.

Tyler bolted up from beside me, running in the opposite direction, straight for the Drimlor. He had a knife held high in the air over his head.

What was he doing?

I hid behind the tree for a moment, peaking around to see what Tyler was doing. Something moved on the ground next to the Watchman and then jumped, grabbing hold of the Drimlor's back leg. I realized it must be Stroder.

The Drimlor bent his leg and lowered his weapon as he roared angrily up toward the moon. He lifted Jill higher and gripped tighter around her neck. She looked like a beautiful offering to some Drimlor God.

"No!" I screamed as I pressed my fingers against the bark of the tree.

Tyler leaped from the ground and jumped wildly toward the beast while something moved up the Drimlors back.

Tyler's body slammed into the creature's side at full force, not even beginning to knock it off balance. He wrapped his legs around its body and sunk the knife deep into the base of his rib cage.

I gasped.

Thick blood gushed from around the knife and a roar exploded from deep within the Drimlor.

The sound of the creature was deafening, and I was sure that every soul in Springfield woke from it. I watched on in horror.

The Drimlor swung his massive arm and hit Tyler in the side, throwing him through the air and back against a tree. He slumped down in a heap and just laid there.

The painful roaring from the Drimlor filled every inch of the forest again and again, like the waves of a wrecking tsunami.

He hurled Jill's limp body into the dark pathway, threw his weapon to the ground, and pulled the knife out of his chest.

"Rotty!" he growled as he dropped to his knees, thrashing wildly out of control while trying to reach the middle of his back.

Stroder had to be digging into his backbone.

"Kill, Rotty, kill!" he cruelly ordered into the dark night.

Do something, Timber! I screamed inside my head. I knew his dog all too well and was sure he was close by.

Jill looked dead in the pathway and Tyler still hadn't moved against the base of the tree. The fear was crippling, but how could I sit here and watch the death of my friends?

'*Timber, dear, rise above the fear!*' Unbelievably, I heard a voice inside my head. A familiar voice. It was *her* voice. '*Find your Keeper's courage and do what needs to be done!*'

Grandma's voice filled my mind as if she were reaching back across the valley of death and over the magical pond to speak to me.

I dropped to my knees and reached for the Creshtil-Ball around my neck. "What is happening?" I whispered.

'You can do it, honey!' she continued sweetly. *'But do it… now!'*

Sounds of crackling branches erupted in the distance.

Quickly, I felt the ground for the eyewear, trying to remember where I threw it. But it was nowhere to be found. Then, I felt a wooden handle. *The ax!*

The Drimlor flung a large handful of blood into the trees and dropped to the ground as he gasped through a mouthful of gurgling blood.

Suddenly, he met my stare and scowled vehemently through green, glowing eyes. Then he started to claw and move his way straight toward me.

I tightened my grip around the ax's wooden handle. He pulled closer and closer through the dirt like an angry wounded soldier, never taking his piercing eyes off me.

The moon once again drifted behind a dark cloud and the forest went pitch black.

I felt a surge of power course through my body. My senses sharpened, and even though darkness encircled me, I could hear the acute sound of Rotty creeping slowly through the forest just next to me. I stood and deliberately lifted the ax over my head.

Do I go for the Drimlor or his oversized dog? I questioned myself. Both were ready to destroy me.

'Just swing the ax, Timber!' I heard her say in my head.

I could sense a heat emanating from the scratching Drimlor on the ground in front of me, and I knew exactly where he was. Just to my side, Rotty's breath fell upon me like steaming hot snowflakes. I closed my eyes and deliberately focused on each move I made. I stepped forward and swung the heavy ax with all my might. Using its momentum, I spun full circle, and then the blade connected with the Drimlor's Beast, slamming him sideways with a thud and a whimper. Other sounds came from the darkness. Grunting and heaving, and then an angry groan—scratching noises—then another heavy thud.

I brought the ax above my head and instinctively launched it into the dark. I heard a distinct crack as the ax connected with something in front of me.

I opened my eyes to the shadows in the forest.

For a few moments everything went silent except for the patter of the rain upon the leaves.

Soft, gray light slowly inundated the darkness, and I recognized a familiar form in front of me.

The silhouette flipped his hair to the side as red pillars reflected off the Crystals in the tree above us. Tyler was sitting just in front of me on top of the huge, hairy dog. His normally brown skin looked white and full of fear, and his eyes were like fiery saucers. He was holding a tightly gripped knife that glistened red in the moonlight. It was obvious that he had just killed Rotty. And under them was the Drimlor lying still on the ground with an ax protruding from the center of his skull.

"Are you okay?" a small, yet controlled voice came from somewhere in the shadows.

"Yeah, I guess so," Tyler responded as he deeply exhaled.

"What about you, Keeper?" he asked.

I looked slowly at my hands then shook my head in disbelief. I felt as though I were waking from a dream-like trance. My vision was swimming.

Tyler pulled me to the ground and wrapped his arms around my shaking body. It took me a moment to realize that I was sobbing.

"It's okay, Timber!" Tyler said, his voice deep and comforting. "Everything is okay now."

I quickly curled up under his arms, pressed my face to his chest, and continued crying.

Minutes passed before I could breathe. "What just happened?" I managed to ask.

"You finished him, Timber!" Tyler whispered incredulously. "I can't believe it, but somehow you really did it!"

I sniffed and quickly wiped my tears.

"It's beginning!" Stroder said from just within the shadows. "Just so quickly. Timber, as you spend more time at the pond you will receive more of the Keeper's gifts. It's just, I've never seen it happen so fast and you move just like her."

"Who, grandma?" I asked.

He nodded.

It was her voice that led me through that situation. Was that a Keeper's gift, too, to hear a voice from the dead? I thought to myself.

"Tyler," Stroder suddenly ordered. "Get the Keeper to the pond, then help me find Ayden."

"Ayden? Was Ayden here?" I asked, then noticed the empty pathway. "Where's Jill?"

"I took her to the pond," Stroder responded, "She'll be fine—she was still breathing. And yes, Ayden was here. We just need to find him...fast!"

"I never even saw him," Tyler said, looking around the shadows of the forest.

Rain continued to dot my skin and rattle the leaves overhead.

I noticed Stroder as the moonlight moved across the floor of the forest. He was covered from head to toe with a thick blackness that had a shade of crimson to it. "He fought by my side the whole time," he said, looking up at both of us with his small, dirty face. His voice sounded different to me, almost defeated. "We were both on the Drimlor, but when I started stabbing his back, Ayden just disappeared. Maybe he fell off."

"Wait!" I said, pointing into the shadows. "I saw the Drimlor throw something over there! I thought it was blood!"

Tyler and Stroder moved quickly.

"Go to the pond, Keeper!" Stroder hollered back. "And check on Jill."

"You don't think—" I started to say but could not finish the sentence.

I stood up and stared at the dead Drimlor with an ax jutting out of his head. *I can't believe I did that!* I said to myself as I moved around his huge, lifeless body with his dog, heaped upon his backside.

As I entered the pathway, soft red pillars of light emanated from the glowing Aspids overhead.

I wanted to see Jill, so I ran the rest of the way.

The most horrible sight caught me completely off guard.

"Jill!" I screamed and ran to her lifeless body. She was lying on her stomach, half on the sand and half in the water. She looked like she had drowned. Her head and arms were floating as her hair swayed gently in the movement of the water. I dropped to my knees and started to lift her up by her shoulders, but I noticed how the muscles on her back were moving up and down. She was breathing water from the pond. The sight was haunting, like she was *feeding* on the pond. But then realization settled in upon my tainted thoughts. *She is healing!* I let go of her shoulders and watched her body sway gently back into the thick water where she relaxed into a steady mode of breathing. *This is what Grandma needed when her heart stopped,* I thought to myself sadly.

"Grandma, are you still there?" I asked quietly. I reached for the sphere around my neck and wondered if, somehow, this is what connected her thoughts to mine. I waited a moment. But there was nothing.

"I know I heard your voice, Grandma!" I whispered. *"If you can hear me—and I wasn't dreaming—I just wanted to thank you for your help!"*

Still nothing.

I looked up to the beautiful moon peaking between the clouds.

"I miss you, Grandma!" I said quietly to myself.

Peace filled my heart at the edge of the pond as I sat next to Jill. I couldn't help but notice the intermittent raindrops sink into the water releasing hundreds of disappearing little rings on the surface.

Tyler and Stroder caught my eye at the end of the pathway. Tyler's hands were cupped together, gently holding a little crimson mass out in front of him.

I gasped.

"Ayden!" I screamed.

"Keeper!" Stroder called out. His hand was firm in the air like he was ordering me to stop.

I ignored him.

"Is he okay?" I asked, searching Tyler's brown eyes. Then I looked back at Ayden.

"I don't think he made it," Tyler responded quietly.

I could feel my eyebrows pull together tightly and rage moved like a fire up the back of my neck.

"You would like that wouldn't you, Tyler!" I screamed, shocked at the cutting tone of my voice.

"No!" Tyler said defensively as I pulled Ayden's fragile, crimson body from his hands and ran to the pond.

I dropped to my knees and held him just under the water. I glanced at Jill and saw her chest moving stronger up and down, then looked back at Ayden. Clouds of blood drifted off his perfectly still body.

"I didn't even know he was there! Why did he come?" I demanded as I stared desperately at his beautiful little face just under the water. His long golden braid floated and made its way gently around my thumb.

"He will be fine. I know it!" I said as I started to feel emotions welling up inside of me.

"Keeper," Stroder said, in a calm and steady voice. "The water of the pass can only heal those who are *still* alive."

I flipped my eyes at Stroder.

"Stop it!" I said sharply. "He will breathe! I know he will!"

Stroder dropped his head.

"I could not feel his heartbeat, Timber," he whispered.

"No!" I screamed. "No one else is going to die!"

My tears burned as they welled up in the corners of my eyes.

I lifted Ayden's body up out of the silky, thick water. His arms hung lifeless over the sides of my hands. His features seemed to melt into my palms as I looked at him through blurry eyes. My tears began to drop freely upon his chest and mixed with the water of the pond.

"Live, Ayden!" I whispered. "Please live! You *must* live!"

Then, Ayden's chest heaved, and he gasped deeply.

I blinked and looked up at Stroder.

"I don't believe it," Stroder said in almost a whisper, then loudly ordered, "Put him in the water now, Timber!"

I did as he said. The water lapped over my hands and covered Ayden's face. His chest moved up and down. He began to breathe in the water, just like Jill.

"I have heard about this, but never saw it with my own eyes," Stroder said slowly, with deep amazement in his voice.

"What are you talking about?" Tyler asked.

"Umm. Oh, it's nothing," Stroder said, shifting uncomfortably.

"Come on, Stroder. Tell us what you're talking about," Tyler demanded. "We both knew Ayden was dead. We checked him by the tree. He had no heartbeat."

Stroder looked at me and then at Tyler.

"Well, there is a legend in Mandoria," Stroder said slowly. "When a Noceans heart has stopped beating, their soul begins to fly across the pass and into the high country. The elders say that there is one thing that could bring it back, and one thing only."

Stroder paused.

My eyes were fixed upon Ayden as he continued taking in the healing water of the pond.

"The ancient records tell of it happening many generations back. I only wish Catherine would have been here when her heart stopped," Stroder said regretfully. He hung his head as he spoke her name.

"The legend is that when two souls destined to be together are near the pass and one dies, they can be brought back as tears fall upon them from their *one true soulmate.* The tears must mix with the water of the pass."

I looked straight at Stroder.

"What?" Tyler blurted skeptically. "That is crazy! Ayden was probably not even dead, then. And Timber is not destined to be with Ayden." But even as he spoke, I could hear the uncertainty in Tyler's voice.

I looked at Ayden. *Could that be true? Was I Ayden's one true love? I would have to become a Nocean for sure!*

"Tyler, you were right. When we found Ayden, he had no beating heart," Stroder said as he started to lap the water onto his arms to wash off the Drimlor's blood. "Life had completely left him."

"You don't know that for sure!" Tyler said desperately. "And legends. They are just made-up stories. And not even true!"

"You wanted me to tell you, Tyler, so I did."

"Quiet you two! I think they are waking up."

Jill pushed up on her arms and water billowed off her hair and back into the pond. She took a deep breath and gently shook her head as she sat back on her knees. Ayden began to awaken too.

"What happened?" Jill asked, dazed.

"It's okay Jill. You're safe. The Watchman is dead," I said placing my arm gently on her back.

"Where is Stroder? Is he okay?" she asked weakly.

"I'm here, Jill," he said as he began to walk closer to her.

Within minutes, both Jill and Ayden were sitting up and color had returned to their faces. We told them all that happened.

"We did it," Stroder said incredulously, shaking his head. He had a wide grin on his face, something I had not seen before. "We killed another Watchman!"

"That was a first for me! To help kill a Drimlor in human form, at least!" Ayden joined in, a little boastfully. "You did this once before, Stroder, didn't you?"

"Many years ago," he said.

The look in his eyes made me wonder if that experience had anything to do with a young girl who grew up to be my grandmother.

Stroder looked thoughtfully at Jill. "I couldn't stand by and allow you to get killed tonight Jill."

Jill's beautiful green eyes flashed down at Stroder. She smiled as a pink color flushed over her face.

"Thank you!" she said.

"You guys did most of the work," Ayden added. "I wasn't much help at the end."

"Come on, now," Tyler interrupted thoughtfully. "*Everyone* helped to slow that Drimlor down. It took all of us tonight."

"But Timber, you finished him off," Stroder said.

"I can't believe it!" Jill exclaimed looking straight at me. "I never thought you had it in you."

"I didn't either," I joined in, shaking my head. "Something just came over me and I knew I had to move."

"Timber, you were chosen to be the Keeper by Catherine," Stroder said. "And when you put the golden eye into the tree the first time, it accepted you. Only a Keeper with a pure and honest heart can do this. The tree will not take the key from any other hand. And now, you are able to access the Keeper's gifts."

"What are those gifts, and how does she get them?" Jill asked.

"They develop over time and are different for each Keeper," Stroder answered. "As she learns to move through her fear, the gift will lead her to do what needs to be done. It's extremely powerful but usually takes years to gain access to and develop."

"She's a natural!" Ayden said proudly.

"Once she gets passed her fear!" Jill exclaimed, chuckling to herself.

"But at least you weren't like me, held up like a wilted flower by the grip of the Drimlors' hand!"

Everyone laughed.

"It's not funny, though," Stroder said soberly. "Jill could have died tonight. Anyone of us could have. But Timber, don't worry about accessing your gifts. They will come on their own. And when they do, just move with them. Try not to let them scare you."

I nodded at Stroder. *If he only knew I heard her voice.*

"Even Catherine was petrified at first. You'll get used to these situations," Stroder concluded.

"I hope so!" I said wearily.

I leaned over to Tyler.

"Thank you, bodyguard, for helping with all of this!"
I whispered.

Tyler grinned and looked into my eyes.

"Anytime, Keeper!" he said as he leaned over and
kissed me on the forehead.

My heart fluttered again in my chest, and I felt that
same warm feeling bounce around inside my ribcage.

"You will become the best Keeper yet," Ayden said
with adoration.

I smiled at him.

"Hey, how did you guys know that we needed
your help up here?" Tyler asked, looking at Stroder. "I
thought you were going to wait for the Aspids to rain
down."

"We wondered if something was wrong since it was
taking you so long."

"Well, some of us overslept!" Tyler mumbled sarcastically. He winked and playfully glared at me and Jill.

I laughed as Jill puckered her lips and mimicked
Tyler's words under her breath. Tyler laughed too.

"But when Ayden and I swam to the top of the
pond, we could not believe what we saw," Stroder said.

"Oh yeah!" I said, pointing to the trees in the distance.
"Look at those beautiful glowing Aspids!"

"I need to apologize to you, Tyler," Stroder said. "I
don't know how you did it, but you figured it out. So,
what did you do differently?"

"We added sugar," Tyler said. "We discovered the
pond needs sugar."

"What's that?" Ayden asked.

"Sugar is a sweet substance that tastes good," Tyler said. "It mainly comes from a plant called sugar cane. After it's harvested and processed, it can be used in many ways. Usually, it is white and comes in little granules or cubes."

Ayden looked at Stroder. "Like sweet stalks?"

Stroder smiled. "We have plants in Mandoria called sweet stalks," he said. "They are extremely hard to find, but I wonder if they are like your sugar cane?"

"Maybe," Tyler continued. "But when we did the experiment, I lost the packets of sugar, so we used Timber's favorite candies instead. They are full of sugar! They are called Lifesavers, and they come in all different colors."

"So that's why there were different colors," Ayden added.

"The Keeper will need to put a cup of sugar into the water each time she comes to Mandoria, and the trees should flourish with Crystals!" Tyler concluded.

"That's wonderful!" Stroder exclaimed.

"Later, we can try planting sugar cane next to the pond. Maybe years ago, it grew here naturally."

"Okay," Stroder agreed. "And we will tell the elders to record this news. I have a lot of respect for you, Tyler, and I am sorry I didn't trust your judgement. Your name will *forever* be remembered among our people.

"You also have much courage. I couldn't believe how you ran at the Drimlor and stabbed him with your knife. You definitely slowed him down so Timber could finish him off. And, if it weren't for you, his dog would still be alive."

"Thank you, Stroder," Tyler said respectfully.

"Yeah. Thank you so much Tyler!" Ayden joined in.

We paused, reflecting on all that had happened.

"But we still have a big night ahead of us," Ayden continued. "We should probably get to chopping a tree down."

"That is true," Stroder agreed. "Why don't you go with Timber and Tyler and get started on that. Jill could help me dispose of Boden and his dog before the Drimlors' sense that something is wrong with their Watchman."

I felt a chill skip down my spine.

"What happens when they find out that he's dead?" I asked.

"The Drimlors are awake during the nights in Mandoria," Stroder said. "They roam the area for any Noceans to kill. That is why we hide.

"Usually, they don't need to come to the rocky hillside that leads to Creshtil Pass because the Watchman is here. Basically, it is far from where they usually roam. That's why the Noceans that are waiting at the Pass right now should be fine."

"The Runners are on guard, anyway!" Ayden piped up, confidently.

"But" Stroder continued, "when the Drimlor scout returns to the area, which they do every so often, they will sense that something is wrong and they will know the Watchman is dead."

"Then what?" I asked.

"Sometimes we go to war," Ayden interrupted.

"But no matter what, a new Watchman will be ordered," Stroder said. "And he will take Boden's place immediately."

I felt sick inside. A Keeper's job was never meant to be as easy and safe as it felt right now.

"You have to know something, Keeper. Every Watchman is different. And all of you will need to be extra careful, for a while as you come and go to Mandoria."

I nodded along with Jill and Tyler.

"So, how do we dispose of the Drimlor?" Jill asked.

"We just drag the beast to the pond," he said. "And it will burn him up as long as he does not have the key. It won't take long at all."

"Well, let's get the ax first and then get started on the tree," Tyler said looking at me and Ayden.

We all walked back through the pathway and Tyler got the ax out of the Drimlor head. Jill and Stroder drug the Drimlor and Rotty to the pond as Tyler and Ayden and I headed for the three shimmering trees in the distance. I put Ayden on my shoulder so he wouldn't have to run and tightly gripped my fingers around Tyler's warm hand. He responded with a smile and a quick squeeze of his grip. I was beaming with joy to be with the two people who I grew to love so deeply. I hoped nothing would ever change!

"So, what color of Aspids do you want to eat for the next ten years?" Tyler asked Ayden as he swung the ax with his other hand over his shoulder.

"I like the way the yellow one's glow in the moonlight," Ayden answered thoughtfully.

"Okay. The middle tree it will be!" Tyler exclaimed. I could tell he was proud of his crystal experiment. "So, Keeper, do you want the honors, or will you delegate your tree chopping authority to me?"

"Ty, I think you deserve the credit for this decade of Aspid Rain," I said. "But as the Keeper, I would love to chop the first tree down. It's just I'm not sure I can do it."

Tyler stopped at the base of the tree with yellow glowing Aspids. "That's your first problem, Timber," he said. "You need to believe in yourself. Here, let me show you."

I sat Ayden on the ground as Tyler held out the ax. I took hold of the handle with both hands.

"Here, Timber," Tyler said. He put his arms around me and showed me where to place my hands. I couldn't help but turn and look into his big brown eyes. He smiled a slight grin then quickly got more serious.

"Timber, now listen," he said. "This is serious. You don't want to hurt yourself. You lift the ax back like this and swing as hard as you can in the same place on the tree." While holding onto my hands, he slowly moved the ax toward the tree placing it gently on the trunk.

"Okay. I got this," I said. "I did finish off the Watchman, Tyler. I think I know how to do this!"

"Yeah, but no offence Timber," Tyler said carefully, "you didn't even make a dent in the tree when you tried it before. Which was *good* because we didn't want to chop it down after all."

I puckered my lips and glared playfully at Tyler.

"Just swing the ax as hard as you can," Tyler said, stepping back quietly chuckling to himself.

I grabbed the ax, lifted it back, and swung it with all my might.

Whack!

Whack!

I leaned down and looked closely at the tree. There wasn't even a mark on the bark.

Whack!

'*Grandma, are you there? I need some help here.*' I said in my mind. There was no response.

Whack!

Whack!

"What am I doing wrong?" I asked Tyler.

"First, you need to swing it in the same place and get the wood to splinter a little," Tyler explained. "Then you need to come down from the top a few times, then switch and come up from the bottom. That way you will chop out little wedges, as you go.

"Timber, do it like Catherine did," Ayden said.

"How could *she* do it?" I questioned as I swung the ax again.

Whack!

"She was probably using her *Keeper gifts!*" I exclaimed almost sarcastically.

Whack!

Whack!

"Wait," I said setting the ax on the ground. "Grandma used to chop wood all the time in her back yard. It was for her fireplace."

"Yes," Ayden said. "I remember her saying she did that so she could become good at chopping trees down."

Whack!

I stopped and leaned down to look closer at the tree. Only a few small marks were slightly visible. "Okay, Tyler," I said looking back at him.

Tyler was standing patiently with his arms folded. He had a cute little smirk on his face.

"You're right Tyler, I'm not even putting a dent in this one either," I said, defeated. "I guess I will need to practice!" I mumbled jokingly but knew the truth behind my statement. "Would you please help me with this?"

"I'd be honored to do this for you, Keeper. I will try to get it where it needs to be, then we can both push it into the pond, if that is okay?"

"Perfect," I said, realizing how big of a task this really was.

"Have a seat, my lady. I will try to make you proud."

I loved Tyler's playfulness.

"We will!" I said as I sat down on an old tree stump that had probably been cut down years before by another Keeper. I put Ayden carefully on my knee.

I was caught off guard by the hissing and bubbling sounds that came from a little way off. Jill and Stroder were in the distance pulling the Watchman and Rotty into the water.

The sharp sound of the ax resonated throughout the forest as Tyler worked steadily on the tree. I felt great joy and relief in my heart knowing the Noceans would live and be safe for centuries to come.

Tyler's arms swung the ax over and over, splintering the wood just like he had explained. He flipped his loose brown hair to the side after each blow. He was my bodyguard, my protector. I thought of the kiss, and a shiver moved through my spine as I smiled wide to myself. I sighed quietly. That moment will live in my memories as one of the greatest experiences I have ever had. He was so much more to me than just a bodyguard—he was almost like my boyfriend.

I smiled and glanced down.

Ayden sat on the edge of my knee, leaning back on his arms. He was relaxed and pleasantly watching Tyler, who was working hard for his people. He was my little friend, kind and strong and valiant. I smiled as I watched him move his long yellow braid over his shoulder and flip it behind him. It thrilled me inside to think that he liked me, too. And if our souls were meant to be together, like the legend said, then I knew one day we would be. The thought felt strange yet wonderful at the same time.

I couldn't see Jill or Stroder anymore and wasn't sure where they were. It would probably be years before Stroder would see Jill as anything more than a kid sister, but one thing I did know was that Jill was an unstoppable force when she set her mind to something. And ever since looking into the Creshtil-Ball, she had set her mind on Stroder. I was not sure how she could so easily be willing to let go of her life in the outer world, which included her family and me, but I knew that someday she would be begging me to change her into a Nocean. This was a decision I was not confident about making yet.

I was grateful, however, to still be the Keeper and to have the chance to learn the job, like my grandmother did. And I was thrilled to be able to hear her voice again, even if it was just in my mind. I wasn't going to tell anyone yet, but I knew it was real and I knew she helped me. I was also excited to be able to make the choice one day for myself. One thing was for sure, I would live in Mandoria—I just needed to decide when. I looked at Tyler and then back to Ayden and thought about each of them. The choice would be a difficult one, but I would not make the same mistake Grandma did. I love her dearly, but she waited too long, something I refuse to do.

"Almost there!" Tyler shouted. His voice interrupted my thoughts.

Ayden slid down my leg as I stood up.

The tree was teetering on a little wedge of wood that was still connected at the base. Tyler set down the ax and motioned for me to come.

"This is *your tree*, Keeper!" Tyler exclaimed wiping perspiration off his forehead. "You need to be the one to do this!" His voice was exhausted yet still full of great excitement. I ran quickly to Tyler's side and couldn't help but notice the beauty resonating from the golden Aspids in the tree above us.

"Ayden," Stroder called out as he and Jill moved swiftly to the water's edge. "As soon as the tree hits the water, you and I must swim to the bottom."

"Well, you better get ready cause she's about to drop!" Tyler called out.

Excitement filled my whole being as I put both of my hands gently on the tree. I couldn't help but think about how Grandmother must have felt the night I was born. Oh, how she must have looked as she pushed the tree down and called out my namesake.

Ayden looked up at me and whispered excitedly, "See you tomorrow!"

"Okay," I responded with a nod and a loving smile.

"Now, go save Brindle and the rest of the Noceans!" Tyler yelled.

The surface of the pond was full of movement as drops of rain continued to fall. Stroder and Ayden smiled at us as they readied themselves at the water's edge.

Tyler braced his feet against the ground and placed his hands on mine and together we pushed on the huge heavy tree. The wood began to splinter and pop as the tree burst free from the last bits of wood holding it to the stump. The sound cracked and echoed throughout the forest. The power was intense as it fell straight for the water.

In unison, all of us yelled at the top of our lungs, "*Timber!*" I smiled and could almost hear grandma's voice join in from within my mind.

A rush of cool air blew forcefully against us as the enormous tree crashed into the pond. A huge wave heaved out from around the large trunk and branches. Golden shimmering crystals instantly began to descend into the pond as tiny bubbles filtered upward and moved wildly on the surface.

I laughed to myself. The pond looked like a glass of sparkling water with a fizz bubbling on the top of it. It was the most beautiful thing I had ever seen!

Ayden and Stroder dove into the sparkling pond. I could see them spiraling down to the bottom.

Tyler and I ran to meet Jill along the edge of the water that was now full of even greater commotion. Golden crystals were falling like tiny stars, and a village of Noceans were moving jubilantly throughout the water. We watched in amazement.

I looked at Tyler and then to Jill. Here we were, our lives forever changed. Tyler was no longer the boy who just moved into grandma's house. He was my protector and bodyguard. Because of his knowledge and courage, we were able to save the people of this wonderful hidden world. Jill was no longer just my best friend. She had a new heart, the heart of a Runner. She was now a warrior, ready to fight for the cause of the Noceans.

And then there was me, the Keeper of the Key. There's so much to learn about the role I played in all of this. But somehow, I felt confident I would discover and conquer this too. And I knew grandma would show me the way and would be forever in my heart. I was happy to give my life to this amazing new world that each of us had become a part of.

We stood and watched. We were different. We were ever needed in protecting Mandoria. And we each had a special part to play in it.

Tyler grabbed my hand and Jill grabbed the other. We laughed and playfully kicked the water while watching the Aspid Rain from the shimmering edge of Mr. Seller's Pond.

ABOUT THE AUTHOR

Sherri Grimaud grew up on a farm in Kansas and later attended BYU-Idaho and then Salt Lake Community College in Utah. She began writing while raising her children and is currently living in Idaho Falls with her husband and grandson.

CPSIA information can be obtained
at www.ICGtesting.com
Printed in the USA
LVHW082101230421
685378LV00030B/715/J